A SMUGGLERS' T

The
Moonrakers
of Avon

To Dominic
Your Godmother tells me how much
you enjoyed reading my first book.

J.A. Ratcliffe

hope you enjoy this one!

J.A. Ratcliff

HSP

© 2016 Julie Ratcliffe
Published by High Sails Publications
PO Box 7575, Christchurch, BH23 9HJ
Tel: +44 (0)1202 471097
www.highsailspublications.co.uk

First published 2016 by High Sails Publications

ISBN: 978-0-9568572-2-4

British Library Cataloguing in Publication Data
A catalogue record for this book is available from the British
Library

Illustrations and cover artwork
© Domini Deane www.dominideane.com

Author photograph
© Amanda Clay www.clayphotography.co.uk

Set by www.beamreachuk.co.uk
Printed by www.beamreachuk.co.uk

Acknowledgements

I would like to thank what has become my 'team' for all the help and support in the production of this, my third Smugglers' Town Mystery. My husband, Michael and my family for continuing to believe in me; my friend and author, Judy Hall, for her help and editorial guidance; Gwynneth Ashby, friend, author and amazing nonagenarian. Also, my thanks go to the Village Writers, who are a great support; my friend and historian, Michael Andrews, for keeping my muskets and carbides in their rightful places, and my brilliant sisters, Susan Robertson and Wendy Edmond, who always see what I don't. I'm particularly thrilled that once again the fabulous Domini Deane has provided the lovely cover and illustrations.

For Michael

Contents

Cast of Characters

Cliff House
Sir Charles Tarrant
Lady Elizabeth Tarrant
Edmund Tarrant
Kitty Dover, guest

Household
Joseph, butler
Clara, maid
John Scott, stableman, coachman
Ben, stable boy

Bay House, Muddiford
Jane Menniere, cousin to Sir Charles Tarrant
Yves Menniere, Jane's husband
Perinne Menniere

Household
Miss Ashton, Perinne's governess
Lucy Scott, maid

Townsfolk of Christchurch
The Reverend William Jackson, Vicar of Christchurch
Adam Jackson (his son)
Will Gibbs
Meg Gibbs, Will's mother
Beth Gibbs, Will's sister
Nathan, Will's friend
Sam the dog
Isaac Hooper, the Gibbs' neighbour, smuggler
Adam Litty, brewery worker, smuggler
Caleb Brown, blacksmith, smuggler
Bessie Brown, Caleb's wife
Guy Cox, fisherman, smuggler
Joseph Martin, landlord of the George Inn
David Preston, Poor House Master, smuggler

Judith Preston, Poor House Mistress
Henry Lane, smuggler
John Cook, Mayor
Edward Allan, Commissioner of Customs
Joshua Stevens, Chief Revenue Officer
Toby Cox, Riding Officer

Burton Village
James Clarke, right-hand man to Sir Charles Tarrant
Hannah Clarke, his wife
Jack Clarke, their son
Danny Clarke, their son
Sarah Clarke, their daughter

Hinton
John Hewitt, former sailor, smuggler
Mary Hewitt, John's wife, sister to Hannah Clarke
Betsy – John and Mary's daughter
(Danny Clarke's aunt and uncle)

Ringwood
Meekwick Ginn, venturer

The Moonraker Gang
Ethan Byng
Mokey
Ambrose
Ben Lambert
Others

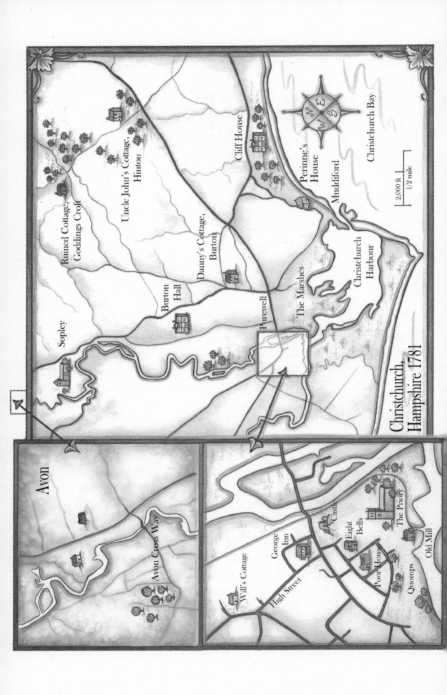

Christchurch,
Hampshire 1781

Sopley

Ruined Cottage,
Goldings Croft

Uncle John's Cottage,
Hinton

Burton Hall

Danny's Cottage,
Burton

Cliff House

Perinne's
House

Muddiford

Purewell

The Marshes

Christchurch
Harbour

Christchurch Bay

2,000 ft

1/2 mile

Avon

Avon Cross Way

Will's Cottage

George
Inn

High Street

Eight
Bells

Castle

Poor House

Quomps

The Priory

Old Mill

Chapter 1

Arrested

'Arrest them!'

The roar of voices broke the silence of the night, as the revenue men burst from the shadows. Soon they were splashing into the black water. Behind them, on the riverbank, silhouetted by the moon, dragoons sat on shuffling horses. The boat had just passed under the bridge. There were two men on board. The blacksmith, a huge man, knew he had no chance of getting out of the boat and running away. His friend was fit for an old man, but could see no way of escape. They lifted their arms, resigning themselves to the fate that awaited them.

'Out of the boat,' a gruff voice bellowed. 'There's just two,' he called out towards the nearby bridge, where the grey shapes of two people watched on.

The blacksmith stepped into the river. He yelped as the icy water reached up his legs and over into his boots.

'Get a move on. Get to the bank,' the gruff-voiced man ordered.

The sound of the horses clattered on the gravelly road and faded as they moved away. The dragoons could see no help was needed; their job done. The second man jumped out of the boat and ploughed speedily to the muddy river's edge. Both men, wet and shivering, were tied up and led away, pistols pressed into their backs. The town was in darkness, any rush lights along the street had long been put out. Ahead the figures who'd been on the bridge were walking away by yellow lamplight towards the revenue officer's cottage.

The blacksmith closed his eyes. The half-moon had tipped the ripples of the choppy water with dancing lights. He'd been relaxed as he'd breathed out a mist of breath into the chilled night air. He'd caught the scent of his friend's tobacco; heard the waterfowl muttering in their roosts. It had been another good night's work. His strong arms had made an easy task of heaving the oars of the tub boat. He'd pulled them hard to keep warm and to speed their return. But now his arms were chained together at the wrists. His feet, still wet from wading in the river, felt as cold as his anvil. He'd returned from the trip dreaming of the cosy fire that would welcome him home. But he wasn't home, he'd been pushed into a cold, damp cellar alongside his old friend, John Hewitt.

There'd been three of them, taking barrels to Avon. Probably of brandy, he hadn't asked. Once there their instructions were to leave the barrels in a pool. This was not their first trip and tonight's job had been as before. The pool was black, only moonlight glinting off the water to guide them. The nearest home was some distance away, keeping prying eyes from their task. The goods had been dropped overboard into the shallow water, no doubt for collection later. He'd no idea who by. Isaac had jumped off the boat to find the boulder where their payment was hidden and had passed him the purse. The money was to be shared the next day. They'd left Isaac Hooper up river, close to his tumbledown cottage. It was when the wharf was in sight that the shouts had gone out.

'What'll we do, Caleb?' John said, as he blew the icy fingers of his manacled hands. 'What's this all about?'

Danny Clarke climbed down the stone, spiral staircase and left through the wooden door into a bitterly cold afternoon. As he cut across the graveyard towards the street, his daydreams of Christmas, and especially Twelfth Night when the family gathered, were broken by shouts and screaming flying about the air. Across the old town bridge he could see dozens of people outside Joshua Steven's cottage. Stevens was the chief revenue officer and Danny wondered what had happened. He stepped up his pace.

When he reached the edge of the gathering, Danny stretched on his toes to try to see what the fuss was about.

'What's going on?' he asked a boy.

'Smugglers, caught last night.'

'*No, no…*' a woman's voice screamed. It was shrill, as if she'd seen a sudden terror.

'*Shame on you.*' '*Let them go.*' The crowd bayed across the biting air.

A red-coated dragoon on horseback came out from the alleyway beside the cottage. The animal snorted, pushing aside those standing in its way. A pair of horses emerged directly behind it pulling a cart. The voices of the onlookers rose to screams; clenched fists punched the sky. A baby was crying somewhere and dogs barked. Two revenue men, wearing thick, dark coats and brimmed hats, were on the cart's seat. Their coats had leather belts each

3

holding two pistols. Danny craned his neck to try to get a better view and gasped as he saw the hulking shape of Caleb Brown, the kindly blacksmith. His gasp turned to a shriek of horror as the cart moved further forward.

'*Uncle John*!' Danny pushed hard to make his way through the jostling men, women and children. The cart was making slow progress as the crowd tried to stop it getting any further. Joshua Stevens stood at the door, his wigged head topped with a black tri-corn hat. His face gave away a hint of fear despite him being safe. To his right was a dragoon, his carbine rifle in hand. On his left a man with a long nose pointing to a dimpled chin stood stiff. His nose had a round mole on the side. That was all Danny could see. The rest of his face was hidden between his high collar and hat, which was tilted forward. He was wearing a navy customs officer's uniform. As the cart emerged another two horses carrying soldiers appeared.

'*Uncle John, Uncle John*, what's happening?' Danny yelled.

Everyone surged towards the cart. The soldier beside Joshua Stevens primed his rifle. The two horsemen at the rear of the cart tried to form a barrier. A man lunged towards Stevens. The soldier pointed his rifle first at the man and then to the sky. The rifle blasted out over everyone's heads with a boom making one of the horses rear onto its hind legs, scattering the people around it.

'*Uncle John*!'

The crowd was blocked by the dragoons from moving up the narrow road. On the cart both Caleb Brown and Uncle John gazed out at the crowd with wide eyes.

'*Help, Danny*. Go to ye father. Tell him what's happened,' John Hewitt cried out, his face pale with lines of worry etched across it.

One of the revenue men turned and shouted something to him, threatening him with his pistol. Danny watched with despair as the cart was pulled further and further away. He had to get home. He had to find his father, he'd know what to do. But the cart would be going the same way. He couldn't get by. The water meadow was too wet at this time of the year for him to make a dash that way. He stood, bouncing on his feet, his body tight, as if he were tied to the end of a rope like a nervous horse waiting to break away.

Some of the people were making their way back towards the high street. Others remained, jeering for Stevens, who'd disappeared into his cottage. Danny moved forward.

'Ye traitor, Stevens.' A thin, old man was pushing his face up to the cottage window. Danny recognised him as Isaac Hooper, the neighbour of his friend, Will Gibbs. Isaac also knew Uncle John.

'What's happening, Mr Hooper? Why have they taken Uncle John and Mr Brown?'

The old man looked drained. His face creased, as if in pain.

'Danny, get ye father, as quickly as ye can, lad.' Isaac was swaying, he'd been drinking.

'I can't get past.'

'The dragoons'll let ye. Yer only a boy.'

'Where are they taking them?'

'Winchester.'

'But why?'

Isaac pushed his nose against the glass again.

'Tell me.' Danny pulled at Isaac's jacket. 'I need to know what to tell father.'

Isaac was shaking. 'He were, er… out on the river last night wi' Caleb.'

'And what happened?'

'We don't know. We can only think the revenue men must've stopped 'em.' He rapped on the glass again. 'Can only be for smugglin', what other reason could there be?'

'But father says Mr Stevens often lets the smugglers go.' Danny didn't think Isaac was telling him the whole

5

story. Then a voice spoke behind him.

'Your uncle's in trouble, Clarke.'

Danny felt a lurch in his stomach. He knew that voice. It belonged to someone he hadn't seen for a long time and certainly hadn't missed. A bully. Edmund Tarrant. He was the son of Sir Charles Tarrant, who owned much of the land locally and was the man his father worked for. Danny thought Edmund Tarrant was horrid. It was Edmund's fault that his friend, Will had run away the year before. He'd taunted Will, just for being poor. And just because Edmund's father had praised Will and himself, Edmund had set on Will, cutting his face.

'Can't think what to say, Clarke?'

'What do you know?'

'I know what your uncle's done.'

'What? Tell me.'

'You should know, your family are all criminals.'

'That's not true and my uncle's done nothing wrong.'

'So you think, Clarke. Well I can tell you now, he'll hang for what he's done.'

'Jump in the river and drown.'

'How *dare* you speak to me in such a way.' Edmund shoved Danny into the road, making him stagger and fall on his back, just missing a woman walking by with a baby. Danny leapt up and ran forwards, punching out at Edmund and catching him on his arm. Edmund swung a fist towards Danny's head; Danny ducked and threw a punch into Edmund's stomach. Edmund sucked in air with pain and swung his hand, his ring catching Danny's cheek. Danny was about to launch himself at Edmund again when he was grabbed from behind.

'Now, boys. I don't know what your row be about, but there been enough bother 'ere today.' Danny recognised the man's face, but couldn't remember his name. Isaac had also stepped forward. Both men kept their distance from Edmund, then walked away.

'When Sir Charles finds out about the coins he'll dismiss your father - if he ever gets home.'

'What do you mean?' Danny wiped his face with the back of his hand, a streak of blood made a line across it.

'You'll find out soon enough, shorty.' Edmund stared directly at Danny, spat on the ground and strode off holding his stomach.

The cart carrying Uncle John and Caleb was no longer visible and the dragoons were letting people move by. Danny needed to get home and speak with his father. What did Edmund Tarrant know about what had happened? Edmund was now mounting his horse. He turned to give Danny one last smirk and galloped away.

'Codshead!' Danny yelled after him and ran home as fast as he could.

Chapter 2

Who can help?

'*Mother*! *Father*!' Danny slung open the door of his cottage. It smelled smoky from the small fire crackling in the grate, so someone was home. He scanned the place, it was only small; mother must be outside. He rushed through the short passageway that led to the kitchen, shouting again.

'Danny, is that you?' Hannah Clarke appeared at the door.

'Father, where's father?' Danny slumped against the cupboard, panting.

'Whatever's the matter? What's happened to your cheek?'

'Uncle John. Uncle John's arrested, taken away, to Winchester.'

'What?'

'Yes. And Mr Brown, the blacksmith. Uncle John shouted to me to tell father. Father'll know what to do, won't he?'

'Well, yes, but …'

'Where is he? Is he at Cliff House? I, I can run there.'

The colour drained from Hannah Clarke's face. Her blue eyes filled with tears.

'Mamma.' Danny's sister, Sarah, had appeared at his mother's side and was tugging at her skirts.

'Mother? What is it? Shall I go to Cliff House?'

'No. No, Danny, your father's not there. He's gone away for a few days.' Hannah ran her hand through the hair under her white mob cap.

'What should we do, mother?'

'Let me *think*,' Hannah snapped. Sarah started to whimper.

Danny bit on his lip. 'What about Aunt Mary?'

'Oh, Mary, my poor sister, she needs to know.'

They heard the door open with a crash.

'That'll be Jack, he might have news, mother.' They rushed to the other room. 'Jack. What are people saying? What do you know?'

'They're saying Uncle John's been arrested. It doesn't make sense, mother. They say he's been smuggling, but they don't usually take them away so quickly. The whole town's talking about it.'

'I saw it. I was there. The revenue men took them. There were dragoons guarding them. I saw Uncle John and he shouted for help.'

'Let's get father, then.'

'Father's gone away.' Danny hung his head.

'We need help. We should go to Cliff House and ask Sir Charles,' Jack said. 'Come on.'

'*No*. He's the magistrate, he would have agreed the arrest.' Hannah lowered herself into the old rocking chair beside the fire.

'Can we send a message to father? Do we know where he's gone?'

'All I know is that he's gone with Monsieur Menniere.'

'Perinne's father? Perinne will know.' Danny's face brightened, Perinne was his friend. 'Shall I go there?' He lifted the latch on the door.

'Wait.' Hannah made towards the kitchen. 'We need

to tell your Aunt Mary. She may know someone who can help.' She reappeared with two lamps. 'Go, both of you. Take these to light your way.'

The winter sun had not appeared all day but now, in the late afternoon, the gloomy shroud had lifted to expose a jet-black sky. The air was as sharp as a needle prickling the skin. The two boys, wrapped warmly, followed the gravel track away from the village of Burton towards Hinton.

'I wish we had a pony,' Jack said. 'We'd get there much quicker.'

'Uncle John's cart must still be in town,' Danny said. 'Shall we go and get it and then go to Aunt Mary's? We'd have something to get about in.'

Jack stopped. 'It's an idea, Danny. But where would it be?'

'At the blacksmith's?'

'What if he hadn't taken it? Come on, Dan, we're wasting time. Let's run.'

Danny stumbled. Running on the rutted road was difficult. The night was clear, but the moon had yet to rise. The light from their lamps was of little use at speed. He found his feet then waited to catch his breath, which was streaming into the frosty air. It wasn't far to his aunt's now. He could see Jack's dark shape just ahead. He'd begun to ache from his scrap with Edmund Tarrant. He felt his cheek, the blood had dried. His mother hadn't asked any more about it, too shocked at the news he'd brought.

'Look, Dan. Cousin Betsy's there, that's her horse and cart.'

Chasing after Jack, Danny could see the cottage ahead, grey whispers of smoke rising over the thatch.

'*Betsy*!' Jack shouted.

'Jack, what are you doing here?' Cousin Betsy was outside wearing her coat and hat. 'And Danny too.'

'Is Aunt Mary home?' Danny asked, breathless.

'Yes, come on in.'

Aunt Mary was sitting beside the fire. 'Have you news of your Uncle John?'

'My father hasn't been home since going to town last night,' Betsy added. 'Mother's worried. Luckily I called around.'

Danny and Jack shot each other a glance. Danny began to shake.

'Uncle John's been arrested by the revenue men, Aunt Mary,' Danny said, his voice now quivering. 'He's been taken to Winchester.'

Aunt Mary gasped, bringing her hand to her mouth. Betsy dashed over to her, putting her arm around her mother, her own mouth wide with shock.

'I saw him taken away from the revenue officer's cottage. The dragoons were there. There was a big crowd. Everyone was shouting to let them go.'

'What have they said he's done?' Betsy asked.

'Smuggling, we think,' Jack answered.

'Was he alone?'

'He was with Mr Brown, the blacksmith,' Danny said.

'Caleb? But he's an honest man.' Aunt Mary was shaking her head. 'They both be. We need to go an' see Joshua Stevens, find out what this is all 'bout.'

The thought of whether you could be a smuggler yet still be honest flashed through Danny's mind, but he dismissed the idea; that didn't matter, they needed to get help, and quickly.

'Does your father know?' Aunt Mary asked.

'He's gone away,' Jack put in. 'Mother thought you might know someone who can help.'

'Then we must see Stevens.'

'It's getting late, it's dark.' Betsy wrapped her arms around herself and rocked to and fro. 'What will become of father?'

'We'll stop this, Betsy, we'll get to the bottom o' it, and I'm not waiting till the morning. This be fearful, Betsy. We'll borrow your cart. You stay here. Come on, boys. Let's get going.'

Betsy's little pony had struggled with the weight of the three, so Danny and Jack walked alongside the cart. Danny's back was aching where he'd been pushed into the road earlier. His legs were tired, too, after all the day's running, but he wouldn't let anyone know. He gritted his teeth and forged ahead. He had to help Uncle John.

It took over an hour to get to Christchurch. The darkness hadn't helped their journey though soon they'd reached the first wooden bridge that led into the town. Rush lights had been lit ahead and were casting flickering golden shadows across the road. Aunt Mary pulled up the cart and climbed down before Danny or Jack could help. She strode directly to the door where Danny had earlier seen the dragoon fire his rifle above the crowd. There was no sign of any soldiers now, but light from a candle could be seen through the window.

'Joshua Stevens, *open this door*.' Aunt Mary banged it with her fist making the handle rattle.

Danny had never seen Aunt Mary angry. Then Jack joined her, hitting the door hard then rapping on the window. The sound of the latch lifting made Aunt Mary step back. She put her hands on her hips and stood firm, her mouth pressed with purpose.

'What is it? What do you want?' A man's face appeared

through a small gap. It wasn't Stevens. 'The officer isn't here.'

'Then where be he?'

'I don't know.'

'Then let me in an' I'll wait till he gets back.' Aunt Mary tried to push open the door, but the man held it firm.

'Go away, come back in the morning.' The door closed and a bolt was pulled across.

'*Come back, open up.*' Aunt Mary pounded the door.

'It's no good, aunt.'

'What now, Aunt Mary?' Danny asked.

'Let's go an' see Bessie Brown, see what she knows. We can check the *George* too, you can be sure that Joshua Stevens be in an ale house. Gloating over his handiwork, no doubt.'

They found the entrance to the lane where the Browns had their smithy. Ahead Uncle John's cart stood, but the pony was gone. Behind was darkness, but for the dim glow colouring a small window close by. Aunt Mary approached the door and knocked urgently.

'Bessie, are you there? It be Mary Hewitt.'

Danny tried to peer through the window, but a curtain had been drawn. Mary rapped again, even louder this time.

'*Bessie.*'

The door opened and a round face appeared from inside. The woman pursed her lips, her face was red and blotched and she was stifling tears.

'Oh, Mary, Mary, it's awful, just awful. Come inside, tis bitter cold. I'll put a log on the fire, warm you up.' Bessie Brown opened the door wide then stopped as she saw the boys.

'It be me nephews, Jack an' Danny.'

They moved inside. Danny scanned the small room. The table was on its end. Chairs were piled into the corner and the rug was folded back. Candlesticks, cups and plates were strewn on the floor. It was a mess.

'Whatever's happened?'

'They came last evenin', the revenue men.'

'They did this?' Aunt Mary moved her hand in an arc. 'Whatever were they lookin' for?'

'I don't know it all, Mary. Caleb don't tell me everythin',' Bessie sighed, looking at Jack and Danny.

'You can speak, they knows what goes on,' Aunt Mary said. 'John's the same. He just said he were coming to town an' that were that. But we got to find out what's happened.'

Bessie sniffed and dabbed her eyes. Danny fetched her a chair. 'They went up river. Caleb spoke of takin' barrels to Avon. But it isn't the smugglin' - it's worse than that.' Bessie sat and put her head into her hands, shaking it from side to side. 'They pushed me about, askin' where Caleb was an' when I expected him back. I didn't know. One got angry, don't know who he were, I hadn't seen him before. Tall he was, had a kerchief tied across most of his face, but his eyes burned into me, like he were tryin' to look straight through me. Then Stevens came in, didn't say a word, even though we've known him fer years. They searched everywhere; the house, the smithy an' the stables. Turned everythin' upside down. They found moulds in the stable.'

'Moulds?' Aunt Mary stumbled backwards, catching hold of Jack. Both boys held her arms to stop her falling. 'That's not true - is it Bessie?'

'What are the moulds for?' Danny asked.

'For making things, Dan,' Jack answered. 'Like coins.'

'They were hidden at the back, with cuttin' tools an' metal an' pipes. I were there when they pulled 'em out. But I can't believe Caleb would do that, I can't, Mary. He's an 'onest man. But they found those moulds, an' the men've been taken away. What'll we do?'

'We must do somethin', Bessie or they're sure to hang.'

Danny fetched ale. It was all he could find. He felt helpless. His head spun thinking that he might never see

Uncle John again. Maybe he should go to Winchester, but that would be of no use, he doubted they would let him into the gaol. He needed to find out more of what had happened and what Edmund Tarrant had to do with it all. He hadn't mentioned Edmund to anyone yet.

'We'll go to see Philip Sweetland,' Bessie said, sipping her drink.

'Who's that?' Aunt Mary asked.

'The attorney.'

'Attorney? We can't afford that.'

'I've some money. What this means for Caleb, it'll be the same for John.'

'How will he help, Mrs Brown?'

'I'm not sure, Danny, but hopefully he knows the law enough to say what we should do.'

'Well, I'm not going to wait until morning, Bessie, I'm going to find Joshua Stevens, he'll know exactly what the charges are. There's been a misunderstanding, I'm sure o' that. We just need to put him right.'

Danny shifted on his feet.

'Are you all right?' Aunt Mary asked. 'Do you know something else?'

Danny nodded. 'Edmund Tarrant was there. When Uncle John was taken away. He said Uncle John would hang. He knows something.'

'But he be a boy, just like you,' Bessie said.

'He's not like me at all, Mrs Brown,' Danny snapped, touching his cheek.

'Did he do that?' Jack asked.

Danny nodded.

'Not a fight?'

'He said we were all criminals and Uncle John will hang for what he's done.'

'He'll be teasin', lad,' Bessie said. 'We'll find Stevens, I'm sure he'll explain.'

'He wasn't teasing, Mrs Brown.'

Jack screwed his face with distaste. 'If Edmund Tarrant's involved, then there'll be trouble.'

'I remember now,' Danny scowled. 'He mentioned coins. How did he know about that?'

Chapter 3

Edmund makes plans

Danny and Jack followed Aunt Mary and Bessie towards the *George*. If Joshua Stevens wasn't there they could speak with Joseph Martin, the landlord; he might know something. Bessie spotted him ahead near to the stables talking to the ostler.

'Come on, Mary, let's see if he's anythin' to say 'bout last night.'

Danny moved to follow the women, but Bessie stopped him. 'You boys stay here an' wait.'

Jack hunched his shoulders. Danny peered around. People didn't seem as jolly as usual, they were simply sitting and chattering. Most huddled beside the fireside. He looked for Beth, his friend Will's sister who worked here. She often overheard things, maybe she knew something, but he couldn't see her. Joseph Martin was shaking his head, his face tilted and his hand on Bessie's shoulder. Now Bessie was nodding. She then said something to Aunt Mary, who returned to the boys.

'I'm going to stay with Bessie tonight. Take the cart an' bring it back in the morning. See, you can get to work an' to school quicker.'

'But Aunt Mary, what's going to happen?'

'Joshua Stevens is nowhere to be seen, Danny. There's nothing more we can do 'til morning. Better for you to get home.'

'But…'

'Come on, Dan, do as Aunt Mary says.'

'But what should we tell mother?' Danny stood firm.

'Just say that I'm staying in town an' will go an' see the attorney with Bessie. Now go. It's getting late an' you boys shouldn't be about.'

Edmund Tarrant glanced across the table at his father, who was chewing on a piece of beef. He had him to himself, maybe for a few weeks. The meddling servant, James Clarke, wasn't around to get in the way of his plans. He'd been home from school for two months and a tutor had just been hired. Father had been angry about the school expelling him. It wasn't his fault, setting fire to the boat house hadn't been part of his plans. Once home, he'd asked to be allowed to go on a tour, visit France and Italy, maybe other places, but his father had refused. He couldn't understand why he'd have to wait, he was seventeen next year and surely father would be glad he was out of the way. Then he'd stumbled across the papers whilst looking for a book in the library, which doubled as his father's study. His father was careless, or maybe wasn't used to having him home again. What he'd seen could pave the way for him not only to go, but to have plenty to spend. Better still, he could leave Cliff House for years.

Sir Charles finished chewing. He pushed his fork around his plate in search of another mouthful.

'Edmund…'

He'd start with a year in Paris. Book rooms, tour the region, collecting paintings, silverware. Travelling in France didn't appear to be a problem for Yves Menniere. Edmund sneered to himself. At least that awful girl, Perinne and her mother had moved out.

'*Edmund*.'

'Er, yes, father?'

'You will help to organise the hunt at Christmas? We'll have a full house.'

'If you wish, father.'

'You can help with the delivery of the gifts,' Lady Elizabeth put in. She was picking at her food. 'The tenants rarely see you. Or we could provide a meal this year. You could do that.'

'Yes, mother.' He looked at her. She was frail and thin, the opposite of her round-faced husband who was tucking heartily into his meal. He remembered going with his parents each Christmas taking food to people living on their land. He'd managed to avoid the task as he'd got older, but perhaps it would be a chance to find someone he could use.

'It's time that you learned about the estate and the tenants. How to organise the servants. Deal with the purchasing.' Sir Charles wiped his lips with a cloth and took a sip of wine. 'James Clarke will arrange this.'

Edmund closed his large grey-green eyes. If he were being allowed more freedom and control of things it might make it more bearable being here. He'd have to put up with the servants. Although as soon as he was in charge Clarke's time at Cliff House would come to an end.

'I'm tired, may I take my leave and retire to my room?'

Lady Elizabeth leaned over and touched the back of Edmund's hand. Her fingers felt cold and bony. 'Of course, Edmund. Come to me in the morning and I'll show you what we need to do.'

Edmund climbed the wide staircase. Portraits of past

Tarrants hung on the walls. One showed him as a child with his parents. He stopped. He could still recall the time that it was painted. He was seven. Each morning when the artist was present, his mother had him dressed by his nurse in the green silk suit of the picture. On one of the mornings he'd slipped past the servants and gone out to the stables. Ursula, a gun dog, had had puppies and he'd wanted to play with them. When he'd been found the suit was dirty and the lace of the collar had been snagged. Father had been furious; that was the first time he'd hit him. Father had little patience with him, but as he'd grown this had lessened. The last time he'd been struck was over a year ago.

When he reached his room he closed the door behind him and crossed to the window. Coal was burning in the grate and the smell from this and the burning candles filled the gloomy air. He pulled the curtain aside. Outside the moon cast a pale shadow across the grounds. To the left he could make out the entrance to the ice house. Joseph, the butler, was climbing the steps, lamp in one hand and a basket in the other. Joseph had been kind to him, but his kindness had cooled recently. He undressed and climbed into bed. Tomorrow, once he'd found out what mother wanted him to do, he would take a ride, maybe as far as Ringwood. His father was weak. With Clarke out of the way it had been easy to persuade him to sign the warrant for the arrest of the men. Meekwick Ginn would be pleased with him.

John Hewitt could see a muted glow ahead and guessed that it was from the city of Winchester. They'd travelled in silence, the revenue men halting any conversation. They'd been given blankets, even their captors had to wrap up. At least they hadn't wanted us to freeze to death, he thought. It had been a long drive. Signs of life had burst from alehouses as they'd passed through villages, but as the night wore on it had faded to shadowy silence. Now people began to appear, even at this late hour. From windows dim candle light glimmered. He had a watch, but it was too dark to check the time.

'Who passes?' A voice shouted from the darkness of the city's south gate.

'Prisoners.'

'How many?'

'Two.'

'Carry on.'

'Caleb,' John whispered, nudging his friend, who had dozed off. Caleb, woke and shivered, making the cart sway.

'Keep still,' a shout came from the front.

Rush lamps that had lit the roadway so far were now replaced with oil lamps and there were pavements. Houses in the new style lined the road, others were in the process of being built. John had been to Winchester, but not for a long time. Soon the cart was waiting by a set of gates. The sound of keys rattling were heard before a figure appeared to heave first one side, then the other. The driver took the cart through and John heard a clatter behind them as the entrance was secured again.

'Get down.'

John's legs were stiff with both cold and sitting for so long. Caleb also climbed shakily down. The two revenue men each stood beside one of them. Another man appeared, a tall, long-faced man with a thick brown coat and wide-brimmed hat.

'This way.'

They were led through a door and along a dim corridor lit by candles, which were set in sconces along the walls. The air was a foul mix of sweat and tallow. The building was quiet except for the occasional sound of coughing that echoed about the high ceilings. At the end of the corridor to the right was a small room, brightly lit, and with a fire in the grate. A man was sitting behind a desk. The first man led them in and then signalled to the revenue men, who turned and left.

'What be we here for?' Caleb snapped.

'Quiet. Speak only when the gaoler demands an answer,' the tall man growled back.

'I think you know very well.'

John gave Caleb a worried glance. He knew people who'd been in prison. He'd heard it was easiest to go along with things.

'The charges against you are high treason. If found guilty, you'll no doubt hang. And …'

'What charges?' Caleb's face had turned red, his eyes wide and fearful. 'We ain't been told. We've a right to know.'

'I told you, *quiet*.'

John took a deep breath. 'Master Gaoler, it's true. We were seized, taken to a cellar, kept there till we were brought here. We've not been told what the charges are.'

The gaoler checked the men in turn. 'I have instructions. I will speak to you both tomorrow. I advise that until then you think about your crimes and tell me the truth. Take them to the cell.'

'But.'

'Hush, Caleb.'

'Follow me, no speaking.' The man who'd brought them in ducked his head as he stepped through the door and led Caleb Brown and John Hewitt away.

The cell was small. There were two low beds and little else. The floor was stone and there was a single narrow window. The only light came from the candles in the passageway and the milky hue from the moon.

'What about a drink and somethin' to eat. We been

travellin' hours.'

'You'll be brought gruel at first light.'

'An' a blanket, we'll freeze in here.'

'You want favours, you have to pay for them.'

'How much? Bread, ale an' a blanket.'

'Shilling. You'll get bread and a towel tomorrow. There's some pie, ye can have some of that.'

'Shillin'?'

'Yes. Each.'

'Fer two? Sixpence be enough for that.'

John dug deep into his pocket. Luckily he'd been paid for another job just before they'd set out to Avon. He gave the man the coins. The man checked them, feeling their weight and inspecting the image of the king then left, locking the door behind him.

'Treason, John. What do he mean, treason? What are they sayin' we done?'

'I don't know.'

'An' what 'appened to Joshua Stevens? He be there one minute, then gone the next and turns up again by the door watchin' us go.'

'That's a strange one, Caleb. Stevens is a fair man. But it's best we do as they say.'

The man returned with the blankets and food, then left, snuffing out the candles as he went. They ate by what little light the moon gave them.

'Better try to get some sleep.' Caleb had pulled his hat down over his face so that only his beard was showing beneath it. His coat then the blanket wrapped tightly around him, it was as if he'd crawled into his own cave, shutting out the horror of where they were.

The damp clung to John Hewitt's skin like sodden stockings. Whatever would befall them from now on? It was something that he dared not think about.

Chapter 4

London, December 1781

'The revenue men at East Parley seized the brandy and were taking it to the customs house when the brutes struck.'

James Clarke watched as Yves Menniere raised his eyebrows as if in surprise. Their trip to London had been uneventful, but the real purpose of their journey would soon be revealed. They knew of this event. It had been reported in the newspaper. His son, Danny had pointed it out to him. They let the man continue.

'The gang was on horseback, faces blackened or covered, at least twelve, if not more. They all had weapons, blunderbusses, muskets and pistols. Many officers were injured and the gang snatched back their goods. But we'll catch them, the rewards have been set.' The man banged his fists onto the arms of his chair. 'Smuggling all along our coast is a big problem. It's costing much-needed revenue. The war in America means our armies are too stretched to get the problem under proper control. And your town, well, it's the perfect place for this criminality. A large harbour and miles of beaches make for easy getaways. A lot to patrol.'

'There is an office and a commissioner. The chief

revenue officer, he also seems to do a good job,' Yves said.

'Hmph. We know the man. It's obviously not enough to stem the lawlessness there, it spreads across the New Forest and the heaths of Dorsetshire. The coast there has no protection. You need a barracks at Christchurch. I'm sure you'd agree?'

'I have been at the town not two years, it is a quiet place, but I do know of problems with the smuggling gangs.'

'Well, it's a subject that needs attention.' The man let out a *tss* of breath. 'What I have to tell you about is even more serious than barrels of wine and spirits and bales of tobacco.' He rose and began to pace the room, wringing his hands as if washing them. The room was large and square with good furniture. The walls held shelves full of leather-backed books. James' eyes followed him. He was well dressed and wore a short, grey wig. His face ruddy and serious. Behind him, through the leaded window, the shape of Westminster Abbey was set against a brightening sky. How long would the task agreed by Sir Charles Tarrant take them? He'd want to be home for Christmas or, if not, most certainly Twelfth Night. That gave them just two or three weeks. If travelling was involved, it would take time.

The man became still, his voice low and urgent. 'What I am about to tell you is of great concern to the king and to parliament. Nothing must be spoken of it outside of this room other than between the two of you.' The man drew a deep breath and pursed his lips. 'Like others from towns similar to yours, Edward Allan, the Commissioner of Customs at Christchurch, was asked to listen for news of unusual cargoes and activities or new gangs. We did not give a reason only that it was most important to pass on any information they came across. Allan sent a message. He said that since the summer he'd been made aware of more frequent loads being transported up the river to a place called Avon. At first there was nothing to suggest that this was illegal activity, though he had officers keep watch. It turned out to be only a small tub boat crewed by just two or three local men. Then he was called to the town hall. The mayor said he was concerned that forged coins were being passed at the local market and it seemed to be more frequently over the past months. Allan wondered if it were coins that we were seeking. We thought there might be a link between this and our problem. We asked him to come to London, bring some of the coins. We have an expert, Mr Young. He would look at the coins, ask questions of Allan. He was here yesterday. They weren't what we were seeking, but shortly after this a messenger arrived saying two men were to be arrested at Christchurch.' The man looked down at his feet, he was twisting a ring on his finger round and around. 'Large amounts of forged coins, mostly gold, are getting into the country. We now believe they come in through your town, then brought here to London. We think they're concealed in barrels to avoid danger of theft on the turnpikes. This is not simply a few now and then, but in large quantities.' He lifted his hand and rubbed the back of his head.

'What is it that you want us to do?' Yves spoke.

'Visit France. Monsieur Menniere, you have contacts in Paris and indeed much of the north of the country. One of our agents has uncovered details and says he's close to finding out where the coins are coming from and who is behind this. He also says people are getting suspicious of him and he wants nothing more to do with it. I will give you an address in Lille. Our agent will send a message and arrange to meet you. He will tell you all he knows. We need to find the people responsible and stop them.'

'We might better find a needle in a bottle of hay,' Yves said. 'What of the French authorities, are they to be informed?'

'We are still at war with France, though half-way across the world. We hope to do this quietly, with only a few agents and pay rewards to informants. First we need to find out who they are. If the coins are coming in through Christchurch there could well be a local connection. You might recognise names.' The man sucked in a deep breath. 'King Louis himself could have agreed the forgeries to damage our economy.' He gazed out of the window and, after a pause, continued. 'We believe you to be the best men for the task ahead. Monsieur Menniere, you are a respected architect and it would not be unusual for you to be travelling with a manservant. Sir Charles Tarrant speaks highly of Clarke. Who could think you are anything other than visiting or on business, though the task is not without its dangers, I'm sure you realise.'

James held his breath. As a servant of Sir Charles Tarrant it was not his place to speak, but the task sounded folly for ordinary men like him and Yves Menniere. A gang like this would be ruthless.

The man noticed the change of expression on James' face. 'We are not asking you to take action, simply assist in identifying the culprits.'

Yves looked directly into the man's eyes. 'Then we need to know more of who it is safe to contact and of the arrangements for our travel - if we are to take on this mission.'

'You will go?'

'Clarke and I will need to discuss this.'

'Then make a quick decision. You'll be well paid, and more if you find the culprits and they are caught and convicted. I have a coach leaving for Dover tonight. You need to decide now.' The man moved towards the door. 'I will have some drinks brought and perhaps a bite to eat.'

A few doors away, two boys stepped out into the street. The frosty air nipped around their faces. One, tall and handsome, was frowning. The other, a black boy, was pulling a hat over his ears.

'What do yu expect, Will?'

'They need to listen.'

'He didn't say no.'

'He didn't say yes.'

'Come on, Sir George said it will take time.'

'But they're not listenin', Nathan. They're laughin' 'cause we're boys.'

'Let's go and get some coffee.'

'Let's not.'

'It *freezing*.'

'We need to save our money. It's not goin' to last the way we're spendin'.'

'We'll speak wi Missus Cooper at the anti-slavery group. We see about delivering de pamphlets and what dey want us to do. She said we'd be paid.'

'Hmmph, errand boys.'

'Come on, Will. Yu losing heart now?'

Will stopped dead and glared at Nathan. 'No, but ye are.'

'Dat not true. Yu know what it means to me. But we are boys, Will. Like yu say, dey won't listen. We need to find folk who want to change things and help dem - like we doing with Missus Cooper.'

'Sorry, Nathan.' Will stopped and leaned against a nearby wall.

'I know yu want to do dis, I do too, Will.' Nathan put his hand on Will's shoulder. 'Dis country already say slaves cannot be sent back to owners, things are happening here. We saw Mr Sharp speak. He's doing good work.'

'I know, it's just the beginning.'

Nathan faced his friend; he sighed. 'We tired, Will. It's been three months. The group can manage without us for a while. Let's go back to Christchurch. What about your mama? She need yu home. Yu promised your father, yu told me dat lots when we were in America.'

Will nodded in agreement and hung his head. Before his father had died, he'd promise to look after his mother, despite his young age. That was over four years ago, when he was eleven, now he was fifteen. He should be with her.

'We take dat room again. We find jobs.'

Will's face brightened as thought filled his mind. 'It'd be the first Christmas since father died that mother won't need to queue fer bread at the Priory.'

'Queue for bread?'

Will sniffed. 'We were poor when father were alive, Nathan. When he died, it got worse. The town gives bread to the poor on Christmas mornin'.'

'Sorry, Will.'

Will stood away from the wall, stretched his back and gave Nathan a look that told him Will had made a decision. 'I 'ave money now, an' you're right, we need to find work.'

'Have we enough for coffee?' Nathan smiled, pleased to see his friend perk up.

The boys crossed the narrow street and pressed their faces against the window of a coffee shop. Inside was a cloudy sky of grey wigs amongst a fog of tobacco smoke. They shook their heads and carried on towards the riverside. They stopped beside a low wall and watched the watermen carrying people and goods to and fro on the Thames. One ornate boat approached a set of river stairs nearby. A queue of people moved aside as a sedan chair, carried by two men in golden clothing, set it down. A man stepped out followed by a small boy. The boy was also dressed in gold and wore an elaborate gold hat with feathers. It was a black boy.

Nathan hissed through his teeth. 'That boy may be well fed and clothed, but he's just a pet, he's not free.'

'An' that's why we need to do this work, you should know, look what happened to you.'

'Hmm, Massa Williams, when he found me he was angry. I was lucky. He told me I was a boy like any other boy. That I should learn to read and write and have a job and do what I want to do.'

'See, we need that for everyone and for slaves to be free people. We'll help with the pamphlet then go home. We can learn from this, make our own pamphlets; spread the word.'

'We won't let this go, Will. Look, there's a chestnut seller, let's get some.'

Will rolled his eyes. 'We'll never be rich.'

The warmth of the brazier kept the boys close by as they chewed.

'It'll be good to see everyone again.'

'Wonder if Danny has had any more adventures?'

Will laughed. 'He does seem to attract trouble, e'en if he doesn't mean to. An' maybe Perinne 'as moved out of Cliff House.'

'Yu sweet on her, Will?'

Will gave Nathan a playful punch on the arm and grabbed the last of the chestnuts. 'C'mon. Let's get back to our rooms. We'll see Mrs Cooper in the morning when we've finished. Tell her what happened today.'

A sudden noise made the boys turn. A man with a cart which had turned and spilled its load was shouting after a coach and horses that was speeding along. The boys stepped back as it rumbled past them.

'Dey in a hurry.'

Will's face widened with surprise. 'That were Danny's father, an' Perinne's too!'

Chapter 5

Where is Joshua Stevens?

Danny shivered and pulled his blanket around his shoulders.

'Come on, Dan, get up.' Jack tugged at the cover, but Danny clung on. 'Come *on*. You'll be late.'

'I'm not well.'

'Mother won't fall for that one.'

'It's too cold.'

'The fire's lit downstairs, can't you smell it?'

'How can I go to school after what's happened? We need to help get Uncle John back.'

Danny threw off the bedclothes and grabbed his shirt and breeches. Once dressed he went to the small window and drew the curtains apart. He peered into the darkness. He hated winter mornings. The school room would be freezing, besides he wouldn't be able to concentrate. He opened the nearby dresser drawer and took out woollen stockings. He pulled them on. They felt soft against his legs, which soon began to warm.

Downstairs, candles flickered and the face of the clock showed it would soon chime seven. Danny grabbed some bread from the table and sat in the rocking chair by the fireside. It had been his grandpa's chair. Grandpa had died in the summer. He stroked the chair arm, then his heart jumped at the thought that he could lose Uncle John, too.

'You'll need to wrap up today, Danny,' his mother said, handing him a cup of weak tea.

Danny breathed in the steam, lifted the cup to his lips and sipped. The liquid slipped down his throat in a welcome burst of warmth.

'I've put two pairs of stockings on, mother.'

'A good idea. I want you to come home straight away today, no lingering with your friends. With father away I need help.'

'But what about Uncle John?'

'You said Aunt Mary was seeing the attorney with Mrs Brown today. I expect Joshua Stevens will be able to explain things. There has to have been a misunderstanding. I'm sure it'll be sorted out soon.'

'But I could help.' Danny cast a worried glance at his brother.

'We could ask other people questions, mother. Some of the, er, fishermen and old Isaac. Danny saw him yesterday and he's a friend of Uncle John's.'

'You boys are not to get involved.' Hannah's voice raised as she wagged her finger at her sons. 'Haven't you learned your lesson, Danny Clarke? And you, Jack, you shouldn't encourage your brother. He's been too close to some bad people recently.'

'Yes, mother.' Jack bit on his lips and looked down at the floor. He was wrapped up and ready to set out for town where he worked for Mr Oake, a watchmaker. He tipped his head to beckon Danny. 'I'm going, Danny. Cousin Betsy's pony needs to be hitched to the cart.'

Danny drank the last of his tea and carried the cup into the back room. His coat was hanging up behind the door and felt cold, so he lifted it off the peg and carried it with his things into the parlour. He opened the coat and held it in front of the fire. When the coat had warmed he slipped it on, wrapped his scarf around his neck, and, lastly, topped his fair, curly hair with a woollen hat. He stepped outside. Bare-branched trees formed lace with the light of the dawn. Jack was ahead, driving down the road. Danny called out and ran to catch up. Some cottages were still burning candles and wood smoke hung in the still air. The journey to school was quick in the cart. The pony trotted briskly and they were soon close to the first of the two bridges that took the road into town over the River Avon. Here the smoky smell from homes mingled with the hops stewing in local breweries. Jack stopped close to the pathway leading to the church. Danny made to jump off the cart, but held back. The school entrance was a short walk away. He would be leaving in the spring and an apprenticeship was being sought. Reverend Jackson was their tutor again. Back in the summer it had been a man called Thomas Walton. It had turned out that Walton had also been working for a man called Stone from Gloucestershire, trying to make money from smuggling. Walton had tricked Danny into helping him and he'd been in fear of his life until he'd told his friends, Will and Perinne, of what had happened. Perhaps his mother was right, he should leave things to the grown-ups.

'It's early. I think I'll come with you to take the cart. I want to see how Aunt Mary is.'

'All right.'

A man on horseback was coming alongside. Jack let him pass by then set the pony moving again. Both the rider and the cart turned into the lane towards the forge. Bessie Brown appeared from the door as if she'd seen them all approaching. The man spoke out as the boys drew up the cart.

'No fire Mrs Brown?' The man asked.

'I'm sorry, Mr Jenkins, Caleb aint 'ere today.' Bessie inspected the man. She knew him from previous visits and wondered why he didn't know of yesterday's events. Everyone else seemed to have heard.

'Pity, he's the best blacksmith around and Lampeter here trusts him like no other.' He patted the horse's neck. 'When will he return?'

Bessie shrugged. Perhaps she should say something.

'Are you all right?'

'Caleb were arrested, Mr Jenkins. He were at the revenue officer's cottage, but he's been taken away on a charge we know nothin' about. I'm off to see Philip Sweetland, this mornin'.'

'What does Joshua Stevens have to say? Surely he can explain.'

'Couldn't find 'im. But I s'pose I should try again.'

'Well I have to say that I am most surprised at this. Caleb has always been a good soul.'

'He still is,' a voice chirped behind them.

'Mary, this is Mr Jenkins.'

'Sir.' Mary Hewitt bobbed her head.

'Try Stevens again. Where is he being kept?'

'They,' Mary put in. 'My husband's been taken too.'

'Winchester.'

'Then the matter is indeed serious. I am most sorry about this, Mrs Brown. I have to get a shoe for Lampeter somewhere, but if I can be of any help, just ask. I live in the cottage next to the well at Stanpit; send a message.' At that the man nudged the horse's haunches and rode away.

'Who be he, Bessie?'

'Not sure. Nor how he'd be able to help. But his idea of goin' seein' Stevens again is a good one. I'll just feed the pony and we'll get our coats on. It's bitter again. The Lord only knows how poor Caleb and John are.'

The two boys had climbed down from the cart. 'What shall we do with the pony, Aunt Mary?' Jack said.

'Walk him into the stable,' Bessie said. Me an' yer aunt have business to do.'

'We're off to see Stevens.'

Danny opened the stable door and Jack took the pony from the trap and hitched him inside the stalls. Danny wheeled in the cart. When they'd done they said their goodbyes.

'That's the man who answered the door to me yesterday,' Mary said, pointing to a figure leaving the revenue officer's cottage and making his way towards them. He passed without speaking, head down.

This time the door was opened promptly.

'Ah, Toby Cox.'

'Mrs Brown.'

'I wish to speak with Joshua.'

'He's not here.'

'I don't believe that. I called yesterday, he must be back.'

'Well, er…'

'Be he still abed?'

'I, er...'

'Go an' fetch 'im; *now*.' Bessie held her hands firmly on her hips and scowled.

'I don't think…'

'Now.' Mary stepped forward.

Cox disappeared into the building, returning minutes later surprise drawn across his face. 'He isn't here. His bed hasn't been slept in.'

Danny was relieved when school was over. He'd tried to work hard so as to make the time pass quickly. He jogged down the high street. Despite his mother saying he'd not to get involved, there was one person who might know something. He knew where Isaac Hooper lived, next door to Will. He wished Will were here. At least he'd know people to ask and no one would bother him or make him go home and do chores.

He turned down the little lane. No one was about. Isaac's cottage looked scruffy next to Will's, which had been repaired last year as a reward for Will helping to solve a mystery and find the parts to a mysterious machine. What adventures Will had had. Gone to America, met Nathan his new friend and was now in London. Maybe he should go to London instead of staying here in Christchurch, perhaps there were more interesting apprenticeships there. He reached Isaac's cottage and knocked on the door. He rubbed at the glass of the dirty window and pressed his nose against it.

'He's not there,' a voice called. 'Well, it be young Danny.'

'Mrs Gibbs, are you well?'

'I heard 'bout yer uncle an' Caleb Brown. Terrible, can't be true.'

'I'm looking for Isaac. To ask him if he knows anything.'

'He'll be out lookin' fer work. He'll start at the *George* I expect. Have ye tried there? He's been stampin' about, he's mighty upset. Beth's there, call in and see 'er.'

'Thanks.' Danny set off, then turned. 'Have you heard from Will, Mrs Gibbs?'

She shook her head. 'Not for a while. 'Bout time he came home.'

Danny couldn't spot Isaac at the *George* and Beth was busy, so he thought he'd go to the Brown's forge next. Aunt Mary might still be there and he wanted to find out what the attorney had said. He didn't want to be too late home. His mother would be angry. He rapped on the door and Bessie Brown appeared. She let him in.

'Ah, Danny, your aunt's about to leave. Jack will take back your uncle's cart later. Come in.'

Aunt Mary was standing in the small room beside the fire putting on her coat.

'What's happened? What did Mr Sweetland say?'

Aunt Mary shook her head. 'He is going to find out what the charges are, but no one can find Joshua Stevens. He's the one who made the arrest, but he's gone missing. There were another officer there that night, an' when Caleb were taken away. He's from Poole, not sure what part he played. Without Joshua Stevens we don't know what to do next.'

Edmund spotted Simon Slate's horse. He rode across the gravelly headland track towards the Haven Inn where it was tethered. Simon, a fair-haired boy, was crouched at the edge of the water. The sun was out now, but the day was still bitter.

'Simon!'

The boy turned his head, saw Edmund and returned to staring into the water.

'*Hey*, Simon.' Edmund dismounted and led his horse to the edge of the harbour entrance at Muddiford. The water rippled and a wake washed ashore as a coasting vessel made its way through the narrow channel.

'How long are you home for?'

'For good. I'm to have a tutor. Don't know why, I don't need one,' Edmund laughed. 'What about you?'

'Return after Christmas. Why aren't you going back?'

'Not seen you for months. What are you doing?'

'Just thinking. You haven't answered my question, Edmund.'

'Got thrown out.'

'Again? What for this time?'

'Setting the boathouse on fire.'

Simon stood. 'What? On purpose?'

'A sort of, er, accident,' Edmund smirked.

'You're getting worse, Edmund.'

'Well, I won't be around here for long. I'm going on a tour. Europe. For at least two years.'

'What, with your parents?'

'No, I was hoping you'd come with me.'

'Me?'

'Why not?'

'I don't have the money for one thing. And we can't go alone at our age.'

'I'm nearly seventeen. And I'll pay.'

Simon laughed. 'You're sixteen. And how will you pay? I don't know how much your father gives you, but I'll wager it won't be enough for two of us, not for that long.'

'Don't worry about that. I have some money and plans for a lot more. We'll go next summer, I'll pay for my tutor to come, that way father has no reason to say no.'

'Apart from wanting to know where you got the money. Where are you getting it from?'

'Can I trust you, Simon? Can you keep secrets?'

'I've kept plenty for you so far.'

'That's true.'

'Well, are you going to explain?'

Edmund tied the horse's reins to a nearby tree and sat down on a boulder. He scanned the bay, breathing in the fresh air.

'Do you know what goes on here, Simon?'

'What do you mean?'

'On these beaches and in this harbour. Smuggling. There's big money to be had, and I'm going to have my share.'

'Smuggling?' Simon lurched into a cackling laugh.

Edmund kicked shingle towards his friend. 'I don't mean I'm doing it, fool, I'll be investing some money to make even more.'

'And how are you going to do that?'

'I have a contact.'

'For goodness sake Edmund, grow up. Those people are bad, you could get yourself killed.'

'Not if you keep your head and stay out of the way. You just fund it. It's called venturing – and I'm going to be a venturer. I've already started.'

'What do you mean?'

'Those smugglers caught yesterday. That was me. I should get a big reward.'

'That's not venturing.'

'No, but it's getting me known for helping the customs, then they won't suspect me.'

Simon laughed. 'I don't believe you Edmund, you've a head full of dreams. Anyway, what do you mean that it was you?'

'I helped a customs officer, Mr Byng.'

'Edmund, those men are going to hang.'

'Then they shouldn't have been smuggling.'

'But you've said that's how you want to get rich.'

'I won't be doing the smuggling. I'll just be someone who loans money.'

'Where will you get it from to loan out? You're not going to steal off your father, are you?'

'That's the thing. I've got money. All my own.'

'How?'

'I made it.'

'Don't tell me you've got a job.' Simon shook his head and chuckled.

'No.' Edmund looked around him. 'I *made* it.'

Chapter 6

Smugglers meet

Meekwick Ginn found a quiet nook of the Woolpack Inn. He propped his stick against the whitewashed wall and settled down with his back to the door. He didn't want to go to Christchurch, he'd been only a few times in the past year. He was well-known to local smugglers, some had worked for him in the past, but after recent events he needed to keep away. Sopley was close enough. He heard the latch and felt a cold draught around his legs, then he caught the smell of sweat.

'Mr Ginn.'

'Hmmph,' Ginn grunted without turning.

'It's done.' The man drew a stool across from Ginn and sat.

'Tell me more.'

Ethan Byng sniffed and leaned forwards. 'We hid moulds and other gear at the back of the blacksmith's forge. Made sure Stevens found them.'

'How? I told you to keep your head low. The revenue mustn't be able to identify any of you.'

'Note under the door.'

'And the moulds, where did you get those?'

'Your young friend,' Byng sneered.

Ginn made a low growl. 'You find it amusing, Byng? We could all be hung if we're found out.'

'I don't like those men being taken any more than you, Ginn, but if it's not them it'd be us.'

Ginn sniffed. 'The boy's news gave us the warning, we should be grateful for that.'

'He's desperate to help. He thinks I'm with the customs. That uniform I made comes in useful.'

'Hmm. At least that worked, telling him I'd arrange a meeting with an officer.' A smirk creased Ginn's chalk-white face. 'Did the boy say where he got the moulds from?'

'He said they'd been at the back of the stables at Cliff House for years. Probably been seized by Tarrant at some time. That's if he's telling the truth; a snake in the grass that one, if you ask me.'

'I'm not. I hope he doesn't change his mind and go snivelling to his father. If he does, you're on your own.'

'You'll swing with us all Ginn, he went to you, not to me.'

Ginn pushed his face just inches away from Byng baring a row of rotten teeth. 'All I've done is pass on payments.'

Byng grabbed Ginn by his scarf. 'I don't believe that,' his voice lowered to a whisper of foul breath which puffed across Ginn's face. 'You supplied the bad coins for the last payment. My men are doing your bidding.'

'Gentlemen, I'll not have fightin' in here. An' how 'bout buyin' some drinks?'

The pair settled again keeping their eyes locked on each other.

'Brandy,' Ginn hissed. 'And get some wood on that fire, it's freezing in here.'

'Ale for me.'

They spoke no more until the drinks were in front of them.

'Tell me about the men they arrested.'

'They'd delivered the barrels as before,' Byng began. 'They were caught on their return to town. Your young friend had ensured his father signed the warrants for their arrest.'

'Why did you pick them? Why not someone else?'

'Turns out the revenue were having them watched. We didn't know about the gold, when you told us it made sense. If the men had the bad coins and moulds, it would all point to them.'

'They'll talk. They'll deny everything.'

'They're known smugglers. They only know where the drop off is. We're collecting the barrels they sank tonight, so if they do tell, there'll be nothing to find. And the rest, it's their word against the revenue.'

'It was a risk.'

'They don't know about me.'

'Are you sure? The Christchurch gangs work together these days. And what about Stevens? He'll be alert. The men may already have spoken to him.'

'Stevens has been dealt with. No one will hear from him for a long time – maybe never again.'

'*Ah, s*ent him on a journey, eh? An old trick.'

'You said not to harm him. We should have just finished him off, you're too soft on the revenue, Ginn.'

Ginn ran his hand over his pale face and took a deep breath. 'You need to make arrangements for the next shipment.'

Byng took a long drink from his tankard and shook his head. 'You need to help. Find us a carrier, we'll do the rest.' Byng leaned into Ginn. 'And, we want a bigger payment, this is dangerous.'

'Hmmph. When's the next due?'

'Nine days. Plenty of time.' Byng rose. 'We'll wait to hear from you. Then find yourself another gang.'

'Beth, 'ows ye mother?'

'She's fine, Isaac. She doesn't like this cold weather, though.'

'Nor any of us. The *Dove*'s due in, will ye be there?'

Beth smiled. The *Dove* was the name of the coasting vessel that travelled between the town quay and London. Its arrivals depended upon its journey. Her brother, Will and his friend Nathan had managed to get cheap passage to London back in the summer. She hoped he'd return soon, she didn't like him being there, he was only fifteen.

''Ave ye heard from Will?'

'No, not a word.' Beth's heart felt heavy. He should be here with her and their mother. Since their father had died, Will helped bring in income. He ran away to America nearly two years ago and returned in June with a new friend and big ideas.

'Thank you for letting me know, Isaac. I'll walk with you, let me get my hat and coat.'

The little man shuffled on his feet to keep warm, pulling his worn coat around his thin frame. He smiled as Beth reappeared.

'Are you working today, Isaac?'

'Goin' to 'elp with the unloading and deliver coal.'

'It's hard for you, I know.'

'Aye, but I keep meself from the poor house.'

'It's a bad affair about Caleb Brown and the other man.'

'John Hewitt.'

'You know him?'

'For many years, Beth. We were at sea together.' Isaac tugged his collar closer to his neck and glanced behind him towards the end of the gravelly lane. Caleb and John had left him beside the bare willows that grew at the river's

43

edge. He'd been lucky, - not for the first time. And it hurt his gut that John was in such trouble.

'But he's not from Christchurch?'

'Lives out at Hinton.'

'Ah.'

'He's young Danny's uncle, Will's friend.'

'Poor Danny. And Bessie. Coining, that's what's bein' said.'

'Aye, but I don't believe it for one minute.' Isaac's voice raised, then lowered again. 'John Hewitt's a good man.'

'So what's being done about it?'

'Bessie's got an attorney. Some of us are getting together to see if we can do anythin'.'

'Soon I hope.'

'Today, now.'

The pair cut through the graveyard of the church, past tumbling walls and by the old mill to the quayside. There was no sign of the *Dove* yet, but a few fishing boats were tied to posts. A group of men stood by one. It was the *Solomon*.

'Hope Will comes home soon,' Isaac said, as he continued walking.

Beth sat on a low wall beside the watermill and watched as Isaac joined a group of men just a few feet away. The cold seeped through her woollen coat. She rubbed her gloved hands together watching the harbour and listening to the men.

'Isaac, any news from John's family?'

'Mary's been about, Guy, but I ain't seen her. Has Stevens turned up?'

The men shook their heads. The water lapped against the shore, littering it with strands of broken reed. The boat's master, Joe Hardyman, was passing boxes off the side. Guy Cox was loading them onto a cart. The smell of salt and fish drifted on the air.

'Has ye cousin said anything about the charges?' Isaac's

eyes fixed on Guy.

'He's busy after that gang at Parley.'

'Won't have much luck there.' A tanned man with light brown hair stepped forwards.

'Why's that, Adam?'

'You haven't heard? Rewards have been set. They'll be laying low.'

''Til the next time,' Guy said. 'Anyway he's gone to the cottage this mornin', seein' what he can find out.'

'That's the last box, Guy,' Master Hardyman called from the boat.

Guy nodded. 'Can't be long, men. Need to get these delivered around town.'

'So, did Caleb mention coins to anyone?' Adam Litty looked around the gang of men.

'Not to me,' Guy answered.

'Falsehood, lies,' Isaac spat. 'But who's spreadin' 'em?'

'And why?' Guy added.

'What was the job they were on?' Adam asked.

'Somethin' Henry Lane set 'em up with.' Isaac looked around the quayside. There were few people about, none near enough to hear anything said. Beth was still there. She was looking across to the marshes, deep in thought. 'Where is he anyway?'

Guy hunched his shoulders. 'Not seen him. Could it be him?'

Adam put a hand on Isaac's arm. 'Do you know anything else about the job, Isaac?'

'Were a simple job. Word comes in, they met a boat on the 'arbour an' took the goods up river.'

'Where to?'

'Not sure.' The others didn't know he'd been out with John and Caleb and knew where the pool was. He'd keep that to himself for now. He wasn't sure who he could trust.

'Why didn't Henry do it himself?'

'He don't 'ave a boat.'

'Look,' Guy said, 'Henry's here now, we can ask him.'

A man wearing a tri-corn hat and russet-coloured coat walked towards the gang. His grey hair was tied back and lay on his collar. His long nose had broken red lines that ran out onto his cheeks. Isaac pushed himself forwards, but Adam held him back.

'Henry. We were just wonderin' 'bout that job ye passed on to Caleb.'

'Aye. Feel bad about it.' He shook his head. 'It would've been me caught.'

'Isaac was telling us as you came. Where's the place the goods were taken to?'

Isaac glared at Henry. Henry took in a deep breath before answering.

'A pool at Avon. It were barrels. The job was to take them to the pool and leave them in the water. The payment was left under a rock nearby.'

'So, no one saw them collected?' Adam asked.

'Moonrakers,' Isaac snorted.

'Who set it up?' Adam narrowed his eyes at Henry.

'The captain of the *Glory* stopped me one night, 'bout six months since. Said it were brandy and could I take it.'

'And who's paying?' Guy scoffed.

'Don't know. Ginn usually ventures the *Glory's* runs.'

There was a grumble of moans and sighs.

'You know you're going to get paid if Ginn's behind it,' Henry bit on his lip.

'What did ye get involved with him again for, Henry?' Adam rolled his eyes. 'The man's as bad as they get. An' it's always others who get caught.' Adam lifted off his hat, scratched his head and put the hat on again. 'Someone needs to talk to him, but it isn't going to be me.'

46

'We done *nothin'*.'

'The moulds were found in your stable with dies for guineas and cutting tools.'

'My job needs cutting tools, but the rest be put there by the revenue.' Caleb slammed his chain-bound hands onto the table. A gaoler grabbed him from behind and pushed him back onto the stool, which teetered under Caleb's weight.

'Then how did the coins get into your purse?'

'I told ye, they were payment.'

'Payment for smuggled goods. You're doomed Brown, and Hewitt. Smuggling and counterfeiting. It'll be Tyburn for you; may just do it here. They'll hang you both no doubt. Make a spectacle of it, put your body in a cage; a lesson for others.'

'It's all a mistake. I know nothin' o' those moulds an' we were just makin' a delivery.'

'So, you're denying smuggling?'

Caleb bit on his lip. 'I told ye. We were takin' the goods for someone else; took 'em off a boat on the harbour. Then we took 'em to Avon and left 'em in the water. How would we know if they were smuggled or not?'

'Barrels handed to you off a boat, at night then a trip up river. Left in a pool. Do you take us for fools, Brown?'

'We've not done what ye say. The purse was left under a rock. And someone put those things in my stable.'

'Take him back.'

Caleb rose and, even with his legs manacled, managed to kick out at the stool. The gaoler swung a stick across Caleb's back; despite his strength and size he winced. He shuffled down the dank corridor to the room where he and John Hewitt had been since they'd arrived the day before. John had yet to be questioned, but what more could either of them say?

'Caleb. You all right?'

Caleb nodded. The gaoler shoved him, but he didn't

47

move. The door was locked and the two men were left alone. The room was small with a high, narrow window providing a sliver of light. A bucket was placed in the corner and the smell of pee, and more, fouled the air. There was a grate for a fire, but none was lit. Two low cot beds, each with a straw mattress and a single blanket were on either side next to damp, whitewashed brick. John Hewitt was sitting on his bed with the blanket pulled around his shoulders.

'Askin' 'bout those moulds and dies. I swear, John, I don't know where they came from.'

'I know, I know, Caleb.'

'I think Stevens knew that too, he looked mighty afraid.'

'Aye, an' where did he go? He arrested us, then we didn't see 'im till we were taken off on that cart. Did they ask 'bout Avon?'

Caleb nodded. 'But we ne'er met 'em, John, what can we say?'

'It were them who gave ye the purse.'

'Aye, an' a bag full o' bad coins it were.'

'What about Henry Lane? It were 'im who got us the job.'

'Only 'cause he aint got a boat.'

'I'm goin' to mention 'im when they come for me. It could give us some time. And Byng. He offered Henry the job.'

'But it won't be fair if Henry knows nothin'.'

'An' everythin' if he got us in this mess.'

'They 'ave to be linked, John. The moulds and things in me stable an' the coins in the purse.'

John nodded. 'There be somethin' odd goin' on.'

'Let's hope young Danny got back home quickly and James Clarke's sortin' things out.'

'He will, he's a good lad, as is his father an' I fear he's our only hope, Caleb.'

Chapter 7

Moonrakers' bounty

'Oh, Mary, what news is there? Have you found out anything? Get your aunt a drink, Danny. Use the brandy from the cupboard.' Hannah Clarke helped Aunt Mary to a chair in the little parlour where flames danced in the grate. Candles flickered in the yellow warmth and the room smelled of the savoury supper hanging over the hearth. 'Did Philip Sweetland say what can be done?'

Mary shook her head and sniffed. Hannah pulled out a handkerchief from her pocket and passed it to her sister.

'He went to the revenue officer's place but Joshua Stevens wasn't there. Stevens had the warrant an' Mr Sweetland says he'd have had to act on it.' She dabbed her eyes. 'He tried to find out who made the charges an' what proof they had the moulds hadn't been hidden there by someone else. All they'll say is that Caleb had been accused o' makin' counterfeit coins an' John were helping him spread 'em about.' She let out a sob. 'Hannah, that means he'll hang for sure. An' Caleb, both o' 'em.'

'Could Caleb have been making coins?'

'Who knows, but Bessie swears not. She says he's busy an' they've done well this year. Tss, must o' done to afford an attorney. Oh, Hannah, I don't know what to think.' She covered her face with her hands and cried.

'Come on, Mary. We'll sort it out.' Hannah rubbed her sister's back. 'Joshua Stevens must be somewhere. He knows John and Caleb, surely he wouldn't have had them arrested if there weren't real proof?'

'John's done some things in his time, but he wouldn't get involved in that,' Mary snapped. 'Stevens must've been tricked too. An' now no one can find him.'

'If only James were here.'

'Where's he gone?'

'I don't know. He often goes away for Sir Charles. He sometimes says where, but this time he said he couldn't.'

'Here Aunt Mary.' Danny appeared and handed her a glass of golden liquor. Aunt Mary was a strong person and Danny felt a pang seeing his aunt upset like this. 'Shall we go to Cliff House and ask there?'

'Oh, I don't think so, Danny,' Aunt Mary answered. 'Mr Sweetland said that it were Tarrant who signed the warrant. Why would he believe anythin' we say?'

Jack had appeared by the doorway and crossed to stand by the fire. He rubbed his chin. 'Mother, you said yesterday that father was with Perinne's father, maybe she knows where they are, or her mother might.'

'It's an idea, Jack. We can say we need to get a message to James. Madame Menniere's a kind soul. What do you think, Mary?'

'Yes, yes a good idea.'

'Have you eaten? There's broth.'

'Thank you, but I need to get home. Betsy was there an' I didn't go home last night. She'll be fretting. If you could ask an' then let me know.'

'Of course, Mary.' Hannah turned to Danny. 'Did you say where Miss Perinne's new home is?'

'At Muddiford. Shall I go now?'

'It's dark and I need to go too, it's late.'

'But mother, I could go. Jack can come with me.'

'It would be wrong to go at this hour without first sending word. There's no school tomorrow, we'll walk over in the morning.'

Danny watched the lamp on Aunt Mary's cart fade like a spent candle as she drove away into the moonlight. He wanted to scream. Why couldn't he go to Perinne's now? Surely her mother would understand. But the charges were serious and maybe they wouldn't want to get involved. When Aunt Mary had gone to the revenue officer's cottage and banged on the door, he'd never seen her so angry. Now she was full of misery. He hoped that didn't mean she was ready to give up. He needed to do something. No one had mentioned Edmund Tarrant again. How did he know about coins and what had he meant when he'd said *if* father got back? What does he know?

'Weather be on our side tonight, Ambrose.'

'Only 'cos it's dry. It's bitter, Mokey, cold as a stone-walled grave.'

'Moon's waxin'; be nice'n bright if the clouds stay away.'

'Hope this is the last load of the winter. Do ye think it will be? The Cross Way can be tough at the best of times.'

'Maybe it will, Ambrose, but it be good money for a small job.'

'Aye, that's true. Not far to go, we'll cross the river soon. He'll be waiting at the top of the hill.'

'Should get double t'night. The water'll be the death o' us.'

'Will you ask him for more, Mokey?'

'We c'n try,' Mokey sniffed. 'Look, there he be.'

'Be quiet,' a throaty voice hissed from the shadows ahead of them. The sound of a horse shuffling could be heard. 'Pull the cart over; get the leathers and mufflers on.'

The two men, both in dark clothes and black masked faces jumped off the cart seat. One reached into the back of the cart and threw what looked like a bag to the other. They made easy work of covering the cart's wheels and wrapping the metal harnesses of the pair of horses at its front.

The man on horseback, also masked, scanned the moonlit valley. 'When we get there I want as little noise as possible; you know what to do,' he ordered.

The cart started out again. There were few cottages dotted along the narrow road. All were in darkness, their thatches charcoal blocks against a star-glittered sky. An owl screeched. Soon the horses turned off and worked their way across a field. The ground was soft and smelled of salty mud. The path of the horses and the cart's wheels laid dark lines in the frost-tinted grass. They settled the cart and horses in front of a crop of ivy-covered trees, hidden from the road.

'This'll do, you can carry the barrels this far. Do you both have a change of clothes?'

'Aye.' Mokey took off his long coat and swapped it for a leather jerkin.

'Not lookin' forward to goin' in the water t'night.' Ambrose shivered, as he changed. 'Gets in the bones it do.'

The men lifted long rake-like poles from the cart and made their way to the water's edge.

'How many we looking for, Mr Byng?'

'No names,' the voice demanded.

'Well, how many?'

'Eight.'

Mokey and Ambrose approached a pool, looped from the River Avon, whose main course ran close by. The water was a mirror of the night, with the moon floating on the surface, bathing in its own light of silver and pewter. The glass-like picture shattered as the men stepped into the freezing water. They worked the poles, dragging and poking until they struck their bounty. Once found they dug the pole into the muddy bed, lifted the first barrel with a gush and carried it to the waiting cart.

'Stop,' Byng whispered.

The sound of laughter trickled towards them. Byng peered around the trees towards the road and watched. The voices grew louder, then began to fade as they passed by.

'Drunks. Carry on.'

Four more barrels were delivered and the men stopped.

'Three more. It be raw.' Mokey shivered, taking in swigs of brandy from a flask then passing it to Ambrose.

'Will there be any more this winter?' Ambrose asked, wiping his mouth with his sleeve.

'Yes, but not from here.'

'But it be a good spot here at Avon.'

'The revenue caught the men who deliver. They could squeal. Come on, get the rest and we can get home to the warm.'

The men entered the pool again, first one then another barrel emerged from the icy water.

'One more.'

They prodded and raked at the muddy bed.

'Are ye sure there's eight. I'm numb from head to toe.'

'An me hands are like bricks.'

'Try deeper.'

'Why don't you come an' try.'

The click of a pistol echoed. 'Find it!'

Chapter 8

Perinne tries to help

'Are you sure you know the house, Danny?'

'Yes, mother, it's new, it's on the cliff top.'

'At least it's a dry day. We'll need to wrap up, the windows were thick with frost this morning.'

'It'll only take half an hour.'

'Not with your sister. She can't walk as fast as you can. Have you got the letter?'

'It's on the table.'

'It was a good idea of Jack's. If Madame Menniere can pass it on for us, it could be quicker than the post chaise, that's if we can find out an address. We mustn't forget it.'

Danny pulled on his coat and tucked the letter into the pocket. He wished he'd thought about the letter. At least he was helping now. It had been two days since the arrest. Aunt Mary said that there would have to be a trial. It would be the assizes at Winchester. That was a court and it was for the most serious things. This couldn't be happening. He stroked the letter. They had to find father. Perinne's mother would surely pass it on.

The house was square with three floors. The top floor was in the roof and small windows peeped over a short parapet. To the right of the house were stables and a man Danny didn't know was wheeling a barrow through a gate at the side. Trees had been planted and in their shade thorns of ice stuck to the branches. A row of low shrubs grew along the length of the gravel path leading to a tall door.

'Mother, what if the lady is out?' Sarah asked.

'We'll leave the letter and a message,' Danny answered.

'Pull the bell, Danny.'

Danny could see a woman through the window to the right, she looked out at them. He didn't know her either. He guessed that Perinne's family would have all new servants. The sound of the door opening broke his thoughts.

'Lucy!' It was good to see a familiar face.

'Hello, Danny. Mrs Clarke.'

Hannah's voice trembled. 'We are sorry to call unannounced, but would you ask if Madame Menniere might spare us a few moments? There is something we wish to ask of her.'

'I'll find her an' see. Come into the hall, it's freezin' out there. Have you walked from Burton?'

'Yes. It's not far,' Danny put in. 'But Sarah has grumbled about it on the way.'

Lucy smiled, closed the door and excused herself. Danny was pleased to see Lucy. She used to work at Cliff House, but was accused of stealing a brooch back in the summer. It hadn't been her, but a girl from Burton Hall. They'd gone now and the Hall was standing empty. Danny had wondered if Perinne and her family would move there, but he liked this house. It wasn't as big as Burton Hall, he could see through to the other side and it faced the bay. He'd love to be able to sit and watch the sea and the ships. He could hear voices coming from the room to the right, the one where he'd seen the woman. Then the door swung open.

'Danny, it is you. I have not seen you in a long time.'

Perinne seemed to have grown taller since the summer.

Her black hair was plaited and wound tidily around her head and tied with ribbon. Jane Menniere was behind her and the woman he'd seen through the window followed.

'Mrs Clarke, this is a surprise.'

'Madame Menniere, thank you for seeing us. I am sorry to call without sending a note. We wondered if you might be able to help us.'

Jane hunched her shoulders. 'Come, let us go into the parlour, you must be cold after your walk. What can be so important to come so far by foot? Lucy, take the coats then make some tea for our visitors.'

'Sarah, *Stop*!' Danny managed to snatch a vase before it fell to the floor.

Perinne gasped then gave a smile and ran up the nearby staircase.

'I'm sorry.' Hannah blushed, grabbing Sarah's hand and pulling her close.

'No harm has been done. Come through.' Jane motioned towards the door, then spoke to the woman from the window who returned to the other room, closing the door behind her.

The parlour was bright and spacious. Danny had thought correctly, there was a large window and the shore could be seen as far as the spit where Hurst Castle sat. The Isle of Wight was clear today and the white stacks of the needles poked out of the blue.

'Please, sit.'

Perinne appeared with a small, wooden doll and gave it to Sarah, who sat on the rug and danced its feet on the floor. She stood beside her mother. Lucy came in with a tray, served tea and left.

Jane took a sip of hers. 'How may I help?'

'I, er, we wondered if you knew where my husband and Monsieur Menniere had gone. We need to contact James urgently.'

'I'm sorry, I don't know. They were sent on a task by

Sir Charles.'

'Did your husband say how long he would be?'

'I'm afraid not, just that he hoped to be home soon.'

'Are you able to contact them? We've written a letter. We wondered if you might ask Sir Charles to pass it on for us?' Hannah nodded at Danny, who fumbled in his pocket.

'Could you not do this yourself?'

Hannah lowered her head.

'Please, Maman, let us help.'

'Is there a problem with that?' Jane set her teacup down.

Hannah pressed her lips together. Danny stepped forward.

'My uncle has been arrested and taken to Winchester.'

'Danny!'

'It's no good, mother, we have say what's happened. Uncle John hasn't done anything wrong.'

'I don't think I'm able to help with that.'

'Maman.'

'My husband will know what to do, Madame Menniere. We just need to get a message to him.'

'What has the man been accused of?'

'Coining. Making coins and passing on bad coins.' Hannah wrung her hands. 'It can't be true, my brother-in-law wouldn't commit such a crime.'

'It is indeed serious. I should not get involved in such matters.'

Danny began blinking hard. He was fourteen, and couldn't let Perinne see him cry. 'It was Uncle John and Aunt Mary who helped Perinne last year. After those smugglers took her.'

'Maman, please.'

'Perinne, quiet.' Jane took a breath. 'I will pass on your letter to Sir Charles; that is all I can do. I am sorry.'

'That's very kind of you.'

'Drink your tea, Mrs Clarke, you need to get warm before your journey home.'

Lucy fetched the coats. Danny was helping Sarah into hers, but she was struggling. Perinne came over to help. She crouched, a worried expression on her face. She whispered to Danny. 'I will try to help you and your uncle. They were kind to me, but I do not think it will be possible. Are you singing in the church tomorrow?'

Danny nodded.

'I will be there with my new governess, Miss Ashton. You saw her earlier. She said she needed to speak with Reverend Jackson after the service, we will have a chance to talk then.'

'Look, mother, there's a cart outside our cottage. Maybe there's some news.'

Danny sped on ahead of his mother. The journey from Muddiford had been slow and solemn and he hoped there was something to cheer him at home. It was Caleb's cart.

'Mrs Brown. Is there news of Uncle John and Mr Brown?'

'I be sorry, Danny, but no.'

Danny was about to ask if she wanted anything when his mother and Sarah arrived.

'Mrs Brown, what brings you here? Has something happened?'

'Ah, Mrs Clarke. I brought Jack home. He was walking with a heavy bag an' I couldn't let him struggle, it being cold an' all. I'm going to Winchester, to take Caleb some food an' a blanket. I can't bear the thought of him in that gaol, cold an' hungry.'

'Yes, I hear how awful it is in those places. It's bad enough thinking about what will become of them, but for them to suffer whilst waiting.' She let out a deep sigh. 'I heard that there are moves to improve things. Hopefully it won't be as bad as we imagine.'

'Well I mean to find out. I thought to go by Hinton, see if Mary wants to come along an' take some things for John.'

'I'm sure she will. We have a blanket you can take for him. Just in case she's not there. And some bread.'

'Shall I fetch one, mother?'

'Yes, Danny and find your brother,' she tutted. He shouldn't have left Mrs Brown here on her own.'

Danny scrambled up the narrow staircase and found the chest in his parents' room where the family linen was kept. He rummaged under layers and found the oldest blanket. He then crossed to the room he shared with Jack, but he wasn't there. A quick look out of the window showed he was in the small chicken coop collecting eggs.

'Here, mother.' He handed over the blanket. 'Jack's in the garden.'

'Go and fetch him.'

'Has Joshua Stevens turned up, Mrs Brown?'

'Call me Bessie. No, not a sign of him. Some of the town men are goin' to look for him. They're sure he can help, if only he could be found.'

Jack appeared with a basket. 'Eight today, mother. Shall we boil some and send them to Uncle John?'

'Yes. Put a kettle on the fire. Do you have time to wait, Bessie?'

'Aye, but I'll go as soon as they're done. I hope to be there by dark. I'll have to find somewhere to stay. Not sure how much longer I can pay out, without Caleb, there be no money comin' in.'

Danny leaned against the wall next to the tall clock. Another good idea from Jack.

'Can I take the blanket, mother? I could ask Uncle John what happened and whether he has any idea about the moulds.'

'No, Danny, certainly not.'

'But mother, what if Aunt Mary isn't there?'

'I expect she will be, Danny.'

'Or can't go. It would be better for Mrs Brown if she had someone with her.'

'No, I need you here.'

'It's good of ye to offer, Danny, but I can manage.'

Danny sat in his favourite place, on a bench beside the window. He looked out across the fields and listened as his mother told Mrs Brown about their visit to the Menniere's new house and how Jane Menniere had agreed to pass on the letter to Sir Charles Tarrant. Could she let Aunt Mary know this? Soon Jack appeared with a rag parcel.

'They're still warm, Mrs Brown, but they'll stay fresh for a few days, especially in this cold weather.'

'Thank you, Jack, and you Hannah. Now I must be getting on, I've a long journey ahead of me.'

Danny watched as Mrs Brown untied the horse, climbed onto the cart's seat and drove off.

'I'm going to my room, mother.'

Danny put his book onto the small table beside his bed and rubbed his eyes. He couldn't take in the words. Thoughts were swirling in his head, as if someone were stirring it with a stick and any good ideas washed down in the whorl and out through the bottom. He was pleased Mrs Brown was going to see the men. There was still a crust of bread from his supper on a plate next to the book. He hadn't eaten much, he didn't feel hungry. He would try to sleep. He blew out his candle and snuggled down under his covers just as Jack appeared, his face whitened with moonlight from the small window.

'I need to do something, Jack.'

'Like what?'

'I don't know. Try to find out about those moulds for one thing.'

'We don't know Caleb. He might've been coining.'

'You don't believe that, do you?'

Jack shook his head.

'No one seems to be doing anything or asking questions.'

'Mrs Brown said she'd had a visit from Guy something.'

'Guy Cox. He works on the *Solomon*, the boat Will used to mend nets for.'

'She said his cousin was a revenue officer. He was trying to find out what's happened to Joshua Stevens. They're worried about him.'

'I'm worried about Uncle John.'

'We all are, Dan.'

'I wish Will were home. Why did he have to go off to London?'

'Because he wanted to single-handedly persuade parliament to ban slavery.'

'That's not fair. It is horrid and he's right.'

'And he's only fifteen, who's going to listen?'

'I don't know. I just wish he was here. He knows the, er, local men.'

'Smugglers you mean.'

'They have to know something. How did the revenue men know Uncle John and Caleb were on the river that night?'

'I doubt they knew *who* it was, they're always after smugglers.'

'But they did, remember, they ransacked Mrs Brown's house. They were looking for Caleb and Uncle John. Someone must have told them where they'd be, but who?'

'Dan, don't get involved. Haven't you learned your lesson? Go to sleep, don't you have to go to the church in the morning?'

Danny turned onto his side. He knew what Jack meant. It was only six months since Thomas Walton had tricked him. As well as the fight with the smuggler who kidnapped Perinne, that was almost two years ago, but it still scared him thinking how much danger they'd been in. And Perinne said she probably wouldn't be able to help. She was fourteen now, the same as he was. They were growing up. Perinne had more freedom than most girls he knew, though now she had her new governess, she wouldn't be allowed to go out and about alone anymore. But he couldn't leave it, he had to do something.

Chapter 9

In the shadow of moonlight

'Well, did Ginn agree to a meeting?'

Joseph Martin set the tankards on the table and scanned the men. Adam Litty, Isaac Hooper, Guy Cox, Henry Lane, David Preston, Moses Pilgrim. Could one of these men be a traitor, betraying John and Caleb? For what? Money? He'd been landlord at the *George* for seven years now. He knew them all well, or so he thought. His nose told him he needed to be on his guard.

'Aye,' Henry Lane answered.

'When?' Adam Litty gave Henry a long look.

'I'm going to Ringwood. Monday, on Reeks' Waggon.'

'Monday? That's Christmas Eve. Wouldn't he come here?' Adam frowned.

'It was when I could go. You know I don't ride.'

'No boat, ye don't ride. What use are ye?' Isaac grumbled.

'I say we should go now, take him by surprise,' Guy suggested.

'He's a weasel. His mouth'll shut like a sprung trap if we round on him.' Adam took a swig of his ale and licked his lips. 'Guy, any news from your cousin?'

'Nothing. He said the warrant came from Tarrant, but he can't find out who made the claim against them.'

'Tarrant? He don't usually poke his nose into the free tradin',' Isaac Hooper said, scratching his balding head. 'Not unless there's somethin' in it fer 'im. And John's brother-in-law works fer 'im.'

Joseph looked across the room. His wife wasn't around, but Beth Gibbs was busy serving and had everything in hand. The air was clearer than usual. Not many people were out and about on such a cold night. The wood on the fire and the tallow from the candles were enough to take away the smell of sweat from the men, who'd been working most of the day. He still had questions. 'What I don't understand, Isaac, is where the moulds and stuff came from. Bessie swears she knows nothing about them; says they turned the place upside-down. The revenue must have been told there was something to look for.'

'Aye, who's doin' the tellin'?' Isaac sipped at his ale, something was niggling him. He just couldn't think. It was something Caleb had said before they'd left him at the riverbank. A name, what was it?

'None of it makes sense,' Henry said. 'Captain of the *Glory* said it were a simple job, barrels from France. A few taken off an' sent up to Avon. Someone would be in touch. Just assumed it were for a local inn.'

'Did he say who it were for, Henry?' David Preston spoke.

'No.'

'How did it all happen, Henry?' Joseph asked.

'Remember that ship full back in June, just after that wrecking? Then, on the beach. I were with John Hewitt. We were Landsmen. A man on horseback stopped us. He said there was a job he'd been asked to do, but it would be easier for someone in the town who knew the harbour and river. We agreed to meet up. Met at the Eight Bells 'bout two weeks later. An' I've told ye the rest.'

'What were he called?' Isaac asked. He stared hard at him, he must know.

Henry looked over towards the fire. Byng could have him killed. 'He didn't say.'

'Maybe it's nothin' to do with that run,' Moses Pilgrim suggested.

'It has to be, Moses.' Adam opened his arms as if about to preach. 'The search at the forge, then laying in wait for them by the wharf. Dragoons there, too. What did they think John and Caleb would do?'

The men sat in silence, each in their own thoughts, watching the crackling logs spitting orange and yellow sparks in the grate. Adam stood.

'Come on, drink up, tide'll be right now, it's still a good moon. Let's make some money.'

Perinne loved the view from her bedroom window. Even better than from Cliff House, which was further inland. Here, near the cliff top, it was wonderful. The scene was moonlit, the sea appeared washed down the middle in a triangle of creamy light. A line between black and grey marked the horizon and the shadow of the island crouched as if waiting to pounce over the fence of the Needles and into the water. It was late. A ship was in the bay, its sails folded. Dots of smaller boats were peppered around it, with others either moving away or approaching it. Perinne knew these were smugglers. She'd lived at Christchurch long enough to know what went on. The door opened.

'Some coal for the fire, miss.'

'You are still up? It is so cold. I hope your room has coal also.' Perinne hugged a woollen shawl tightly around her.

'I've a nice room, miss. Do you need any help before I

go? I expected you'd be asleep.'

'Non. Thank you, Lucy.'

'Is something wrong?'

'I cannot sleep. I am thinking of Danny. He was so sad today.'

'Yes, miss. I saw he was.'

'And I cannot help. I have Miss Ashton who has to be with me all the time.'

'I'm sorry, miss.'

Perinne's head lowered in thought then returned to the view. 'Look, out at sea.'

Lucy finished scuttling the coals onto the fire and rubbed her hands down her apron, leaving dusty streaks. She came to the window.

Perinne pointed. 'The smugglers are at work. It is wrong, and Danny's uncle was caught. I cannot see what anyone can do about it.'

'Maybe I can find out what's happened?'

'Oh, Lucy, you are so kind. I am pleased Maman let you come to work for us.'

'And I'm happy about that too, miss.'

'It is not fair, I love to ride out alone. My adventures here have been exciting, but I am no longer allowed such freedom.'

'You're growing up, miss. You'll be looking for a husband in a few years' time.'

'Lucy! Do not talk like that. I do not want a husband. I want adventure first. That is, if I want a husband at all. I want to do something that will help people.'

'What have you in mind, miss?'

Perinne scrunched her face in thought. 'I would like to help poor people, or help to stop the slavery, like Will is doing. That would be a good thing to do.'

Lucy smiled. 'Shouldn't you be getting into bed, miss? You have to go to church in the morning. A chance to ride in the new carriage.'

'Yes, Lucy. I will. Do not say anything, but I shall speak with Danny tomorrow, just in case there is something that can be done. Maman is sending his mother's letter to Cliff House in the morning, so it is hoped that it will reach his father and he will return home.'

'I'm also going home tomorrow to visit my family while you're out.' Lucy pulled the curtains together. 'I'll ask if they know anything about what has happened to Danny's uncle.'

'Thank you, Lucy,' Perinne said, climbing into bed and pulling the covers around her. 'Please leave open the curtains.'

Lucy snuffed out the candles, giving the room over to silver moonlight. 'Good night, miss.'

'Goodnight, Lucy.'

James Clarke pulled his collar around his neck. The ship was under sail and moving quickly away from Dover. The cold salt air stung his eyes as he watched the cliffs, lit by the waning moon, fading ghost-like into the distance. He'd heard about the cliffs, but this was the first time he'd seen them.

Yves Menniere rubbed his hands together. 'It will be a good crossing, there is plenty wind to take the sails, though not enough to make it rough. We should reach Calais by morning. It is the first time that you have sailed?'

'I've been in the bay, but that's all.'

'And your thoughts on our task?'

'I didn't think it my place to say.'

'I should like to hear it.'

'It seems, as you pointed out earlier, that we are seeking a needle in a haystack.'

'Yes. But they are paying us very good money,' Yves smiled. 'It will help with the new house and I have also bought a new carriage.'

'It's a fine house that you've built in a pretty position.'

'It is what I enjoy doing best, rather than this spying business.'

James was taken aback. Did he mean what they were doing was spying? He thought they were simply out to seek out information.

'It will be a bonus for your family, no? The payment. More than Sir Charles would pay you.'

'Yes, it will. I'll need to think carefully how best to use it. But we need to earn the rewards first.'

'Let us go below. Try to get some rest.'

Ethan Byng lurked in the shadows of the watermill, his face covered by a black scarf. With each breath he could feel the metal of his pistol, tucked into his belt beneath his coat, pressing into him. He watched as the Christchurch gang climbed aboard two boats at the quayside, their figures lit by dim lamplight. The frosty air skipped across the water as the motion of the boat made tiny waves. With two of the gang taken away they'll be asking questions and Henry Lane knew his name. That had been a mistake, he should never have told him. It wouldn't be long and they'd be asking after him. He'd visited alehouses, keeping his hat low and his collar high, sitting in shadowy corners, listening to the gossip. The two arrested men were clearly well thought of. This wasn't good. The town was uneasy. Two of their own could hang and no one knew the true reason. They didn't believe the one given by the revenue men. People were also talking about the revenue officer,

Joshua Stevens and that he'd gone missing. Stevens would be in France now, taken who knows where and dumped – no food, no money and no doubt unable to speak the language. He was sure Stevens hadn't recognised him and only Ginn knew about him and his gang. Ginn had been against them making sure Stevens never returned, though he'd be lucky to survive the cold. It didn't matter to Ginn whether Stevens found his way back home or not. If and when he did, it would no doubt be too late for the two now rotting in Winchester gaol.

Byng crept away from the mill following the shadows of nearby cottages and narrow back lanes. The customs were also looking for his gang after the fight at Parley. It was one of the largest consignments of brandy he'd brought in. How the revenue found out about it, caught them, and seized the brandy, he'd yet to discover. Their plan to get back the goods had gone wrong. It was supposed to be quick. Overpower the officers and take what's theirs. But there were more of them than expected. The officers seemed unafraid, despite being faced with his gang's many weapons. Some of the gang were wounded, so were some of the officers. He'd insisted that the gang blackened their faces and used masks, giving little chance of being recognised. But others knew them and the customs were offering large rewards for their capture. He stopped at the end of the path, ducking behind a broad oak as he heard voices. After they'd passed he stole down a lane to where he'd left his horse. The sound of a stream trickled by and he glanced at the water. It was a pity about the pool at Avon. It had been a good place and he'd used it often and his father before him. No doubt the arrested men would describe it and it would be watched. The captain of the *Glory* would be in Poole soon, he'd get him to pass on the message that he wanted nothing more to do with the job. He'd bide his time. Once the two Christchurch men were convicted, things would start to get back to normal. He mounted his horse and sped away with one thought remaining. There was one person who could get in the way, the Tarrant boy, who Ginn had somehow got involved with. Landowner's son or not, he could easily see them all at the gallows.

Chapter 10

Winchester gaol

They'd reached an inn on the outskirts of Winchester in the early hours of the morning. After resting and a small breakfast the two women were ready to move on again. The same ostler who'd taken the tired horse with its cart to the stables earlier, was approaching, his feet dragging wearily.

'Mistress, can I help?'

'We need the cart, Master Ostler. We're goin' into the city.'

'Where're you heading?'

Bessie gave Mary a worried glance. Mary stood firm.

'We be visiting family, not far from, er, the church.'

The ostler, snugly wrapped in a thick coat and wearing a felt hat, laughed. 'An' which one's that?'

'What do it matter to you?'

'I'm tryin' to help, mistress. The city's a busy place and there are many churches. And it might be difficult to find somewhere to leave the beast.'

'Sorry. I think it's close to the cathedral, though I'm not sure.'

The ostler took a deep breath. 'Are you lookin' for the gaol?'

Mary's eyes widened in surprise. Bessie bit on her lips.

'It don't matter, mistress, the debtors often have visitors.'

'How could you tell?' Bessie was pleased the ostler either didn't know, or didn't care why the men were in the gaol.

'You've bags of blankets, food, that's what most people take.'

'Is it far?' Mary asked.

'No, not far and best leave the cart here. I'll take care of it, and the horse.'

The women passed through the south gate and onto a long straight road. One side was paved. They held hands as they stepped into the road to pass wooden props where new houses were being built.

'I see what the ostler meant 'bout churches, Mary.'

'Aye, that's the second one we've passed an' that square tower over there must be the cathedral.' She pointed across a spread of red roofs holding up a crisp, blue sky.

The high street was busy with people. A tempting smell drifted from a pie seller carrying a tray of wares and calling out his prices; carts with barrels rattled along. Everyone was wrapped up against the chill. Women with long coats and woollen bonnets; their hands in muffs. The men in thick stockings and coats, scarves and hats.

'Look, over there,' Bessie said. 'They must be the gates the ostler said to look for.'

They were surprised when the ostler had explained that there was more than one prison in the city. The largest, he'd told them, was once going to be a palace and it held thousands of prisoners of war. When they reached the building where Caleb and John were being held, it wasn't as big as they'd imagined. A cart passed carrying barrels and baskets full of loaves. The gaol's gates were opened without the carters getting down from their seats. The two women followed it.

'Stop!' A man dressed in dark clothes and wearing a tricorn hat held up his hand to them. 'Are you here to visit?'

'Yes. Caleb Brown an' John Hewitt. They were brought 'ere Thursday.'

'Follow that path and wait in the room on the right,' the man pointed.

The mouth-watering aroma of the fresh bread was soon replaced by a bitter smell of sweat and rotting waste. They entered a room with painted walls that had benches resting against them. Three other people were already seated. One, a thin man, was reading from some papers resting on a bag on his lap. The others were women. One looked up and nodded to Mary, who had stepped in first. The bright room was lit by a large, sunny window that looked out onto a square yard. Here men walked about as if on a treadmill, their faces long, staring down at their feet. Mary and Bessie sat.

'What happens? Does someone come to us?' Mary asked one of the women, who nodded.

'Yes, the gaoler's man will come and ask who you wish to see.'

Mary smiled weakly.

'Not been here before?'

'No.'

'It isn't as bad as some.'

Bessie gave Mary a worried glance, Mary took her arm and pulled her towards her in a hug.

'Mistress Howden, you may see your husband now.' A voice sounded in the doorway. The head of a man in a grey wig popped inside and looked around, spotting the newcomers. The man reminded Mary of a pigeon. His beak-like nose pecking at the air. The nodding woman got up, smiling kindly as she left the room.

'Who are you here to visit?' Pigeon-man said.

'John Hewitt,' Mary answered.

'And Caleb Brown,' Bessie added.

The head disappeared. The man with the case was now looking across the room at Mary and Bessie, quickly getting back to his papers when he realised they'd noticed him. No one spoke. In the background there was a hum of voices. Occasionally someone would shout. Knocks and bangs from outside could be heard and then footsteps.

'Mr White's ready for you, sir.' Pigeon-man had stepped into the room. He was short and thin. His stockings, that should have been white, were grey and he gave off a sweaty odour. He made a short bow as the man with the case rose and passed him by. Pigeon-man didn't leave the room, instead he looked sternly at Mary and Bessie and spoke.

'The prisoners can be visited now, show me what you've brought.'

Both women opened large bags and the man rifled through them.

'It only be a change o' clothes, blankets an' food,' Bessie said. Her heart began to beat hard in her chest.

'What are ye lookin' for? There's nothin' else,' Mary said.

The man continued his search. Finishing by tearing open one of the loaves and sniffing it. 'Follow me.'

Mary and Bessie were led along a corridor. The floor was stone and the walls white-washed. It led to a set of steps, just five. At the bottom there were two doorways. The first led to a room. The door was slightly ajar. Mary could see the case that belonged to the man in the waiting room set down on the floor. Voices could be heard. The women continued through the second door and along a corridor of cells. It was from here that the smell of dung and urine which hung over the whole building was emitted. The rooms were full. Some were large with several men, some single. Faces of men peered from hollow eyes as they passed. One, Mary noticed, had a desk and chair and a man was sitting writing. At the end and on the left they found John and Caleb and pigeon-man let them inside.

'Mary!'

'Oh, John, whatever's happening to us?'

Bessie and Caleb were hugging, Bessie sobbing.

'Are you all right? How are they treating you?'

'It aint too bad, Mary,' John said, though his slow voice said the opposite.

'It's cleaner than I thought it'd be,' Bessie put in, wiping her face with her sleeve. She was now sitting on the cot bed with Caleb.

'They had us locked in irons, hand an' foot,' Caleb said. 'Better now we're free from 'em.'

''Ave ye seen Danny?' John asked. 'I shouted for him to fetch his father.'

'Yes, it were Danny who came for me,' Mary said. 'He wanted to come with us, but Hannah said no. An' she's right, this is no place for a boy. He's upset enough without him seeing you here an' with...' her face went pale and she took her eyes away from her husband.

'What is it? What's wrong?

Mary took a deep breath. 'It's James. He's gone away, John. We don't know when he'll be back. It could be Christmastime, even later.'

'Oh, no.' John put his face into his hands, his words muffled. 'They're sayin' we've been makin' an' passin' bad coins. Treason, that is.'

'We've told 'em we don't know where those moulds came from. They're nothin' to do with me,' Caleb said.

'We believe you, Caleb,' Mary said as she held John's hand in hers.

'I've hired Philip Sweetland. He's lookin' into it all,' Bessie spoke.

'An attorney?' Caleb shook his head.

'We had to do somethin'.'

'I know, I know, Bessie.' He hugged his wife again.

'What about Joshua Stevens, what do he 'ave to say?'

'That's the strange thing, Caleb, he's nowhere to be found.' Bessie began bringing things out of the bag and placing them on a cloth on Caleb's straw bed. 'Adam Litty called, said the men were tryin' to find out who gave Henry Lane the job up to Avon.'

'What did Henry say?' John pulled a chunk from a loaf and chewed on it.

'Adam says Henry don't know him. Says he were only with him a short time. It were a simple job.'

'He must know somethin', Bessie,' John said. He brushed crumbs from his shirt into a shaft of light that beamed through the window. They fell, making speckles in the dusty air. The sun was as high as it would get that day. It would soon pass and darkness fall onto their plight. Mary broke the silence.

'Hannah's sending a message to Cliff House, asking if Charles Tarrant would pass a letter to James, askin' him to come home. I expect Tarrant will know what it's about.'

'Aye, Mary,' John said. 'He'd have signed the warrant.'

'Danny said that boy of Tarrant's was at the revenue officer's cottage when they took you away. Say's bad things always happen when he's around.'

'He's only a boy, Mary. What could he do?'

'He's a bad 'un,' Caleb said. 'Remember it were 'im who hurt the Gibbs boy.'

'Forget him,' John hissed. 'Best see if the men can find out about Byng, he's the key to all this. And let's pray Philip Sweetland can get us out of here.'

'Byng?' Mary said, puzzled.

'I were with Henry on the beach when he were offered the job. He gave his name as Byng,' John said. 'It were too dark to see his face.'

'Then I met him with Henry Lane,' Caleb added. He rubbed his whiskery chin. 'He kept in the shadows. What I could see of him looked familiar, but I didn't know him.'

'But Caleb, what would he know about the moulds?' Bessie asked.

'I don't know, but he must know who were payin' us with bad coins.'

The man set his case on the floor and sat opposite Richard White. White had been the gaoler here for four years and was mostly left alone, so why this man had come from London just to see him he hoped to now find out.

'Are the prisoners secure?'

'They are, Mr Young.'

'And have they caused any problems?'

'No. They've done as asked and caused no trouble so far. Though they continue to protest their innocence.'

'Caught red-handed I heard, how can they protest?'

'They admit to being on the river that's all. They strongly deny any knowledge of the moulds.'

'And the coins?'

'They say they received the purse as payment for a delivery.'

'Hmm. And the moulds and coins were brought here with them?'

'Yes, as proof, for the trial.'

'And what do you think. You've seen many felons and debtors pass through the gates. Do you think they're guilty of coining?'

White shifted in his seat and sniffed. 'I do have doubts, Mr Young.'

'And why's that?'

'Let me show you.' White left his seat and went to a door at the rear of his office. It opened to reveal a small store room. He disappeared, returning with a box and a bag. He placed the box on the table in front of Young.

'The moulds.' Young opened the box and took out a tray with eight disc-shaped dents. The tray was dusty and scuffed. There were two other trays.

White took a purse from the bag and emptied the coins beside the moulds. 'Take one, Mr Young. And find me where it could have been made in that press.'

Young chose one of the coins and inspected the profile of the King. It wasn't a bad image, and a good forgery. He'd seen many, his job was to try to stop such coinage being made and spread, he feared he was losing that battle. This time the governor at the Bank of England had set him a more serious task. He spun the coin to its tail. This was disappointing, the coin was not even the same type as those he'd expected to find. He'd been hoping these were copies thought to be coming into England from France. He couldn't mention that to White.

'These coins were not made in those moulds,' Young said, returning the trays to the box. 'And it's clear that the moulds haven't been used for some time.'

White gave a satisfied smile. 'My thoughts also, Mr Young.'

'But the men will stand trial still?'

'They had the bad coins. They would have spent them with no doubt.'

'Would they have known they were bad?'

'Who knows? If what they tell me is true, they'd only just received them. But they've admitted to taking barrels up river.'

'I'll take one of the moulds. Maybe I can find out where they came from. When will the men appear in court?'

'The next assizes aren't till Lent. Though if they're not to be tried for coining they could be called to the quarter session. The next one's Epiphany. So just a few weeks.'

'Do the men know this?'

'It's not for me to decide. I'll know soon.'

'Smuggling is a problem.'

'The men are from Christchurch. There's been trouble near there. Revenue men have been attacked. It's getting bad. They could be made an example of. They could still hang, even if they're not charged with the coining.'

Chapter Eleven

The letter

'Where is Edmund? We'll be late for church.' Lady Elizabeth Tarrant stopped pacing the floor and sat on the wooden bench beside the tall double doors of Cliff House. Through the window John Scott, the coachman, could be seen driving the horse and carriage towards the entrance steps.

Sir Charles sighed. He was wearing a green woollen coat that almost reached the floor. He put on his tri-corn hat.

'Edmund!' he yelled up the staircase. Joseph, the butler appeared from a nearby door.

'Is there a problem, sir?'

'See if Master Edmund is in his room. Tell him to come immediately.'

'Yes, sir.'

The ornate hall was chilly. White plaster and porcelain figures reflected in a large mirror doubling their number, standing like frozen ghosts. Soon feet drummed on the staircase.

'Hurry, Edmund.' Tarrant's small eyes glared from his reddened face. 'Where's your coat, boy?'

'I'm not going to church, father.'

'Oh, you are.'

'But father.'

'Get your coat on now. Hurry, Scott's here with the coach.'

'I'll ride, father. I was going to go to Ringwood.'

'Ringwood? What are you going there for on a Sunday?'

'Just to meet a friend.'

'You'll come to church first. Don't be late.'

Edmund watched the coach leave. The cold hall seemed warm against the bitterness pushing its way inside. He closed the doors. He'd ordered Joseph to tell Ben the stable boy to saddle his horse. He knew he'd get his way with father. He was about to go and fetch his coat when he heard voices coming from the rear of the house. Then Joseph appeared with something in his hand.

'What's that?' Edmund pointed.

'A message for your father, Master Edmund.'

'Give it to me, I'll put it in his study.'

'Yes, Master Edmund.'

Edmund took what looked like a packet and went into the library. Now Joseph was out of sight he inspected it. It was two letters, bound by a blue ribbon cord. He untied it. The first was unsealed. It was from Jane Menniere.

Bay House
Muddiford
16th December 1781

Dear Charles,

Mrs Clarke paid me a visit yesterday, and asked if a message could be sent to her husband. I know nothing of the errand he and my husband are undertaking, nor of how long they will be away, so I was unable to help her locate him. She would like him to contact her. I would be grateful if you could pass this message on to him if that is possible.

Your obedient cousin
Jane

The second letter was addressed to James Clarke. Edmund turned it to look at the seal. It had not caught the paper and was open. He unfolded it. A sly smile washed over his face. He read it. It was about John Hewitt, the smuggler caught last Thursday night. It was a plea to return home as quickly as possible to help to gain Hewitt's freedom. '*Accused of coining*' '*a mistake*' it read. It mentioned an attorney. It pleaded, '*please return at the first chance*'.

Edmund knew James Clarke had gone to France. He scowled, if he were to have his share of the reward, then he didn't want Clarke returning and proving the men's innocence. He looked again at the first letter. There was no mention of the second letter, only a request to pass on the message for Clarke to return. Nor was there urgency in it, unlike the second. He stuffed Hannah Clarke's letter into his pocket and retied the ribbon around Jane Menniere's. He would take the Clarke one with him to Ringwood after church. He was sure Meekwick Ginn would be interested in its contents.

Danny could see Perinne on the benches. She was wearing a thick blue cloak and blue woollen bonnet. Her hands snuggled in a fur muff. Beside her was a young-looking woman. It was the one who he'd seen through the window at Perinne's house yesterday, her new governess, Miss Ashton. He was cold. The choir's surplices did little to keep off the chilly draughts that were whispering the smell of must and candlewax through the ancient church. He wanted to rub his arms. The church was not very full, despite it being Advent. He expected people preferred to stay at home and try to keep warm. The Tarrants were there, including Edmund. He'd arrived late and everyone had turned as he'd plodded down the aisle without any care that he was disturbing the service. Close by was Perinne, but not her mother. Perinne occasionally looked up. He watched in case she looked his way and he could catch her eye. He was sure she'd keep her promise and try to speak with him after the service. After what felt like a day, the service finished. The vicar led the choir out and the boys scrambled to replace their cotton tunics with their coats. He thought that Reverend Jackson would most probably speak with Miss Ashton by the west door after he'd bade farewell to the congregation.

Danny left with the others and made his way along the nave aisle towards the back of the church. Perinne was standing with her governess talking with Lady Elizabeth Tarrant. Edmund seemed to be arguing with his father. He didn't want to see Edmund, so held back behind one of the broad stone columns. He watched as Edmund stormed off and Sir Charles made his way towards the vicar, forcing a smile. Once the Tarrants had left he expected the governess would take her chance to speak with the reverend. Lady Elizabeth followed her husband to the door and Perinne glanced around. Danny poked his head from around the pillar and waved. She nodded. Miss Ashton was now chatting so Danny moved out and walked up to his friend.

'Hello, Perinne, it's good to see you. Are you warm enough?' Danny said, loud enough that the grown-ups would hear and see it as two friends greeting each other.

'Hello, Danny. It is very cold, is it not?'

The pair moved a few feet further into the church.

'Did your mother pass on our letter?' Danny asked in a whisper.

'Yes, it was sent this morning. We were going to go to

Cliff House today, to take tea. I thought that I could say something. But Maman is unwell. That is why she sent the letter rather than we take it. Have you heard from your uncle?'

'No, but Aunt Mary's gone to the prison. He's innocent, Perinne, my uncle wouldn't do what they are saying.'

'Your uncle seemed kind and Mr Brown also, but we both know many of the men are involved in smuggling.'

Pain creased Danny's face. 'Yes, I know, but not coining, Perinne.'

Perinne's eyes darted across to her governess, who was still talking. 'I am sorry, Danny, but I do not know what I can do. I am not allowed anywhere without Miss Ashton.' Danny's shoulders fell. Perinne sighed. 'I wish I could. What about Will, is he not home? He would help, surely?'

Danny's face held a worried frown. 'No, he hasn't been heard from. Beth hopes he'll come home soon.'

'With luck your father will get your letter and return home quickly.'

'But what if he doesn't, Perinne?' Head bowed, Danny walked away and out into the daylight. He wondered if he should try to find Isaac Hooper. Isaac might know if any of the local men were trying to help Caleb and Uncle John. His mother would be angry if she thought he was getting mixed up with the smugglers again, but he had to do something. His father was away, Perinne couldn't help and Will wasn't around. There was no one else. He looked behind him. Reverend Jackson was leaving the church. His son, Adam was his friend, he would be home from school for Christmas. He liked Adam, but he doubted he'd get involved.

He pulled his scarf around his neck and dug his hands deep into his pockets. He'd passed the Eight Bells alehouse and squinted through the window. No sign of Isaac there. Apart from the occasional horse and rider the town was quiet. Windows and doors were closed and woody-smelling smoke rose from chimneys into the biting blue sky.

A coach and horses was turning into the George and Danny caught sight of Beth Gibbs peering around the gate. Two coachman climbed down from their seats. One let down the steps. Two men and two women passengers stepped out and into the warmth of the inn. Danny saw Beth again, this time smiling at the newcomers, a smile that dropped as soon as they were ahead of her.

'Beth,' Danny called out and ran across the street.

'Danny, how are things, have you heard anything more about your uncle?'

'No, nothing. What about you? You looked disappointed just then.'

'I always hope that Will is going be on a coach. I wish he'd come home.'

'So do I.'

Beth put her hand on his shoulder. 'You think Will would know what to do, don't you?' Danny nodded. 'I'm sure everyone's doing their best, Danny.'

'But not me. I feel useless.' He sighed, then took a breath. 'Is Isaac here? I thought I could ask him if he knew if anyone's helping.'

'He is, but he's with mother, and they've had plenty of ale between them.' She blew a sigh. 'I'd better get back to work, Master Martin will be stopping my wages.' At that she headed away.

'Beth,' Danny called after the girl. He'd hoped to ask her if she'd heard anything, but she just looked back and waved. It was down to Isaac. He poked his head through another door into a small room. There, close to the fireside, was Isaac and Meg Gibbs. They would normally be laughing and joking, but this time were sitting quietly. Isaac was skinny and small and looked tiny next to Meg. They were picking at a single plate of food. Though Meg wasn't big, the pair reminded Danny of Jack Sprat and his wife from an old nursery rhyme book at home.

'Isaac,' Danny called, approaching the pair.

'Danny, it is, isn't it?'

'I wondered if you'd heard anything more about my uncle and Mr Brown. Is anyone trying to find out what happened?'

Isaac took a moment then leaned forward. 'Aye, aye. Henry's goin' to see Meekwick Ginn.'

'Why? Will he know anything?'

Isaac sniffed, wiping his nose on his sleeve. 'Don't trust Henry. He were with Ginn's gang before ye know.'

'Isaac's very upset 'bout it all,' Meg put in.

'I spoke to Henry after we'd all met on the Quay.' He paused. 'Must tell Adam Litty,' he muttered to himself, then carried on. 'He said the captain of the *Glory* had given him the job, but that's not what John told me. He said he were with Henry on the beach. A man approached an' asked if they'd take brandy up river to Avon for a gang.' Isaac seemed to drift off to sleep for a few moments, then his eyes opened wide.

'Byng.'

'What's Byng?' Danny asked him, thinking he might not get a sensible answer.

'Who, Danny, who.' Isaac leaned back into the settle and inspected the ceiling. 'I've been tryin' to remember. I were with Caleb an' Henry one night. Byng's the one who gave Henry the job, then Henry gave Caleb the job.' He rubbed his eyes.

'What did he look like?'

'It were dark, lad, can't recall.' He wrung his hands. 'Wish I could.'

'Did he mention where he lived or where he was from?'

Isaac waved his hands and pulled a face. 'No idea, ne'er seen nor 'eard o' him afore. But if I get me 'ands on 'im.'

Danny noticed Isaac's eyes. They were not glassy with drink, but had the beginnings of tears.

'Calm yerself, Isaac, now.' Meg stroked Isaac's hand.

'Thanks, Isaac.' Danny knew he wouldn't get any more from the strange little man, but at least he had some information. He was surprised Isaac was so upset. He needed to find out about a gang at Avon and who Byng was. But how?

Edmund rode away from the town. At last he'd got away from the church and his meddling parents. From the talk after the service it sounded like the two arrested men were well and truly caught. He smiled to himself, a conviction meant he'd surely get a generous reward. The customs officer he'd spoken with told him he would, Ginn too, but they'd have to claim it together. He expected Ginn would be at the inn at Ringwood where they'd met before. He'd try there. If he couldn't find him, then he'd go High Town way and ask if anyone knew where he lived. He'd seen Simon Slate and stopped to chat. Simon now seemed keen to hear more about Edmund's plans and they'd agreed to meet on Christmas Eve. That was over a week away. He was now on his way to meet Ginn. If he kept at a canter, he should be there in around two hours.

He cut through the track along the river valley past the scattered cottages of Burton following the winding road. He didn't notice a wide V of hooting geese flying overhead, making for their feeding grounds. Soon the short steeple of Sopley church could be seen. As he reached the nearby Woolpack inn a rider burst from the rear of the building, scattering chickens across the road in a panicking squawk. Edmund looked to see if there was any reason for the hurry. To his surprise, struggling to the top of the steps of a stone mounting block, was Meekwick Ginn. He was being helped by a stable boy who was holding out a hand to steady the man's stooping, cautious climb. Beside the block was a small, but handsome dapple-grey horse. Edmund smirked at the weakness of the man, who made himself out to be so fierce and strong. He nudged his horse and approached.

'Mr Ginn, I was on my way to see you.'

'Hmmph.' Ginn paused his ascent, a frown on his pale face.

'I want to talk to you.'

'What is it? We've nothing to talk about.'

'It's about the matter we spoke of last.'

'I've nothing to say.'

'Yes, you have. Tell the boy to go.'

Ginn let out a squeaky laugh. 'You're only a boy yourself.'

'Should I tell father you helped get the men in trouble?'

Ginn's eyes widened and his mouth opened as if to speak, revealing his rotten teeth. He gave the stable boy a look motioning towards the ground. 'Five minutes and come back.' The boy nodded and helped him back down the steps.

'Don't speak aloud of these matters, fool.'

Edmund's nostrils flared. He took a breath. 'I was coming to see you about the reward.'

'Reward? What reward?'

Chapter 12

A shock for Danny

Byng saw signs of the gang ahead as he made his way through the pines. Broken remnants of last autumn's brambles and the tell-tale U-shapes of horse shoes stencilled into the peaty earth led the way. The horses had been rounded together and a foggy steam rose from their just-ridden backs. The gang was deep enough into the heath that they wouldn't be seen. Few people were about in any case, the Avon valley often difficult to pass over at this time of the year. Occasionally the lookout's head snuck a glance around a crop of gorse, his small hat not much of a disguise. Byng allowed himself a wry smile. Ben Lambert's shock of ginger hair was always a giveaway, but the lad was doing well and learning the free trade easily. The boy's father, Seth and he, had also learned from their own fathers and it was now a way of life. Byng raised a blue kerchief, the gang's signal all was clear, a hand waved above the gorse and Ben appeared.

'Everyone here?'

'Yes, Mr Byng. Apart from father, he's still nursin' his bad leg.'

'He's getting better though?'

'It's still bad, Mr Byng. The apothecary mixed some herbs to see if that helps.'

'He'll get better. Take my horse and tether him with the others.' Byng jumped down and entered a clearing where a large group of men had gathered. Seeing him their chatter stopped.

'You manage to see Ginn?' A man approached. His dark skin and brown eyes just visible beneath a wide-brimmed hat.

'Yes, Ambrose, gather the men around.'

Ambrose clapped his hands together. 'This way, men.'

Ben appeared. 'Do I listen in an' tell father the news, or do I keep lookout?'

'Ye keep lookout, lad,' Ambrose said. 'Did you come with Mokey?'

'Yes.'

'Then Mokey'll go home with ye, an' he'll tell Seth anything he needs to know.'

'All right, Ambrose.'

Byng eyed his motley bunch. 'I have your pay from the last load.' A cheer burst from the gang.

'Ambrose will hand it out at the end, I've news to pass on first.'

'This 'bout Parley?' A dark-haired man with long whiskers asked.

'In part, yes,' Byng said. 'Your pay today includes your share from the goods we seized back from the officers. There'll be two more shipments between now and Christmas. We have to change our operation times and positions after being caught last time. Ambrose and Mokey'll meet me at Seth's place tomorrow evening. Having his leg shot might mean he can't get out and about, but he can still plan. Once we know the movements and deliveries, we'll be in touch.

'How did the revenue know we'd be on that road?' A tall man put in.

'I'm certain it wasn't from this gang, Jed. The revenue got lucky, that's all.'

'You sure about that?' Another voice rose.

Byng scowled across the heads of the men, catching as many eyes as he could, as if warning them one-by-one. 'We've been working together long enough and are paid well, there's no need for any man here to spill our secrets.'

'Have ye seen the reward the customs are offering after the fight? Some might be tempted,' the tall man called out.

A hard frown lined Byng's face. 'This is what I wanted to speak about. Yes, the rewards are good, but any man who betrays any of us will have me to deal with. He won't live long enough to enjoy a penny of any reward.'

The gang began talking together and the voices rumbled around the clearing.

'Men.' Byng brought the chatter to a full stop. 'We stick together and we don't go tittle-tattling to anyone. Even if we don't tell, others might. So take your pay today and speak no more of that fight again, to anyone.'

'Come on, men, listen to Mr Byng. He's always kept his word and we should trust him.'

'Thanks, Mokey. We also have a problem. We can't use the pool at Avon, at least not for the next few months.'

'Thank the almighty for that,' Mokey mumbled. 'Too darned cold.' The men closest to him heard and laughed.

'We need to bring in a special load, one that Ambrose and Mokey've been dealing with. We can't use the pool, so need another drop off place and someone to meet the load off Christchurch Harbour. If anyone knows of someone or somewhere, come and tell me after. Now, Ambrose will hand out the pay and you can go.'

Now that Danny was nearing his village, he didn't want to go home. If he kept walking, he'd stay warm. His thoughts were a soup of questions about his uncle. 'When would the trial take place?' 'Who would be the witnesses?' 'If he's found guilty…' he shuddered, he couldn't bear the idea of losing him. It had been almost six months since his beloved grandpa had died. And now this. He recalled standing beside grandpa's grave and his uncle coming along and giving him a hug. Uncle John's voice spoke in his mind. *'Ye can come an' talk with him anytime. It's not far, is it?'* Danny made up his mind to go to Sopley and ask grandpa what he should do.

Walking briskly, it took half an hour. He heard a buzzard mewling and searched the clear sky until he saw it. It soared, winding its way over the valley with nothing to worry about other than finding its next meal. He hadn't been this way since the funeral. That had been in the summer time and he'd been afraid then. Thomas Walton, his teacher, had followed the funeral procession and, shortly afterwards, had threatened him. Walton had been arrested and taken away; forever he hoped. He hadn't heard if he'd been hung. Why did they have to kill people to punish them? It didn't stop the smugglers and it just made things worse for their families. Father said that they used to send smugglers to America, transportation he called it, but that had to stop because of the war.

He could hear water from the nearby mill rushing through the wheel and the inn came into view. The road passed in front of it. He thought about going inside, if only to get warm, but he had no money and he'd be expected to buy something. As he turned up the lane that led to the church he heard shouting and glanced over his shoulder. He could see two people arguing by the gate to the back of the inn. His mouth fell open. Realising who it was, and not wanting to be seen, he ducked behind a hedge. He couldn't tell what was being said. Crouching, he crossed the road and squatted under a low wall. He could hear now.

'Just keep out of it, boy.' The man speaking was, like everyone that day, wrapped up against the raw, winter air. His voice was squeaky. He was short and leaning on a stick.

'Keep out of it?'

'Yes. Go home, forget it.'

'How dare you. You didn't tell me to go away when I told you about the coins in the letter to my father, the man from the customs you sent told me we'd share the reward.' The colour of Edmund Tarrant's face deepened. He was shaking his hand in the air. He was holding something, but Danny couldn't tell what it was.

'I've told you, no rewards have been set, so how can you have any?'

'Do you think I'm stupid?'

Danny stifled a snigger, everyone knew Edmund was stupid. He wished the man would turn around so he could see his face.

'It was in the *Chronicle* yesterday. I helped you, I helped Mr Byng.'

Danny's eyes opened wide. Edmund knew Byng.

'Look, as far as I know there is no reward. The men are in gaol. They'll face trial. Why would they give out a reward now?'

Danny began to seethe. Edmund had been there when Uncle John and Caleb were taken away. He said they'd hang and now, here he was, talking about rewards. And Byng's name again. Just what had he done to help the man, and who was he?

'Rewards are paid on conviction, they may yet pay.' Edmund drew a deep breath, his face flushed to scarlet. 'You wouldn't know if it wasn't for me. Here, I brought you this.' Edmund thrust something into the man's hand. 'I shall tell father about Byng and what he did, I'll tell him he should write a warrant. I won't help you again.'

The man shouted behind him; 'Boy, bring my horse!' Then he leaned into Edmund. 'You do that and Byng will find you long before any revenue men could capture him. I shouldn't think your father will ever see you again if he does.'

The man turned to make his way towards the mounting block. Danny saw his face, a face as pale as a ghost, white as the down of a swan. That had to be Meekwick Ginn. He was a venturer, he paid for the ships the smugglers used and provided money to buy the goods overseas. No one had ever been able to prove he'd done anything wrong.

No more was said between Edmund and the man. The man climbed the block with the help of the boy. Edmund thrust his foot into his stirrup and launched himself onto his horse. His face raged and the veins of his neck pulsed as he sped away in the direction of Christchurch. Ginn was now on his horse. As he rode out of the yard he threw something onto the ground and took the road that led north. Danny waited until both had disappeared from view and came out from his hiding place. He ran over to the cream-coloured speck in the lane. It was a piece of paper. He grabbed it, quickly pushing it into his pocket whilst checking around him to make sure no one had seen him.

He climbed the pathway to the church and made his way to his grandfather's grave. It had a square of stone. His mother, Aunt Mary and his other aunts and uncles had shared the cost. This was the first time he'd seen it. On it, simply carved, it said: '*In Memory of Benjamin Daniel Hopkins*' and underneath '*Departed this life on 19th June 1781*'. Danny sat on the frozen ground.

'Grandpa, what should I do? Uncle John's in prison. They're saying he's been passing bad coins and he's been helping Caleb Brown the blacksmith to forge them. I don't believe it.' He watched a magpie settle on the next stone along, its black and white feathers a splash against the mossy grey slab. 'Father's gone away and mother says

I shouldn't get involved.' The cold was rising through his body. He shivered. Clouds were gathering overhead, heavy and pale. 'Edmund Tarrant's done something, I know he has.' He remembered the paper and took it out of his pocket. It had been screwed into a tight ball. As he unfolded it specks of red sealing wax fell from the folds. The rest of the seal appeared. 'No, *no*!' Danny's hand trembled. 'Grandpa, it's the letter we sent to Cliff House asking Sir Charles to pass on a message to father to come home. He'll never get it now.' He leaned against the stone and sobbed out loud.

Chapter 13

Thoughts of home

'These are de last ones, come on, Will.' Nathan waved a handful of papers in the frosty air.

Will, huddled into his coat, hands tucked in the pockets, trotted to catch up with his friend.

'Yu going to tell Missus Cooper today?'

'Aye.'

'It's right thinking, Will, yu've been a-grumpy for days. Come on, let's split these and get dem finish.'

Will climbed the steps to the final doorway and rattled the brass-ring knocker. After a few moments the latch could be heard and the door slowly opened. The nose of a girl wearing a scullery maid's cap poked through the gap.

'Will ye pass this on to the master o' the house please?' Will held up a pamphlet.

'Who is it?' A rasping voice sounded out.

'A boy, master.'

A short, plump man in a house coat and cap swung back the door and pushed the maid aside. His face frowned with anger, he was clenching his fists. A damp waft from boiling cabbage hung on the air.

'What do you want? Bothering people on the Lord's

Day.'

Will took a step back from the smell and the fists. 'I've a pamphlet, sir. We've to leave it with ye an' someone'll come soon an' ask ye to sign a petition.'

'Petition? What petition?'

'To stop the slave ships.'

'Pah. Go away.'

The door slammed shut in Will's face. He threw his arms in the air shaking his head as Nathan looked on from the pavement.

'See if it'll push under de door, Will. He look like he just got out of his bed.'

The aroma from freshly baked pies seeped through the door of Ellie Cooper's house, taken over for her *Halt the Slave Trade* campaign. It was a town house, three floors high.

Nathan sucked in the air and licked his lips. 'That smell good, hope there's some for us.'

'All you think of is ye belly,' Will smiled. 'It does smell tasty.'

Nathan rapped on the door. A young woman whose blonde hair was tied up and fastened around her head with a red ribbon appeared.

'Ah, boys, come in, it's such a cold day again.'

The boys stepped into a square parlour. A small fire glowed invitingly from the grate.

'How did you do?' Ellie asked.

'Usual.' Will rolled his eyes. 'Some good, some bad.'

'Did you deliver them all?'

'Yes, Missus Cooper.'

'Wonderful. Sit beside the fire and I'll fetch you a warm drink and something to eat.'

Nathan rubbed his stomach and grinned broadly. Will stood with his back to the fire. He scanned the room. Plain wood panelling and bookshelves filled the walls. There was little furniture. Instead around the walls were tables topped with heaps of papers and more of the pamphlets they'd been delivering for the past week.

Ellie Cooper appeared, pushing the door with her back, carrying a tray. Will rushed over to hold open the door. He knew that whilst she had servants, she often did tasks for herself. Ellie set the tray on one of the tables and passed a steaming bowl of broth to Nathan. Will stifled a chuckle at the look on Nathan's face when he saw it wasn't a pie. Will took his broth and a chunk of bread, sat at one of the tables and tucked into the tasty mutton and vegetables.

Ellie settled on a chair with a cup of tea. 'We are very grateful for your help today. There are just those to do,' she nodded towards the pile. 'I will of course pay you both once the job is completed.'

'Thank ye Missus Cooper.'

'And, after Christmas, you can help with the petition.'

Will shifted in his seat. Nathan opened his eyes wide at his friend. Ellie looked at one boy and then the other.

'I will pay you.'

'It aint that Mrs Cooper.' Will bit on his lips.

'What is it?'

Will put down his spoon. 'I, er, we're goin' home. Back to Christchurch.'

'For Christmas?' Ellie clapped her hands together and smiled. 'That's all right. It will be good for you both. There's plenty of time, we won't do the petition until after Epiphany.'

Will wrung his hands then looked directly at Ellie. 'No, Mrs Cooper, we're goin' home fer good.'

'Oh.' Ellie sat back in her chair. After a few moments she spoke again. 'Is it because of the people who argue?'

'No, nothin' like that.' Will's shoulders sank. 'I, er, made a promise, an important one, an' I've realised I 'aven't kept it.'

'It true, Missus Cooper. Will, he been unhappy some time now.'

'I see. What was this promise? Can it be done and you return afterwards?'

'No. Ye see, when he was dying, I promised me father I'd look after mother. I went away, as ye know, then came here after just a few weeks o' bein' at home. Been away nearly two years altogether. Mother aint getting' younger, her sight's goin'. She won't be able to work fer much longer. I should go home an' keep me promise.'

Ellie put down her cup, lifted her chin and looked first at Will, then at Nathan. 'You boys have been such a big help. We need people like you. But your duty is to your mother first, Will.' She glanced again at the pile of papers.

'We do those before we go, Missus.'

'Thank, you. I would be grateful for that. When do you plan to leave?'

'We need to find when there's a coach.'

'There are diff'rent ones we could get, but we need to watch our money.'

'Our rooms, dey cost a lot.'

'Soon, before Christmas. I'm sorry, Mrs Cooper.'

'I understand. We will miss you, and please, return any time. Now, finish your broth and we'll sort out the rest of the pamphlets.'

France

'Do you think Bertin will turn up, sir?'

'Who knows? I think it is likely that he will, though later, when it is dark.'

'Hopefully not too late. It'll be good to get to bed tonight. The journey has been a hard one so far.'

'Yes. I fear that it will get worse. I expect snow soon.' Yves eyed the darkening clouds through the window beside the small table where they were sitting. 'It will make further travel difficult.'

'Let's hope we can finish our job here in Lille. I have a bad feeling about all of this.'

'I think we are only beginning our work. The smugglers have agents all along the French coast and up to Holland. Bertin is no doubt among them.'

'Why would he put himself at such risk by helping the English government?' James knew of such agents and Yves answer was as expected, money.

'No doubt a large reward for conviction is the reason. People here are only too pleased to supply the smugglers with the goods and there are willing helpers. Just as it is too easy for men to be hired in your town and all along the British coastline.'

James let out a long sigh. He wondered about the men who'd been arrested recently. Some men deserved to be caught, but many were simply trying to make a little extra money to put food on their families' tables.

'And it has been too easy for our children to become caught in their work,' Yves continued. 'Perinne's kidnapping last year and the problems poor Daniel had with his teacher.'

'Yes, sir, I would have expected my son to be safe at school.' He held in another sigh. He'd been surprised how easily Danny and his friends had got themselves mixed up with smugglers. Whilst the Gibbs boy had a good heart, he lived amongst people happy to join in bringing in goods. There was also his brother-in-law, John Hewitt, though John had kept his promise to not let Danny and Jack know he worked with the gangs.

'Please, when we are not carrying out our task and no one is about, call me Yves.'

James smiled. He wished he were home. He lifted his cup of coffee to his lips. A luxury, and probably not what a servant would have normally enjoyed as part of their duties. If only he could break away from having to work for Sir Charles Tarrant, but what else could he do? He was a secretary and organised much for his employer, he was better paid than most servants. It was important that Jack and Danny should have a trade, be free to make their own destinies. He studied Yves Menniere. He had a handsome face, dark eyes and tanned skin. He'd never seen him in a wig, his hair was thick and tied neatly back. People were suspicious of him, yet the authorities trusted him to do this work. He was an architect, of that he had no doubt. But was he more? He'd mentioned spying before. He shook the thoughts from his mind.

'What will we do if Bertin doesn't appear?'

'I think that he will. If he is in danger of being discovered as we have been told, he will want to pass the risk on to us and flee; that is, if he has any sense.'

The girl was speaking again. Joshua Stevens strained to hear, his head still cloudy and sore. He wished he knew what she was saying. He tried to push away the fear he'd felt on waking, but yet he trembled. The room was nothing more than a shack, rough wooden walls and damp air. There was a bench and on it a pitcher and basin. He could see it was daylight through a tiny window. The girl's face was kindly enough, though lines of worry crossed her forehead. She hunched her shoulders and pointed to the rough wooden table beside the straw bed where a tin plate held some bread and cheese. The cheese smelled strong and scented the small room. Beside this a pewter tankard held some kind of liquid. A lump came to his throat. The girl's clothes were worn and torn, she looked as poor as the worst he'd seen arrive at the poorhouse in Christchurch.

Yet she'd given him a bed and food, even though she looked afraid of him. Slowly, he managed to shift his body sideways and reach the drink, though each movement brought a stab of pain. He sipped; it was some kind of ale.

He'd heard French and thought that this was what the girl spoke. He rubbed the back of his head. He'd been hit hard from behind then given potions to keep him asleep. He knew of stories where smugglers would sometimes take officers like himself and abandon them in France. Is this what had happened to him? The girl pointed towards the food, as if to say it was safe. Stevens tried to turn his legs over the side of the bed, but a pain ran through his back. His foot was in some form of splint. He wondered if the girl would help. She held back. He realised he was still wearing his customs officer's uniform, maybe this was what she feared. He pressed his elbow into the straw and pushed himself around to sit. His head was throbbing. The girl gave a hasty, forced smile and left. He listened for a key turning in the lock, but the door was simply closed and footsteps heard on gravel, slowly fading. He wasn't a prisoner; at least that was good news. Though more likely whoever she was and whoever she lived with, could see he would not be able to run away, even if he'd wanted to.

'What day is this?' Thoughts scrambled in his head. The last thing he remembered was going into the customs cottage after Caleb Brown and John Hewitt were taken away. Those moulds had not long been in Caleb Brown's stable. He knew Caleb. Yes, he was a smuggler, but not part of any large gang and made a good enough living to not clip coins or make forgeries. Someone had placed the moulds there on purpose, to get him in trouble. Or, more likely, to take attention away from the real culprits. And who was the commander who demanded so much of him and had men hold a pistol to his back? Edward Allan, the commissioner, had been sent to London and was still away when it all happened. He pushed his face into his palms, rubbed it and ran his fingers through his hair. He needed to speak with someone who knew English, but could he make himself understood to ask for someone? Wherever he was, he needed to get home soon or Caleb Brown and John Hewitt would surely hang.

Chapter 14

Uncle John's secret

Danny stomped along the snow-flecked road. His face, just visible between his woollen hat and scarf, showed the markings of a scowl. His hands were pushed deep into his pockets, fists clenched. Luckily he was too late for his mother to send him to church for the evening service, he wasn't in the mood in any case. It was just two days before Christmas when he would have to attend the Priory both in the morning and evening. The singing was all right, but he didn't like standing in the cold whilst Reverend Jackson took to the pulpit to deliver his long sermons. What he wanted now, more than anything, was that his father were home, because he was furious.

Mother had sent him to help Aunt Mary and he'd been at Hinton for the past two nights. She'd caught a chill from her visit to the gaol a week ago. He'd been sent to do chores for her, especially collecting wood for the fire to keep her warm. He'd happened across a fallen tree and had taken Uncle John's axe and cut up a large branch. It had been hard work, but it should keep his aunt's fire going for a week or more. Cousin Betsy had made a large kettle of broth, and had been running between her mother and her own home.

'I'm much better today, Danny,' Aunt Mary'd told him that morning. 'Much better. I'm going to take the pony an' cart into town tomorrow.'

'Are you sure, Aunt Mary?'

'I must find out if there's any news from Winchester. It's been ten days since the arrests. There's been no word about a trial.'

'Was the gaol awful?'

'The place were cleaner than I thought it would be. The men were given bread an' a clean towel every day.'

'What did Uncle John say? About why they'd been arrested.'

'Said they knew nothing of the coins an' told the gaoler as much. Said he'd had a look o' sympathy about him when they'd both insisted.'

'And you're going to see the attorney again?'

'Yes, an' ye must be getting back home.'

As he moved swiftly along the gravel track his head spun with a tale Aunt Mary had told him about Uncle John's time at sea. Whenever Uncle John had told him stories, they'd been fantastic tales of enormous waves and colossal animals. He was sure a lot of the stories were made up, but those thoughts had gone and now his aunt's story haunted his mind.

'John went to sea at 11. He started out on a coasting vessel, a bit like the *Dove* that runs coal between Christchurch an' London. He worked from Lymington, taking salt to places, all over. When they were at sea he'd watch the mighty navy ships an' East Indiamen with their billowing white sails an' began to dream of travelling around the world. He were 14, 'bout the same as ye are now, so he made his way to London an' joined such a ship as a cabin boy. He worked his way up to boatswain, in charge of those sails he so admired.'

Aunt Mary had allowed herself a smile, something

Danny had not seen her do since their problems had started. She told him Uncle John had come back to the land for a while, and they'd met, got married and had Betsy. As they sat in the pale, yellow glow of the fire, she continued. 'But the lure of the oceans were too much. Being skilled he could earn good money, to help keep me an' yer cousin, so he went to sea once more. His last ship was the *Coledale,* three decks an' a hundred an' fifty feet long. It had sixty guns an' a hundred an' thirty crew. More than two years that voyage took. He came home safe, just, but changed, diff'rent. It was on the *Coledale* that he met Isaac Hooper.'

Danny was spellbound. He'd not heard about how Uncle John and Isaac had met and hadn't realised they'd been friends for so long.

'John told me this story twenty years ago, or more. It were the first, an' last time he spoke o' it. It were as if he needed to pour out the memories so they'd ne'er wash around in his head again. Nor has he been to sea since, only in the Bay.' Aunt Mary pulled a woollen shawl around her arms and looked at the flames flittering in the grate. Danny could hear her breathing in and out, just like she was about to start running, or to climb a hill.

'It were on the journey home. They'd been to Bombay, that's in India. Had a cargo of silks from the east, spices, things I've ne'er seen nor heard of. Altogether the cargo were worth a fortune. He said they had to be aware o' pirates, near Malabar, ready to chase after them an' take the ship. They've spies, ye know, tell the pirates the best ships to go for. Captain doubled the watch. John had to ensure they moved as quickly as they could. They were making good sail, the weather was perfect, though John said the heat made every man sweat to soaking an' thirsty as if they were being drained. The smell were bad, it were best to be upwind o' the men.

One afternoon the captain were on the deck. It were a clear day, nothing surrounding them but a deep blue sea, capped with pearly tips an' a curved horizon breaking onto a sky blue as a sapphire. It were all peaceful until suddenly the light chatter o' the crew doing their work, an' voices singing below, came to a sudden stop as the screech o' a man falling from the rigging split the air. He tumbled, catching his arms on the lines o' ropes. John gasped, holding his breath, waiting for the worst to happen. A man could get caught by the neck, fall to the deck an' break bones – or die. Instead the man made a lucky landing into a web o' netting. It were Isaac Hooper. He were drunk. The captain, who'd ordered every man on board to keep alert for the pirates were furious an' ordered his flogging. Well, ye seen Isaac, skinny as anything.'

Danny nodded. Isaac made him laugh, he was often drunk, dressed in strange clothing and was, as Aunt Mary described him, very thin. He was also short, in fact he was now shorter than Danny.

'John knew it'd be bad for him. Isaac were a good sailor, quick on the masts an' one o' his best men, so John pleaded with the captain. He said the men needed to drink due to the heat, but Isaac had to go through with it. The crew were gathered an' he were whipped with a cat o' nine tails. His back cut up, the sores were bad an' he ended up so ill they all thought he'd die.'

'Did the pirates attack?' Danny's eyes were wide, this was the best story ever.

'No. Not a sight o' them at that point, they were passed the worst, but they could strike anywhere. It weren't pirates to blame for the tragedy that struck.'

'Oh, no, what happened?'

'One night, 'bout six weeks into the journey, the ship blew up, burned an' sank.'

Danny gasped, pulling his hand to his mouth.

'John weren't certain why, but he thinks the wet curtains in the magazine where they store the gunpowder had dried out an' a spark from a lamp outside set 'em on fire. The curtains must have set a barrel alight or there'd been some spilled powder. The magazine went up an' blew the ship apart. John were blasted into the sea along with those on the deck at the time. The orange glow o' the flames lit the frame of what were left o' the ship. It were like a scene from hell. John couldn't bear the screams piercing the night. The only other light were from burning bits of wood an' there were a vile smell o' gunpowder an' flesh. He swam through the fiery debris, the heat searing his face so much that he kept under the water as much as possible. He reached the fo'c's'le which were broken an' drifting away. The deck were alight an' loud crashes an' bangs thundered 'round his ears. John managed to climb aboard. The screams were coming from the crew decks where people were trapped. He managed to force open a hatch an' terrified men scrambled up the ladder that had, by God's will, stayed in place. Dozens spilled out, pushing their way through the flames and leaping into the water.'

'Uncle John did all that?' Danny lifted his hands onto his head, his mouth held agape.

Aunt Mary nodded, 'There's more, Danny. Then John remembered Isaac, sick in his hammock. He climbed down inside. It were a jumble of wood an' smashed walls. A canon had fallen through from above an' lay in a hole in the floor which was slanted down. Flames were making their way along what had been a ceiling, an' around the canon. Water were gushing through holes an' the wooden hull cracked loud like a massive lightning strike an' thunderclap. The limbs of crew crushed an' dead could be seen between the broken boards. Through a hole ahead, John could see hammocks swinging. Without thinking o' his own life, an' me an' Betsy ...' Aunt Mary paused, biting on her lips and her eyes beginning to fill. Danny was frozen, he knew how things turned out as Uncle John and Isaac were alive, but how had Uncle John rescued Isaac?

'He could see more dead men. After a frantic search,

there, rolled in a blanket an' caught up in a spinning hammock, were Isaac. Uncle John clawed his way over the rubble an' flames an', drawing a knife which was still fastened to his belt, he cut Isaac down, tossed him over his shoulder an' pushed his way back through the fiery hatch an' out into the water.'

Danny sat back and blew out his cheeks in a loud whistle. 'Uncle John saved Isaac's life.'

'He saved many lives, Danny. They were lucky that they were close to an island, though they couldn't see it during the night as they clung on to wreckage. John managed to put Isaac onto a wooden plank to keep him from drowning. People from the island had seen an' heard the explosion. They'd taken to small boats an' had already rescued many, but they hadn't seen yer uncle. As soon as dawn came those still in the water were able to swim to the shore. John pushed the plank with Isaac to the sands an' the islanders took them to nearby huts an' brought food an' drinks. They nursed Isaac an' the rest of the sick an' injured back to health an' sent word of the wreck. It were four months afore a ship came to bring 'em home.'

'Uncle John's a hero, Aunt Mary. But he's never said anything.' Danny felt a tide of pride for his uncle rising in his chest.

'He saw some dreadful things, Danny an' he were hurt too, burned. He wanted to forget, forever.'

'Burned?'

'Have ye noticed that he always keeps his back an' arms covered? That's to hide his scars. The islanders tended his burns, he were very lucky, he might have died.'

After recalling his aunt's story, an anger rose in Danny through every nerve of his body making his heart beat as if it were pushing him from the inside out. The story explained why Isaac was so upset. Danny ran and ran until he could see his cottage ahead in the fading light. The sky was heavy grey, it would snow again soon. A candle shimmered in the window, so someone was home. After all Uncle John had been through, what he'd done to save those lives, it was wrong that he should hang over a few coins and Edmund Tarrant's lies. Whether father was home or not, he was going to confront Edmund and force him to tell the truth.

Chapter 15

Puzzles for Danny's friends

'Ringwood. White Hart!'

Nathan blew out his cheeks. 'I'm glad we here, me bones are a-rattlin'.'

Will laughed. 'This were supposed to be one o' the better coaches.'

The door opened and the driver drew down the steps bringing a chilled draught of early morning air through the sweaty cabin. The boys allowed a couple with their daughter to dismount then followed them. They stamped the stone flags to shake the numbness from their legs while the driver and mate lifted luggage off the tail board.

'Only a bit of snow here, Will,' Nathan said.

'Then probably less in Christchurch. Let's find the ostler, see if he knows of anythin' goin' there today.'

A stout man dressed in a long coat and boots appeared and began unhitching the horses from the coach's shafts. He gave Nathan a long look and addressed Will. 'Good morning to you, was it a good journey?'

'A bit shaky,' Nathan said, as he took a trunk from the driver.

'We're glad to be 'ere, master ostler,' Will answered,

'but our journey's not over yet. Would ye know of any waggons or coaches goin' to Christchurch today?'

The ostler held the reins of one of the large horses and patted it. 'There'll be coming and goings, it being Christmas eve and all, but nothing for passengers.'

Will looked at Nathan and pulled a face. 'Don't much want a ten-mile walk with that.' He pointed at the trunk.

'There is someone you could try.' The man rubbed his whiskery chin. 'Davey Brook. He said he was delivering some cheeses to Christchurch. He might find room for you. Or he could take the trunk, make your walk easier.'

Will's face brightened. 'Where'll we find 'im?'

'Follow the road,' he pointed. 'Past Lonnen and turn right. There's a cottage across the road. Davey's dairy's just up the lane beside it.'

'Lonnen?' Nathan shrugged.

'Grand house at the end, you can't miss it.'

'Thanks.'

'It's busy,' Nathan said, sniffing and catching aromas of brewing and baking. A boy rushed past pushing a trolley laden with barrels.

'The gentry make a fuss of Christmas. Lots of games an' feastin'. He'll be deliverin' those somewhere.' Will puffed. 'This trunk's heavy. Are you sure we only put clothes inside?'

Nathan hitched his side up. 'Yes, that's all. Hope these handles don't break.'

'Holly?' A woman shouted out. She was standing beside a table laden with prickly green boughs covered in red berries.

Will shook his head. 'I promise ye, mother'll 'ave a bough over the fire, but it'll be from the fields.' He smiled, then nodded towards a tall, red-bricked building. 'That must be the house the ostler means.'

The boys found the small cottage and a narrow alley beside it where the smell of cheeses hung in the air. Davey

Brook was wearing a felt hat and woollen coat. He was in a stable brushing an attractive grey horse. Will had seen dapple greys before, but not like this. Its hair was a charcoal colour with spots of a brighter but not light grey. There was no white. Its mane and tail were both long and black. It was typical sized yet heavily built. A perfect carthorse, though it would be difficult to see in the dark.

'Hello, Mr Brook?' Will called out. 'The ostler at the White Hart said ye might be goin' to Christchurch today. Would ye have room to take us?'

'And that?' The man pointed at the trunk.

'Aye.'

'Shillin'.'

'Sixpence.'

'Help me load the cart and sixpence'll do. Come back later, I'm not goin' till this afternoon. You can leave your trunk.'

'Let's find an alehouse, keep warm.'

'We passed one earlier.'

'There's one.' Will trotted across the track to a thatched building where barrels were piled outside. A streak of smoke rose into the grey sky. He poked his face at the window then darted away, pressing his back into the wall.

'What is it?' Nathan caught up with his friend.

'Meekwick Ginn.'

'Who dat?'

'A venturer. Puts money into smugglin'.'

Nathan snatched a glance through the window. 'He's very pale. Who's dat with him?'

'Don't know.'

'Do he know you?'

'He saw me once, last year. He was talkin' to Isaac. Doubt he'd remember me, but can't be sure. Let's go in.'

'Don't forget, everyone'll look round when dey see me.'

'Aye, which means they won't look at me. Come on.'

The inn was just one small room with a low, beamed

ceiling. Logs crackled on a roaring fire and smoke from pipes being sucked by those inside hovered in the air. Will spotted a table close to Ginn, who was facing the window and to one side of his friend. They took their seats, Will with his back to Ginn's. Nathan removed his hat and scarf and undid his coat. Will kept his hat on. The mutterings that had met their entrance had returned to the normal chatter of an alehouse. A girl approached and they ordered small beers. Ginn and the man were talking.

'...to Christchurch, but the Tarrant boy may be a problem.' Will pricked up his ears. He motioned to Nathan with his eyes and mouthed to him, 'they're talking about Edmund Tarrant.'

Their drinks arrived. Nathan leaned forward across the table and Will took his tankard and sat back. They listened.

'Don't bother me with him. He's your problem,' Ginn hissed.

'You got him involved,' the other man said. His voice was slow. 'You could have ignored him, just told me the revenue were getting close.'

'He wants money, he's after a reward.'

'What does he want rewarding for?'

'The arrests,' Ginn scoffed. 'Said you'd told him so.'

'It was them or us. They were good men.'

'Were?'

'Well they're bound to hang.'

Ginn leaned closer to the man. 'That's your doing, having the moulds planted. The Tarrant boy helped with that. He could still get a rope around your neck too. I warned him you'd get to him first if he said anything.'

'We're picking up the barrels tonight. They'll be the last until we hear from France. Word is that agents are closing in. It might need to go quiet for a while.'

'Henry Lane came to see me this morning. The town's bothered about those men who were arrested. I'd stay away if I were you, Byng.'

The man called Byng stood, lifted his coat from the chair and put it on. 'I've told you now, tonight's the last lot. We'll be done with Christchurch after that. And I can't stop those men going to the gallows can I? If I speak I'll take their place and I'm *not* going to do that.' He slammed on his hat, brushed past Will and stormed out.

Ginn sniffed and leaned over to pick up his stick that had fallen to the floor as Byng had passed. 'Bess, get the boy to bring my horse and fetch my coat.' He finished what looked like brandy, pushed himself to his feet and made his way through the rear of the inn. Will watched under the brim of his hat until he'd disappeared then lifted it off his head.

'What is it, Will, yu gone pale as him?'

'Did ye hear that?'

'Some of it.'

'Somethin's happened an' Edmund Tarrant's part of it.' Will clenched his fists. 'It sounds like men have been arrested at Christchurch.'

'They say anythin' else?' Nathan asked.

'Somethin' 'bout moulds. Never heard o' that man, Byng, but he's just said that the men will hang. I wonder who they're talkin' 'bout?'

'Why won't Papa be home for Christmas? Why do we have to go to Cliff House? Can we not stay here in our new home for Christmas?'

'Oh, Perinne, all these questions.' Jane Menniere looked up from her book.

'I miss Papa.'

'And so do I, Perinne. Maybe he'll be home soon.'

Perinne scanned the bay. There were ships out at sea

and small boats making their way towards the harbour entrance. It had been strange to see the tide washing away glistening white snow instead of sand.

'Maman, perhaps Uncle Charles knows.'

'Yes, perhaps. Now, go to your room and I'll tell Lucy to help you dress and put up your hair. We must be going soon.'

The coach pulled up at the stone porch of Cliff House. Perinne peered up towards the window that had been her bedroom for over a year. Someone was watching, a girl. The face was familiar, but Perinne couldn't recall where she'd seen her before. Scott, the Tarrant's coachman pulled on the doorbell cord and returned to help Jane and Perinne. Lucy the maid stayed inside the coach. Lucy had worked at Cliff House until moving to work for the Menniere family. John Scott was her father and she gave him a broad smile.

'Thank you for coming for us, Scott,' Jane said.

'My pleasure, Madam Menniere.' Scott bowed. He took down a box that had been beside him on the coach seat and carried it behind the visitors who were now passing into the hall.

'Mistress, Perinne welcome back. Your rooms are ready, follow me please.' Joseph took the large box from Scott who left, closing the high wooden door behind him. The chill from outside drifted away and the smell of burning coal filtered around.

They climbed the staircase and passed along the corridor. Perinne tried to catch a glance through the door of her old room, but couldn't spot its occupant.

'Who is here, Joseph?'

'Perinne! You will find out soon enough,' Jane chided.

'Sir Charles and Lady Elizabeth will greet guests at dinner at five o'clock, Madam Menniere. It's just gone two. Sir Charles has asked to see you in his study at three. Might I tell him you'll attend?'

'Perhaps he has news of Papa.' Perinne jumped with

excitement.

'Perinne, please. Yes, of course, Joseph, I'll make my own way.'

Perinne's room was across the corridor from her mother's and looked over the back of the house towards the courtyard and stables. The coach was now stopped by the coach house and Lucy was speaking with her father, who hugged her. Lucy made her way into the building, but it was a while before she was with Perinne.

'Sorry I've been so long, miss. It's good to see Joseph and Susan again and I've been given my orders for the next few days. I'm sharing a room with Clara and I'm helping with the feast tomorrow.'

'Feast?'

'It's instead of gifts. This year Sir Charles is using the big barn and all the tenants are invited on Christmas Day to a feast. Master Edmund's organized it.'

'Ah, the tenants were given gifts last year. But Edmund? He would not like doing that.'

'I don't think he had a choice.' Lucy's eyes twinkled with mischief.

'What do you mean?'

'I shouldn't say it, miss, but he's been in trouble again. Thrown out of school. He's home for good now.'

'This does not surprise me.' Perinne stopped as voices sounded from the hall below. 'That is Maman, she is meeting with Uncle Charles. I must go, I want to see if there is any news of Papa.' She dashed to the door.

Jane had already reached the library where Sir Charles Tarrant had his study. Perinne saw her tap on the door and step inside. Scrambling down the stairs she stopped outside, the door was ajar and she wondered if she should go in. Her mother was speaking.

'Have you news of Yves, Charles? When should we expect him home? Perinne's been fretting.'

'I really cannot say. They, that is Yves and my servant,

Clarke, are undertaking King's work.'

'What kind of work?'

'I don't know too much about it myself.'

'Were you able to pass on Mrs Clarke's letter?'

'Letter? I know of no letter.'

'Why, I sent it over a week yesterday, last Sunday, when we were supposed to visit, but I was unwell.'

'I'm sorry, Jane, I did see your note. I was going to write to London. I don't know of another letter. I'll ask Joseph.'

Perinne stifled a gasp. Danny's letter was missing, he would be so upset. It meant his father was unaware he was needed at home.

'What was the letter about?' Sir Charles continued.

'It was asking her husband to return home as soon as possible.'

'Ah, the arrests.'

Jane dipped her head and rubbed her hands together. 'I do not approve of what they've done, but the truth of the matter is being questioned.'

'What do you mean?'

'From what Mrs Clarke said and from servants' gossip, it seems someone has hidden moulds on purpose to get the men into trouble.'

'Gossip is all that it is. I'm surprised at you, Jane.'

'But the men, one is the man who brought Perinne home after those awful smugglers snatched her from here last year. The other saved the girl in the church in the summer.'

'That doesn't mean they've not been coining.' Sir Charles rose and stood beside the fire, holding his hands to the warmth of the flames. 'It's more than that, Jane.' He took a deep breath and rubbed his chin. 'This is most secret and not to be repeated.' He paused, staring into the grate, as if conjuring words from the flames. 'Someone is forging coins and bringing them into England through the harbour. The men are part of the gang taking the goods onwards. Edmund found out and he fetched the warrant to be signed.'

Perinne slumped onto a chair close to the door and ran her fingers through her hair. Despite the chill of the hall, she felt her face redden. It couldn't be true about Caleb and Danny's Uncle John and if Edmund had played a part, nothing could be believed. But what could she do?

Chapter 16

Angry Danny

Danny wove his way through carts and people, who were dashing in all directions like ants escaping from a nest. Edmund Tarrant had to be here somewhere. The town clattered as folk rushed around carrying baskets filled with breads, meats and fruit. Two boys were standing under the arches of the town hall crying out, 'holly for sale'. The afternoon sun was losing its fight; the occasional spot of blue was being swallowed by the darkening cloud falling over the town like a grey blanket.

It was Christmas Eve and Danny would have to return at midnight to attend the Priory. Jack would go with him, mother had to stay at home as it was too late to take Sarah out and about. The layer of snow that had covered the ground that morning had melted away. He hadn't slept well. There'd been no word of his father and he couldn't stop thinking about Uncle John and what he'd been through. How must he be feeling stuck in a smelly gaol waiting for his fate to be decided? He had to get him out of there, and he was certain in order to do so he had to find Edmund Tarrant and make him talk.

He made towards the end of the high street trying to

think where Edmund could be. He reached the brewery across from where the old Bargate had stood and propped himself against a wall. He pulled his scarf around his neck and tucked his gloved hands deep into his pockets. The chilled air was a sickly mix of hops and wood smoke. He watched the faces of people scurrying about, it would soon start to go dark. A shout blew through the door of a nearby shop and a boy jumped into the street laughing. Danny recognised him, it was Simon Slate. The first time he'd seen Simon was on the beach. He was with Edmund and they'd all fought. Simon had attacked Will at Edmund's command. He'd seen him around the town now and then, but had never spoken to him. But he would now.

'Simon?'

'Who are you?' The boy looked down his long nose. His dark hair showed in waves from under his round, brimmed hat.

Danny took a breath. He hadn't remembered him. That would help. 'I'm looking for Edmund, he said he'd meet me.'

'Oh? He didn't say. He's supposed to be meeting me.'

'Er he said here, I've been waiting.'

'He's not meeting me here.'

'Do you know where he is?'

'He's gone to the custom's cottage, something about a reward, anyway he'd surely have told you that. Are you …'

'Sorry, got to go.' At that Danny sped away.

'I can see the river, should be a good place to leave the horses.'

Ambrose took his white clay pipe from his mouth and

pointed with the stem. 'There's a stable lad by that brewery, we can ask him to guard them.'

'I'll go.'

Ambrose watched as Mokey crossed the road, spoke to a young lad and reached into his pocket. He gave the boy what was probably one of the coins they'd spent the day before clipping the edges to save the metal. Soon the men were heading towards the high street.

'Tis busy.'

'Good, no one will notice us,' Ambrose answered, tucking his pipe into the inside pocket of his coat.

'Do we know what this boy looks like?'

'Fifteen-ish. Son of a landowner, not many o' those in Christchurch. Look for one well dressed.'

'Need to get him away from these crowds.'

'Remember, Mokey, we're only warning him.'

'I know.'

'Then we got to get down to the main business. Won't be long afore dark.'

'Look, Ambrose, coming up that street.' Mokey pointed his short, stubby finger.

'That could be him, though he's not in as much a hurry as that young lad.' Ambrose motioned towards the figure of a fair-haired boy running towards them.

'Could that be him?'

The boy passed them and turned the corner, stopping dead in his tracks. 'Edmund Tarrant, I want to talk to you,' he yelled at the taller boy, poking him in the chest.

Ambrose gave a wry smile when he saw the scuffle. 'There ye are, Mokey, our job done for us. Wonder who that other lad is?'

'He looks mighty angry. He's yelling loud now, let's get closer.'

'What have you been doing Edmund? What lies have you been telling about my uncle?' Danny gave Edmund a shove.

Edmund leaned back and smirked. 'Don't know what you mean, shorty Clarke.'

'Yes you do. You were there when he was taken away.'

'So.'

'You knew about the coins.'

Edmund scoffed.

'You want money, you were asking about a reward. Is that for lying about my uncle, don't you have enough money already?'

'That's none of your business, Clarke.'

'Why did you have our letter?'

'What?' Edmund's eyes widened, then screwed his face in a scowl.

'And you're mixed up with Meekwick Ginn.'

'You don't know that. You're guessing.' Edmund pushed Danny, who stumbled backwards.

Danny snorted, finding his feet again. Then, with a deep breath, grabbed Edmund by the coat and bellowed, 'who's Byng? Tell me. I want to know where to find Byng.'

Edmund grabbed Danny's coat, the boys' chests almost touching. 'Shut up!' he hissed into Danny's face. 'What you all staring at?' He screamed at the crowd, which had gathered around the pair. Faces appeared at the upstairs windows of the town hall. One of the boys who was selling holly was standing on a crate, the other craning his neck to get a better view. Mokey and Ambrose pressed into the crowd.

'Get him, Edmund.' It was Simon's voice.

Breaking free of Edmund's grasp, Danny kicked out striking Edmund on the shin, then landed a punch on his stomach making Edmund suck in air. Edmund gained his breath and leapt onto Danny, spinning him around and flattening him onto the ground. He thumped Danny's back. Danny let out a yelp, he scrunched his fury-filled face and with a huge breath heaved himself up, sending Edmund tumbling onto his backside. Both had mud seeping into their clothes from the churned gravel of the street. Danny's stockings were ripped and his hat squashed from falling onto it. They were both upright again and tugging at each other to try to get the upper edge.

'*Desist. Stop, boys*, *now*.' Reverend Jackson pushed through the crowd. 'You're acting like a pair of drunken ruffians, you should both know better.' He was followed by a boy. The vicar took Edmund's arm and the boy pushed himself bravely between the enemies. It was Adam, the vicar's son.

'He started it,' Edmund spat.

'He's been spreading lies about my uncle. I wager he was the one who put the moulds in Mr Brown's stable.'

'Liar!'

Simon appeared and stood beside Edmund.

'Tell them, Simon. Tell them I've had nothing to do with smugglers and everything else these peasants get themselves involved in.'

Simon nodded.

'Master Edmund, you should go home. You Clarke, I expect you here for midnight mass prompt and tomorrow you help to serve the alms to the poor after morning service. Now go, both of you.'

'Come on, Danny.' Adam put an arm across Danny's back and led him nearby to the *George*, sitting him on a bench.

The crowd began to disperse. The vicar was stern faced as he spoke to Edmund. Simon disappeared, reappearing a few minutes later with two horses. From inside the *George* Beth Gibbs appeared.

'You think Edmund hid the moulds?'

Danny hunched his shoulders. 'Did you hear?'

'Half the town heard.'

'I don't know, but he is involved. I heard him with Meekwick Ginn and Isaac mentioned that some of the town's men were looking for someone called Byng. You know what he's like, don't you Adam?'

Adam nodded. 'But I can't get involved, Danny, father won't allow it.'

'He knows something. He's part of it. He was laughing at me until I mentioned Ginn and Byng. Why would that make him so angry?'

'Well, that was interesting.'

'We're not going to get to speak with the Tarrant boy now, Mokey, look, he's heading away.'

'He's got a loose tongue. How did the other boy know about Ethan Byng?'

'And he mentioned coins. He's still there, look. Maybe we should find out.'

'A bit risky that, Ambrose. He's looking for information and he'd want to know why we're interested.'

'Yes, ye're right. We need to report back an' see what Mr Byng wants us to do. Let's sort tonight's shipment an' then we've no need to come back here. Unless we need to sort the Tarrant boy.'

'Perhaps we'll need to sort the other boy too.'

Chapter 17

Danny discovers more

Flecks of snow skipped across Danny's face as he trudged his way home. He was too angry to feel sore from his scrap with Edmund. Shadows from candles were softening the late afternoon gloom. One was winking through the window of the revenue officer's cottage. Danny stopped in his tracks, as if the sight had lit a light in his mind. He took a step back and rapped on the door.

'Yes?' A man wearing the blue uniform of a riding officer looked Danny up and down. 'What've you been up to?'

Danny instinctively brushed his hand across some of the dirt on his coat. 'Is Mr Stevens here?'

'No, no one's seen or heard of him for days.'

'I wanted to ask him something.'

'Ask me.'

Danny scanned the officer. He was bright faced and appeared the cheerful kind. Maybe he would answer his question about something Simon Slate had said. He thought he knew the answer, but maybe there was more. The only way to find out was to ask.

'Edmund Tarrant was here a while back. What did he

want a reward for?'

'Ah, him,' the man chuckled. 'He thinks the customs owe him money for catching two men smuggling a few nights back.'

Danny held his breath and counted in his head to try to stay calm. 'And did he? Will he get a reward?'

'Come inside, the cold's getting into the cottage.'

Danny took off his hat, shook away flakes of snow and stepped indoors. The cottage had a low ceiling supported by dark beams. A fire was lit and there was a desk and chair in the corner beside the window. A door led to what Danny imagined was an upstairs and also down to a cellar, where prisoners were probably held. There was no one else about. Perhaps it was why the man was happy to talk.

'The reward?' Danny pressed.

'Well, that's the problem. No reward was set. He's not happy about it. He'd come here nearly two weeks' since. Said he'd seen some moulds at the blacksmiths whilst he was waiting for his horse to be shoed. He'd heard from his father men had been coining and said he could get a warrant signed if we wanted. He was very keen and Joshua was most interested. I think Joshua knew something else, but wasn't saying. I was with him on the night the men were caught. It should be Joshua getting any rewards, if only he could be found.'

'So...' Danny paused. His heart had quickened in his chest. The man was giving him good information, if he stayed calm he might keep him talking.

'Yes? If there's nothing else, I'll bid you good evening.'

'Er, just one thing. What were the men smuggling?'

The man shrugged. 'There was nothing on the boat. They'd done for the night.'

Danny forced a smile. 'Thank you.'

'Oh, and, if you're interested things have been brought forward. We've heard they'll go before the judge on the third of January.' At that, the man opened the door, it was time for Danny to leave.

Danny stood in the snow unable to move. He shivered, it was fully dark now. He guessed it to be about five o'clock. His mother was going to be fuming. Late, dirty and with torn stockings. He thought about what the man had told him. It meant two things. First, it had been Edmund who'd told the revenue men about the moulds and second, he had just ten days to find out the truth and rescue Uncle John and Caleb from the hangman.

Chapter 18

Home to bad news

Whilst Danny had been with the riding officer, a cart passed by. Huddled on the seat along with the driver, Will and Nathan saw shadows of the ruins of Christchurch castle and the old house appear dim from the glow of nearby rush lights. Will smiled.

'I love this view, Nathan. When I see the ruins, I know I'm 'ome.'

'My first stop's just here, boys,' the driver said. 'The *New Inn*, the *George* and then *High Street*.'

'We'll get off first stop,' Will said.

The boys lifted their trunk from the cart and handed Davey Brook the sixpence he'd asked for. In exchange Will was given a small package.

'Here, this is for Christmas Day.'

Will sniffed it, it was cheese and smelled sour and earthy. He grinned at Brook. He did wonder earlier why he was setting out so late in the afternoon at this time of the year. But during the ride he'd told Will he had something to bring back, then winked. Will knew whatever it was, it would probably come in through the harbour after dark.

'Thanks, Davey. Come on Nathan, let's get 'ome.'

'How long to the rendezvous?'

'High water's not 'til ten. We're meeting them by the head. We'll need to set out before nine to get out of the harbour and around the sand bar.' The man lifted his tricorn hat and ran his hands over his grey hair.

'And we're all right here until then?' Mokey looked around the boathouse. The single candle lit a web of ropes and a rowing boat. Their horses were shuffling beside the closed doors, brought inside so there was nothing to be seen that could betray the old building had occupants.

'No one will come this way now. But stay quiet and only one candle, keep it where it is.' The man's face was serious.

'This place yours?' Mokey asked.

'No. It's Caleb Brown's. The blacksmith, who's in gaol for delivering your barrels.'

'Not ours. We're just doing a job, same as you.' Mokey crossed his arms, any of them could meet the same fate as the two Christchurch men.

'Ye're being paid well for tonight,' Ambrose added. He was sitting on an upturned box barely visible but for a speckle of light, like a glow-worm pulsing as he drew from his pipe.

'Aye, and once it's done, I'm doing no more for Ginn. I've finished with him. Here's some food. I'll be back later.' At that the man slipped through the door and onto the snowy riverbank.

'Mother!' Will called out, lifting the latch and pushing open the door of the tiny cottage. A brown and white dog with long, brown ears appeared, its tail flicking back and forth and barking snappy woofs of greeting.

'*Will*, oh Will, I can't believe ye're home an' on Christmas Eve.' Meg Gibbs threw her arms in a hug around her son, squeezing him until he had to gently pull away.

'You're here, you're home.' Beth Gibbs appeared at the top of the steps which led to the attic where the family slept. 'And Nathan's here too.' She scrambled into the room and launched herself at her brother who lifted her by the waist and spun her around.

'Careful,' Meg squealed with delight, 'ye'll knock o'er what bit o' furniture we 'ave.'

Beth lifted Will's coat from his shoulders and knocked off his hat. 'Come, take off your damp things and sit by the fire. You too, Nathan.' She held out her arm. 'Did you arrived by coach? Mr Martin said the last had arrived this afternoon.'

'Smell de clothes, Beth,' Nathan grinned.

Beth lifted a coat to her nose, then scrunched it. 'Cheese?' Sam the dog joined in, sniffing the air.

'We got a lift from a cheesemaker, bringin' deliveries from Ringwood. Here, he gave us some fer the Christmas table.'

'We got there dis mornin' on de coach from London.'

'How long are you home for?' Beth asked, hanging the coats behind the door.

Will's face beamed in the soft, ochre candle light. 'Fer good.'

'This be wonderful. We'll 'ave some tea, good an' strong.' Meg took a small, wooden box from a dresser then opened a drawer under the counter top. She lifted a key with a grin and disappeared into the room at the other side of the fire, which was burning briskly. A kettle, already steaming was hanging over the fire.

'Ye've a good blaze, an' a decent pile o' logs,' Will said, as he and Nathan jostled playfully before the flames in an effort to get warm. Will pointed to a holly garland stretched across the mantel. 'Told you,' he mouthed to Nathan.

Meg reappeared with a tray carrying four china cups and a matching tea pot. Will knew it wouldn't have been used for a long time. His mother would have been given some tea to keep in the box, probably by Isaac. The caddy had been a gift when his parents were married.

'Isaac found that firewood. He's been workin' so hard.' Meg set the tray down.

'Isaac? Work hard?'

'He's been miserable, he's tryin' to take his mind off things.'

'Oh, *mother*,' Beth exclaimed. 'Will won't know.'

'Know what, Beth?' Will paused. He glanced at Nathan. 'Is this about men being arrested?'

'You've heard about it? In London?' Beth's brown eyes were wide.

Will pulled a chair close to the fire. Sam settled at his feet. 'No, we overheard Meekwick Ginn talkin' with another man at an alehouse in Ringwood.'

'Jus luck we were there. Wastin' time waitin' for the cheesman,' Nathan said.

'Meekwick Ginn? Might've known he were part of it.' Beth pulled a face as she spoke the name.

'They were talkin' 'bout Edmund Tarrant. Somethin' 'bout moulds. They mentioned Henry Lane, too.'

'An' somethin's happenin'. Tonight. Dey gettin' some barrels.'

'That's nothin' unusual, Nathan.' Meg pressed her lips together.

'So, who's been arrested?' Will asked.

Beth gave her mother a worried glance. Then turned to Will. 'It's Caleb Brown and John Hewitt, Danny's uncle.'

'*No*! Not *them*. What's happened to 'em? Where are

they now?'

'Why they be in Winchester gaol. The charge is coinin' an' smugglin'. It be bad, Will.' His mother's face wrinkled with concern.

'Danny's in a bad way,' Beth said. 'He had a fight with Edmund Tarrant this afternoon. It's not for the first time. He said they'd also fought the afternoon the men were taken away.'

'What's Tarrant been up to now?' Will gritted his teeth. Edmund was an old enemy.

Beth looked directly at her brother. 'Danny thinks he hid moulds in Caleb's stable, then the revenue officers found them.'

'Why would he do that? What does Joshua Stevens say? He's a fair man.'

'He may well be that, Will,' Meg replied. 'But no one's seen 'im since the aft'noon John an' Caleb were taken away.'

Will blew out a whistle; his eyebrows lifted.

'Poor Danny,' Nathan said. 'It not long since dat school massa treated him bad.'

Will sprung to his feet. 'We've got to go and see him, Nathan. See what we can do.'

'Yes, we must.'

'Not *now*,' Meg squealed. 'It be dark an' snowin'. You can't do anythin' now.'

'He'll be at the Priory tomorrow, won't he?' Beth said. 'It being Christmas morning.'

'Aye,' Meg put in. 'Wait 'til tomorrow, Will, please. We've not seen ye fer months.'

Will slumped back onto the chair and blew out a long rush of breath. 'All right, mother, but we must go an' see 'im tomorrow. Poor Danny.'

Perinne's old room at Cliff House had seen little change. The dressing table with the carved edges and legs had been moved to the opposite wall, which remained a mix of wooden panels and a grey-green wallpaper. The bed's silken red canopy had been dusted in readiness for its latest occupant, Katherine Dover. The girl, who said to call her Kitty, was sitting on the bed. She was taller than Perinne and her fair hair was without any of Perinne's curls and waves. Perinne was beside the window leaning against the casing. She remembered Kitty now from the masked ball held in the spring last year when she'd been kidnapped by the smugglers. It was all that Kitty wanted to talk about, until Perinne had asked her to stop asking questions. It was not something she liked to think about. Kitty's father was a diplomat and spent most of his time with her mother in Italy. Kitty had to board at school. Kitty looked up from her book.

'Il sera dîner bientôt.'

'You do not need to speak French,' Perinne replied. 'Clara will tell us when dinner is served.'

'Do you not miss France, Perinne?'

'Sometimes.'

'Your family will not return?'

'I do not know. It is not probable. We have our new house at Muddiford now.'

'I wish mother and father would come and stay here in England. I don't like being at school all the time.'

'I have a governess, Miss Ashton. I would not like to be at boarding school.'

'Shall we go down in any case, we're both dressed and ready.' Kitty slipped from the bed and made to the door.

'Yes, I think there must be others here by now.'

'Leave me alone,' a voice shouted as a door slammed along the corridor. Perinne cast Kitty a wry look, rolling her eyes.

'Edmund, *Edmund*!'

Perinne and Kitty slipped back inside the bedroom and stifled giggles as Edmund's father, red faced and puffing, stamped past.

'What's he done now, I wonder?' Kitty whispered.

'It could be anything. He has been out most of the day. Perhaps Uncle Charles is angry, there must be much to do for the meal for the tenants tomorrow. Look, Clara is coming.' Perinne stepped forward. 'Clara, what has happened with Edmund?'

Clara, small and pale, stopped. She was holding a pitcher of water, the handle wrapped in a cloth to keep it from burning her as she carried it. She looked around. 'I shouldn't say, Miss Perinne.'

'You can tell us,' Kitty said. 'We shan't say it was you; we won't tell anyone at all.'

'Emm. Master Edmund's been fighting in town. His face is cut and his clothes muddy.'

'Edmund, he is always fighting,' Perinne tutted.

'He's been fighting Mister Clarke's son.'

'Danny?'

'Yes, miss. I don't know any more. I have to go.'

'Are you sure? You have not heard anything else about it?'

Clara looked over her shoulder and whispered: 'Only that it's something to do with the men caught smuggling.'

The words jolted at Perinne as if they prodded her and woke her from a slumber. She leaned towards the servant girl and whispered. 'Clara, I have something to ask of you.'

'Yes, miss.'

'Anything Edmund might say about the smugglers, that you overhear, anything at all, will you tell me?'

Chapter 19

Smugglers at work

For the second time in almost two weeks Danny was sore and bruised, though he ached more from his heart. He'd expected mother to be angry when he'd returned home, but he hadn't been prepared for her reaction.

'How can you behave like this, Danny? I'm on my own and Aunt Mary's beside herself with worry about Uncle John; your father's away and we have no idea where he is or when he'll be home and all you can do is fight with the likes of Edmund Tarrant.' She sniffed and wiped her eyes with a cloth that she'd been using to clean plates that had been gathering dust on the nearby dresser.

'Sorry, mother, but Edmund ...'

'*Stop* there, I want to hear no more. I've had as much as I can take.'

'Please, *listen*, I'm sure Edmund ...'

'No more. *No more*. Get cleaned up. There's some supper for you before you go to the Priory. Thank goodness Jack will be with you.' She sat down, pursing her lips tight and screwing her eyes into a torment of lines.

'What is it, mother?'

'Aunt Mary came. The trial's soon and the attorney thinks there's little we can do.'

At that Danny's mother took a lighted candle from the mantelpiece and disappeared up the stairs sobbing.

The snow that had fallen in the afternoon had gone. The clouds had moved away, leaving a clear night that would freeze any settled water into glass by morning. Only a few people had braved the night. Their faces dotted the nave of the church, which was lit by dozens of pale yellow candle flames, swaying as draughts whispered by in the icy air. The service was his last task of the day. The thought of his mother being so upset pulled hard in Danny's gut. The idea that nothing could be done made him feel as if he was about to retch. He hadn't been able to sing. His throat caught and nothing came out. He'd been about to tell her of the trial date, but word had already got to her. He felt as helpless, as if he were locked away himself, but he wouldn't give in.

Reverend Jackson had missed at least one hymn and Danny was certain the vicar had speeded his usual steady tongue through the lessons. No one, Danny thought, really wanted to be there. Tomorrow morning's service was to be a little later than normal and all he wanted now was to be home in bed. He knew he wouldn't sleep well, he would toss and turn, thrashing out in his mind ideas of what to do next, as he'd done each night since they'd taken Uncle John away. Even Jack seemed to have given up, saying little on their walk to the service, only vague notions that 'things will turn out' and 'they're innocent, it'll be all right.' Danny didn't believe any of it, they had to fight. He felt so alone.

A dim light broke through the windows of the church as the bell tolled for midnight mass. Three men rowed across the harbour, silently, except for the lapping of their oars. The only other noise came from night birds pipping and piping in the reeds of the marshes. Just eight small barrels laid under a canvas. As they travelled over the water they watched for signs of riding officers who might be patrolling, though it were unlikely tonight, Christmas Eve. If they were about, they were more likely to be close to the quay. It would be a waste of their time, the men would take a different route tonight. The water was ebbing from the harbour as low tide approached. There was little water now, just enough to take the weight of the men and their cargo. It was another reason for the revenue men to think smugglers would have finished for the night. Ambrose and Mokey were glad they had a guide to take them along the channels that wove around sandbanks and walls of the creeks. The snow clouds of the day had cleared and a waning moon shone above the headland spreading a silver lane of light pointing towards the neck of River Avon and the wharf. The clear skies had brought a hard and biting cold that nipped at the parts of their faces not covered with scarves and darkened with soot. Ginn's man had arrived with the cart before they left and would be waiting to carry the barrels away.

Pulling onto the bank just passed the deserted wharf, Ambrose stepped into the icy water taking the rope with him. He was followed by the other two men. Without a word to each other the men quickly passed the barrels they'd brought and stacked them on the cart that had been waiting with its owner at the boathouse. Caleb Brown's sturdy rowing boat was pulled onto the bank, it would be put away once they were ready to move on. No one would know that it had been out on the water again.

'You can go. We'll lay low until the town's sleeping,' Mokey whispered.

'I'm going,' the grey-haired man said. 'Tell Ginn that's it. No more from me.'

The cottage was set on a ledge of land. Its whitewashed walls a deep grey against the black of the night. To the front was the gravelly road that led through Forest hamlets before arriving at Ringwood. To the rear, after an incline, the water meadows spread wide and flat as the River Avon meandered through them on its way to meet the sea. The moon was finding its way to hide behind the thick thatch from where a line of smoke rose out of a single chimney. Only just a sense that there was a light inside showed through the tiny window that faced south. The curtain remained drawn back to allow the occupiers a view of any on-comers travelling from Christchurch.

'My men have risked much in this job, Ginn.'

'Pah, you've been paid well enough, Byng.'

'And we've lost use of our pool here. Been hiding goods here for years, now we need somewhere new.'

'It wasn't me who suggested it, was it?' Ginn's white face appeared jaundiced in the sullen light. 'Didn't need to use it, did you? Plenty barns and shepherd huts along this route.'

Byng let out a long sigh. 'Now I know what's in the barrels, I'm glad it's done with.'

'Getting choosey?'

'There's no pleading on coining; counterfeiting's a death sentence.'

'And fighting the revenue won't also get you hanged?'

'That can't be traced back to my men.'

'Only takes one squealer.'

'My men are loyal.'

'Are you sure about that?' Ginn sneered.

'Why, yes, they're good men.'

'It only takes one and an offer he can't refuse.'

'Look, Ginn. We've done a good job this last twelve months. Where the word's got out isn't from around here. It's where the coins begin, or where they end up; that's where it's gone wrong. That's where you'll find your squealer.'

Ginn sniffed. 'There'll be other jobs, Byng. I'm just like you, a link in the chain. The link's snapped somewhere and that's the end of it. We made good awhile and now it's ended.'

'And two innocent men will hang in the New Year. And there's nothing we can do without putting a rope around our own necks.'

'Daniel Clarke, a few words in your ear before you leave.'

Danny was looking for Jack, who he spotted in the short queue of people waiting to light their lamp from a church candle. His shoulders dropped.

'Yes, Reverend Jackson?'

'You are to help disperse the Christmas alms tomorrow after the service, did you tell your parents?'

Danny's face dropped. 'Father's away and mother was, er… ' His words stuttered out. He closed his eyes to shut off the tears he was holding back. 'Mother wasn't well when I got home earlier. She'll be asleep when we get home.' Danny was waiting for the vicar's voice to raise, but instead felt his hand on his shoulder. Jack had approached and was standing nearby.

'You've had a tough time recently, Daniel, but you must learn to control your anger. It will do you no good to be seen brawling in the streets.' Reverend Jackson stepped back and beckoned Danny towards Jack. 'We do need help tomorrow, it will take only a half-hour to give out the food. You will help, won't you?'

'Yes, Reverend Jackson.'

'Have a safe journey home.' At that the vicar walked off.

'Come on Dan.'

A few rush lights remained alight on the road and the boys' lamp offered only a low glow. Danny and Jack had walked this road many times and knew it well. The track was damp from the snow of earlier. There were few puddles to avoid and of those they could see, ice had begun to whiten their edges. They would be home in half an hour.

'You all right?'

Danny nodded then stopped in his tracks. 'Do you remember when we took Aunt Mary's cart back the day after Uncle John was arrested?'

'Yes.' Jack lifted the lamp to Danny's face as if to see what he would say next.

'Well, there was a man there, he was on the horse wanting a shoe. He was called Mr Jenkins, I think. He said he liked Caleb and that if he could help at all, to send a message.'

'Ah, yes. He said he lived by the well at Stanpit.'

'Well let's go and see him. Maybe he can do something.'

'The attorney says there's nothing more that can be done. Do you not think we should ask Mrs Brown first?'

'I suppose so, but there's nothing to lose.'

'All right, though we'll have to wait a couple of days.'

As he'd spoken his idea, Danny felt as if his steps had become lighter. There was a flicker of hope. Whoever the man was, it was worth a chance.

'What's that?' Jack broke Danny's thoughts. He was pointing ahead.

Danny squeezed his eyes hoping to focus on the sight. There was a cart pulling out of the path that led to the wharf. It was as if it were travelling of its own accord.

'How's it moving?' Jack asked.

'Come on, let's get closer.'

They quickened their step just as the cart passed by a building emitting a beam of light from a lamp. There was a horse, it was definitely there, though it had been invisible in the shadows of the cloudless night. As they watched, the single driver flicked the reins and the horse set off into the darkness at a trot, disappearing once again.

Chapter 20

Christmas morning, Northern France

Bertin entered the coffee house as if he were about to fall into a hole as soon as he made it over the step. He would give them just a few minutes, it was too dangerous to remain for very long. If his messages had arrived, then the two men would be here. He'd pass on the information and leave. He'd worried that being Christmas Day it might be quiet, but, as in the past, the place was busy. He scanned the room. The ceiling was low with oak beams, the air was smoky but had a rich coffee-bean aroma. The place echoed with chatter. The men he was seeking were a Frenchman and an Englishman. Neither, he was told, would be wearing wigs. One signal was that one of them would be wearing a pale blue handkerchief tied at the neck, the other signal was to be words. He could see them, close to the fireplace. A chair was free nearby, towards the window. He preferred a shaded corner, but he needed to be certain it was them. He signalled to the serving girl for coffee and moved to sit down, nodding politely to seated customers he passed by. The two men were toying with their cups in silence. The one wearing the necker-chief had his back to the wall and was dark haired and handsome. Bertin sat, his hands began to sweat. He noticed the man's brown eyes were darting, as if trying to meet his. The other fair-haired man was sitting sideways to him. The girl settled a cup in front of him, steamy vapour rising from the dark liquid. He lifted the cup and sipped. Despite having done this work for many years, his heart was beating hard. This would be his last task, then he'd take his family to the south and make a new life with the payment he would soon receive.

Yves Menniere turned his head as if to look out of the window. He took a long, silent breath and directed his words towards Bertin.

'It is set to be a bad winter, is it not, Monsieur?'

'I fear you are correct, though we hope a good summer will follow.'

'Would you care to join us this Christmas morning?'

'Thank you, I will.'

James Clarke moved to another chair and Bertin sat beside him bringing his coffee. He raised the cup to his lips, drained it and set it in front of him.

'The place you are looking for is Brionne. It is close to here where the items you seek are made. They are taken to ships at Harfleur. You are correct in their landing place in England, but there has been a problem and this will soon be changed.'

'Have you a name?' Yves whispered.

'Here in France, or in England?'

'Both would be of great interest to us.' Yves viewed the room, everyone seemed occupied.

The goods are taken on a lugger, the *Glory*. The captain's man ashore is called Byng. The payments are arranged by a man called Ginn.'

James shifted in his seat.

'You are aware of them? The coins are being forged on land belonging to the Comte de Melaine.' Bertin cleared his throat, placed his hands on the table and rose.

'Merci, Monsieur.' Yves reached into his coat and took out a purse. Checking no one was looking his way he slipped it over the table where Bertin took it and spirited it into his pocket.

'Au revoir,' Bertin said, before weaving his way back through the tables and disappearing out into the street.

Yves raised his eyebrows. 'Let us get back to the inn, we need to discuss what to do next.'

The inn was a short walk away from the coffee house. The two men were soon in the small bedroom overlooking the street. It had started to snow hard and a fire had been lit in the room.

'Is the place far?' James asked, sitting on a chair close to the door and leaning as if to listen for anyone approaching. 'And do we need to go? Surely now we have the information we can return?'

'Our task is to find out who is making the coins and where. The Comte may know what is happening.'

'But you gave Bertin the reward.'

'We will get no more from him. But we have an advantage.'

'What's that?'

'I know the Comte. I built a house for him close to the coast.'

James ran his fingers through his hair and took a breath. 'What are you suggesting, that we simply ask him?'

'I will pay him a visit. Make remarks that may lead him to speak of the matter. It is another chance to get information. Whatever we decide it should be me only, James, not you.'

'What do you mean?'

'The Comte does not like the English. I doubt he would worry much about something happening that would damage the English economy.'

'Hmm. Where is Brionne, is it far?'

'I make a guess that it may be two hundred miles. We will get a coach to Rouen, we should not attract attention. We will go to Brionne from there.'

James sighed.

'Brionne is not far from the coast. There is Harfleur and also Le Havre, we should be able to get to Poole from there and home. Then I can go to London alone, they also need to know that the landing place will change.'

'How long will this take?'

'It is difficult to say. A week perhaps. We'll leave tomorrow if possible, but looking at the weather, we may be stuck here for a few days.'

'I hope it clears. We won't be back for Christmas, but it would be wonderful to be home for Twelfth Night. Our family gathers on that night. It's something we all look forward to and I'd like to be there. It's such a happy time.'

'Monsieur? Ça va?'

Joshua Stevens had lost count of the days that he'd been recovering in the shack. It was bitterly cold and more blankets had been brought. Ice had formed on the water that had been left beside the bed. The people were definitely French, but he knew no more than that. He'd slept well last night for the first time and this morning he felt he was beginning at last to recover. He'd been given wine the night before and some kind of sweetmeat. It was fully light outside. The girl, whom he had worked out to be Hélène, came in carrying a tray. A man followed her. He was tall and well dressed, his face lightly tanned. He wore a heavy woollen coat and felt hat.

'Monsieur? You are English?'

Joshua drew a quick breath, as if the man's words had

pushed him backwards. It had seemed such a long time since he'd heard language that he could understand and he almost laughed with relief.

'Yes, why, yes. I'm Joshua Stevens.'

'Hélène saw me at the market and told me of you. That you were found by her grandfather at the side of the road, badly injured.'

'I can't recall how I arrived here, sir, but in the time I've spent I've received only kindness. The girl appears to be most poor.'

'The family is indeed poor, but kindly. Your injuries are healing, Hélène says.'

'I've tried my foot daily and it's still difficult.' Joshua put his foot to the floor and tried to stand. 'I'm recovering and I'll make sure that their kindness is repaid, sir, but I need to get home first.'

'Where is your home?'

'Christchurch, in Hampshire, England.'

'And do you have any idea of what happened to you?'

'We have problems with smugglers, sir. There was an incident when two men were captured. They were also accused of counterfeiting coins. I no longer believe they're guilty. I think this is why I was taken so the true villains could escape justice.' He opened his arms holding his hands out, his shoulders lifting. 'It's not uncommon that customs officers such as myself are taken and left here in France.'

'I can help you return, once you are well enough. Though it is also getting difficult to travel. There have been snow storms and the roads are blocked.'

'If I cannot return soon, is there a chance you could help me to get a message to England?' A thought sprung in his head. If he could send a message, he would need to be careful to whom it was sent. 'It is important, sir. I fear that if I cannot say what I believe about the arrested men, then a grave injustice will occur.'

Chapter 21

Christmas morning, Cliff House

'I'm too busy. You want me to arrange the servants' meal, I've no time for church,' Edmund bawled, as he ran down the staircase and disappeared through a door.

His father shook his head and sighed. 'Are the visitors down?' he asked Joseph, who was waiting for instructions.

'Yes, sir. Those going to church are in the drawing room with Lady Elizabeth.'

'Tell Scott to bring the coach to the front and instruct the guests' coachmen to follow.' Charles Tarrant went into the study library, pulled the door closed and sat behind his desk. He picked up a letter from a pile in front of him and re-read it.

'*... and it appears that Edmund is the offender. This would explain his actions in the matter of the burning of the boathouse. You would realise the grave nature of the matter if I could explain further, however by letter is not advised. I would urge a meeting here at the school at your first opportunity and before the start of the new term.*'

Your obedient servant
Hugh Taylor
Headmaster

He huffed at the mystery of the headmaster's words. Edmund had been expelled for the boathouse incident. What else could it be that he'd done to be described as 'grave'? If he confronted Edmund he'd deny being part of anything. The boy had become out of control. Perhaps he should send him on the tour, but that would reward his bad behaviour and rudeness. The trip to the school would take three days, he would make an excuse to the family, saying he had business in Bath. It would have to be after the guests left, otherwise suspicions might be raised.

Edmund entered the barn and sat on an old apple barrel wringing his interlocked fingers, frowning beneath his thick brown hair. Danny Clarke's questions had been ringing in his ears since the fight. How had he found out about Ginn? How did he know Byng's name and worst, why did he suspect that the moulds had come from him? It was all going wrong. He'd told Ginn about the coins, helped get the two town smugglers arrested, arranged the warrant, seen them taken away. Yet there was no reward. That can't be right. He should stop worrying about the moulds, Clarke couldn't prove he'd placed them in the blacksmith's stable, he was surely guessing. Ginn was useless, perhaps he should try to contact Byng, though he had no idea how. And now his father was acting strange, giving him long scowls, yet saying nothing. He watched as the last of the food was placed on the tables that had been set up in the barn. The farmers who worked his father's land and their families would arrive soon for their Christmas meal. Perhaps Simon had been right to laugh at him when he told him about making money from smuggling. Perhaps there was an easier way.

Edmund jumped off the barrel and strutted around the table checking the food, not that he cared. He made towards the end where the Christmas box stood. Each farmer would receive a share of the contents. His father put money aside and asked guests staying to contribute. Why give them money? He looked at the tenants sitting on long benches around a table in the centre of the barn. Listen to them, noisy rabble, no manners. He picked up one of the coins and inspected it. The King's head was worn and on the edge was a notch. This had been clipped. Everyone did it. As he turned the coin to tails it caught a shaft of light passing through the nearby window. That was it. He would make coins again. No one would know. He was almost caught last time because his hiding place hadn't been good enough and there were too many people allowed to wander around. That couldn't happen here. There were empty cottages and old shepherd huts on the estate. He was glad he hadn't used all his moulds to hide at the blacksmiths. The others were still hidden in his room. He'd do this; make coins and go off to Europe whether his father agreed or not. He looked up, the servant girl was passing. He called after her.

'Yes, Master Edmund.' Clara made a short bend of her knee. Once she'd turned around she pulled a face. The barn rang with chatter and laughter. The air smelled of spices and orange mixed with the aroma of hay. The tenants were tucking into meats, breads and cheeses as if they hadn't eaten for weeks. She guessed in some cases it might be true. Edmund was in charge, the master and mistress would visit to give their greetings after they'd arrived home from church. Around the edges of the barn a few green boughs of holly mixed with ivy leaves were strewn. Edmund had left everything until the last minute and it had been difficult to help here whilst at the same time carrying out duties in a house full of guests. Miss Perinne and Kitty Dover had offered to help, but Edmund had shunned them. The barn door creaked open and a draft of cold air whistled through, making the decorations sway. It was Edmund's friend, Simon Slate. He brushed past her and made directly to Edmund. Clara watched the other servants moving to and fro with plates and drinks, which clanked and clattered. She filled the pitcher that she was holding with ale from the barrel by the door and followed Simon. Edmund had settled on a box across from the end of one of the benches, she moved towards him. She held the pitcher trying to look as if she were watching out for anyone who needed more drink. She could just about make out what the two boys were saying.

'What do you want, Edmund? I've had to make excuses to leave, we have visitors too. I need to be back home soon.'

'Do you still want to come on a tour with me?'

'Yes, if we can raise funds. But you said the customs weren't paying a reward.'

'Yes. I haven't given up, though. Ginn owes me if nothing else.'

'Then what's so urgent that you need to speak with me today?'

'Remember what I told you about why I set fire to the boathouse at school?'

'You didn't, you said it was an accident.'

Edmund gave him a sly glance. 'Did I?'

'Yes. You said you were going to make money smuggling and that you already had lots.'

Edmund grunted.

'What do you want, Edmund. It's Christmas Day. This could have waited.'

'I said I'd made the money, didn't I?'

Simon nodded, looking around the bustling room. There must have been thirty men, women and children, plus servants looking after them. 'Your father must have plenty of money to do this for his tenants.'

'But he won't pay for the tour,' Edmund sniffed. 'I'll get all that's father's one day, but I'll have to wait. Until then, I'll travel.'

'So, what do you want me for?'

'I'm going to see a man called Ethan Byng. I'm going to go the day after tomorrow. I want to find out if he can help me with a plan.'

Simon took out his pocket watch and checked the time. 'And?'

'If he agrees to my plan I can make a lot of money, but I need help and you are the only person I can trust. Will you help?'

'Do what?' Simon huffed.

Edmund leaned into Simon and whispered in his ear. 'Make coins again.'

Chapter 22

Christmas morning, Christchurch

Danny wanted to shout out loud when he spotted Will and Nathan in the side aisle. Will had waved and made gestures towards the back of the church. The place was packed for Christmas morning. Many people were there to receive food afterwards. He hadn't been bothered much about helping, but now he longed to escape and tell his friends everything that had gone on. Perinne was there too. A large group had arrived with the Tarrants. Danny thought they must be guests; his father had often told them about all the people who came to stay at Christmastime. There was no sign of Edmund though and he allowed himself a smile. Sitting next to Perinne was a girl around the same age. She had a thin face. Her red bonnet set off the small rounds of her rose-coloured cheeks. He was so distracted at the thought of meeting with his friends again that he began another chorus of *Oh, Come All Ye Faithful* when everyone else had stopped singing. There had been a wave of giggles throughout the congregation, but he didn't care, help was here at last.

The bells rang out for the end of the service. The choir

had processed behind the vicar into the cloister where they would rid themselves of their vestments and be free. Danny stopped Adam Jackson, who was to join him in handing out bread and food to the parish poor.

'Adam, did you see Will?'

'Yes, I wonder when he got home?'

'Did you see where he went? I need to speak to him, do you think your father will let me be late?'

'I wouldn't do that if I were you. He wasn't happy catching you fighting yesterday.'

'Oh.' His shoulders sank. 'I need to talk to Will, it's urgent.'

'I know, but surely it can wait another hour, it won't take more than that to hand things out.'

Danny groaned and followed Adam through a stone arched door at the south of the church. At the west door the vicar would be greeting the congregation as they left and wishing them well for the season.

It was grey outside. Snow had fallen overnight and it lay across roofs and covered nearby bushes like white sheets on laundry day. Women, wrapped for the cold in woollen hats and coats, were already lifting baskets from inside the cloister. Danny and Adam would be in charge of the bread. A queue had already formed. There were more people than Danny expected. Many of them looked pale and were not dressed for the snowy day that had met them. He felt guilty. He knew even though his family had nothing to enjoy about the day, they would be well fed and warm. He was counting the loaves in one of the baskets when a voice called.

'*Danny*!' Will tried to push his way through the crowd, but he was jeered back. Danny was about to leave his spot when another voice called from behind him.

'Danny, *Danny*.' It was Perinne and the girl he'd seen with her. His face brightened. 'This is Kitty, she is staying at Cliff House. Maman said we could come and greet you

154

as it is Christmas morning and you are doing good deeds, but we have to be only a few minutes.'

'Our letter didn't get to father,' Danny said, making the best of any time Perinne was allowed.

'I know, I heard Maman ask about it and Uncle Charles knew nothing of it.'

'Edmund. He must have seen it. He took it.'

'You know?'

'Well …' Danny hesitated.

'Perinne, come along.' Jane Menniere appeared and smiled at Danny then beckoned the girls forward.

'Will's home. Can you get to the beach tomorrow?' Danny's voice quickened.

'I do not know how, but I will try.'

'I'll get there late morning, and Will.'

'Perinne, it's time to go.'

Danny watched Perinne follow her mother. The queue now wound around the church. Reverend Jackson appeared and began to give out instructions. Danny saw Will and Nathan waiting, rubbing their hands and moving on their feet. His own feet itched to go to them, but he knew he had to stay. Will waved then pointed, mouthing words. Danny couldn't understand what he was trying to say. People were jostling for their Christmas loaves and he and Adam set about their task. It was busy and the time passed quickly by. When Danny looked up Will and Nathan were nowhere to be seen. His fingers were numb. It was a freezing cold day and he imagined his friends would be waiting somewhere warm. He thought that must have been what Will was trying to tell him. He thought about the direction Will had been pointing, guessing towards the *George*.

Inside the inn a fire blazed throwing heat into the smoky room. Laughter rang around and, in the corner along with Meg Gibbs, Beth and Isaac, sat Will and Nathan. Will jumped up and pushed his way across the crowded floor, a wide smile on his face. The boys hugged tightly. Nathan was close behind and hugged him too.

'I can't believe you're here,' Danny said. His voice quivered with emotion. His eyes blinked and he pressed his lips hard together.

'Well we are an' it's fer good this time.'

'I know you're only just home, Will, but something awful's happened and nothing's being done.'

'Yer Uncle John an' Caleb.'

Danny's face lifted. 'You know?'

'Some o' it. Beth an' Isaac 'ave told us what happened an' we know Ginn's involved too.'

'I saw Edmund with Ginn at Sopley. We need to do something, Will, the trial's soon.' Danny paused, he was desperate to stay and talk everything through, but he didn't want to upset his mother again. 'I have to get home. Come with me.'

'I should stay with mother an' Beth.'

'Then tomorrow. Please?'

'Aye, come 'ere again. We can talk to people.'

Danny's brightened face dropped.

'What is it?'

Danny took off his hat and scratched his head with his free hand. 'I've asked Perinne to meet us. She's at Cliff House for Christmas. I said to meet at the beach if she can get away. She's heard things, I'm sure she can help too, but she's not allowed out on her own anymore. She might not come, but I'd feel awful if she went and I wasn't there.'

'All right, the beach it is.' Will's dark eyes sparkled.

'Shall we meet at the coppice? I want to visit a man in Stanpit. I think he might be able to help, too.'

'Aye.'

'Thanks, Will.' Danny took a deep breath as if to hold in all the emotions he wanted to blurt out.

'I'll try to get as much out of Isaac as I can an' see if I

can find Guy Cox, ask 'im what he knows.' Putting his arm around his friend he added, 'we'll work somethin' out, Danny. I promise.'

Chapter 23

Who was that man?

'Will Perinne attend the hunt today?' Kitty asked.

Jane Menniere gave a hoot-like laugh. 'Oh, I wouldn't expect so, Perinne doesn't like the hunt at all.' She paused. 'Have you seen her since breakfast?'

'She said she was going to check her pony, I'll go and find her.'

The stables were busy when Kitty arrived. The horses were being groomed not only by Ben and John Scott, but also other men who'd arrived with the Tarrant's guests. The animals were snorting in their stalls and there was a chatter of voices as the men worked. Somewhere, not far away, dogs could be heard barking. There was no sign of Perinne there, but as she passed by the dairy house, Kitty spotted her friend. Perinne didn't notice her at first as she stepped into the stone-floored room. It was Clara who saw Kitty first and her conversation with Perinne came to an abrupt halt.

'I've been trying to find you, Perinne. Will you be joining the hunt?'

Perinne spun on her feet. 'Oui, er yes,' she replied with a wide grin, which turned into a look of puzzlement. 'You look surprised.'

'I've just spoken to your mother, she said you didn't like it.'

Perinne approached Kitty and took her arm. She looked back over her shoulder saying, 'thank you, Clara,' then led her friend into the courtyard. 'So, Kitty, are you going to ride?'

'Yes, I've brought my riding clothes.'

'I will ride also.' Perinne lowered her voice to a whisper, 'but not with the hunt.'

'What do you mean?'

'I shall just take a ride. I will set out with the rest, but will go my own way once we are out of sight of Cliff House. It will be good to ride alone and without Miss Ashton. It will be as it used to be, if only for a short while.'

Kitty giggled. 'Oh, Perinne, you'll get into trouble.'

'Only if someone should tell.'

'Oh, I wouldn't.'

'Thank you, Kitty, and if anyone should ask, then I was with you, that is all right?'

Kitty gasped, then giggled again. 'I think I'd like to ride with you. We could say we got separated from the others and then lost.'

'I do not think that would work.'

'Yes it would, Perinne. I'd love to be as free as you've been. You could show me some smugglers.'

'Kitty, it is not a good thing to mix with the smugglers.'

'I was only making a joke. Please, Perinne, let me ride with you.'

'If you do, then you must make a promise.'

'What is the promise?'

'That you will keep everything that we do a secret. Tell no one, is that a promise?'

Kitty jiggled about, clapping her hands together. 'Oh, yes, I do promise, I do.'

'I want your word, Danny that you will not do anything to get into trouble. Aunt Mary and I have written to Sir Charles asking to speak with him about the arrest and the warrant. Mr Sweetland suggested it. We are all doing our best. I've also asked when he expects your father home. We're doing everything we can.'

'Yes, mother. I haven't seen Will and Nathan for months. I want to hear all about London. That's what we'll talk about.'

Hannah Clarke gave her son a long look as he pulled on his coat. He was fourteen and almost as tall as she was. She knew he would talk about his uncle with his friends, it was what they'd no doubt plan to do which worried her most.

Danny spotted Will and Nathan ahead walking towards the coppice. Sam the dog was sniffing at the trees and making his mark. It was a dry, bright winter's morning with cloudless blue sky. The air smelled sharp yet woody from the smoke piping in lines from nearby cottages. The boys were wrapped well in coats and wearing hats and scarves.

'Shall we talk as we walk? It's too cold to stand around,' Danny said, as he approached his friends, his breath leaving a misty trail.

Will smiled, 'aye, come on.'

The boys set out side-by-side, Danny between his friends. The dog edged itself alongside Will's legs.

'De ye think Perinne will come?'

Nathan grinned and widened his eyes towards Danny. 'I think he want to see her.'

Will tutted. 'I've only managed to speak with Isaac an' didn't get too much information. Guy Cox had gone out on the *Solomon*. Joseph Martin at the *George* says he thinks one o' the Christchurch gang is involved, doesn't know who. They thought it were Henry Lane. Henry says he's told them everything he knows. Adam Litty said it were none o' my business.'

'Could it be him?' Danny asked.

'S'pose so; or Guy Cox or John Brown or Henry Lane. They've all been involved with Meekwick Ginn.'

Danny sighed. 'Even if we find out who's involved, and what really happened, how do we prove it? And we'll have to get to Winchester to tell the gaoler – or the judge.'

'What about yu daddy? Have yu heard when he comin' home?' Nathan asked.

'We don't know. It's something for Charles Tarrant and he's gone with Perinne's father, that's all we know. We sent a letter to Cliff House, but Tarrant didn't get it. Edmund had it, I think he saw it and stole it. Mother and Aunt Mary have written again, asking to see him and to ask about the warrant. I think Edmund's involved with that too.'

Will huffed. 'An' who's the man we're callin' on?'

'Don't really know. He called on Mrs Brown when me and Jack were there. He called to get a shoe for his horse, he said he'd help Caleb if he could. Thought I'd ask him if there's anything he can do. It was just an idea. He probably can't, probably just saying it. Must be around here somewhere, he said the cottage was near the well. That must be it.' Danny pointed and broke away from his friends. He stepped up to the door of the cottage. It was a large building, but old with a dark thatch with mossy patches. Smoke was rising from a square chimney and the smell mixed with that of the salty marsh behind it. He rapped on the iron knocker. Will and Nathan stood a little way behind him. It took a few minutes for the face of Mr Jenkins to appear. He gave Danny a puzzled look.

'Yes, young man, what is it?'

'Mr Jenkins?'

'Yes, that's me.'

'I'm Danny Clarke. I was at Mrs Brown's when you called the Friday before last. You said you'd help if you could, with er, getting Mr Brown free.' Danny had begun to mumble. He realised he should have thought more about what he was going to ask.

'Did Mrs Brown send you?'

'Er, no. But the other man arrested with Mr Brown is my uncle. The trial's soon and I know they didn't do what they're saying. I think I know who did.'

'I don't think I can help with that, young man. I was going to help Mrs Brown in more practical ways, getting someone to do Caleb's work so she keeps the roof over her head.'

Danny's shoulders sank. He was about to apologise and bid farewell when he spotted another man. He'd appeared behind Jenkins. He was in smart clothing and was wearing a powdered white wig. Danny didn't know the man, but there was something familiar about him.

'Well, young man, I'll bid you good day. There's nothing I can do for your uncle.'

'Er yes, sorry to...' before he could finish his apology he remembered where he's seen the other man. His heart began to beat fast. He shouldn't have told Jenkins his name and that he knew something. He was sure the man behind him was the same one who was standing beside Joshua Stevens when his uncle was taken away.

Chapter 24

Friends together at last

The courtyard of Cliff House was a bustle of snorting horses carrying riders dressed in blues and reds. White breeches were covered to the knee by polished boots and heads were topped with riding hats, though some had tricorns. The ladies, sitting on side saddles, gown coats draped over their horses, wore hats with feathers. Outside the gates a pack of hounds snapped and barked in readiness for their chase. Sir Charles Tarrant and Edmund were at the front of the group nearest to the gates when the signal was called to move from the house and commence the hunt.

'Keep back, Kitty,' Perinne said as Kitty nudged her dapple pony. The girls waited until most of the riders had moved on then followed, side by side.

'When the 'tally ho' is called we will ride with the hunt to the edge of the field until we reach the trees,' Perinne instructed.

Kitty pressed her lips together. Her brown wool riding habit made her feel hot as she flushed with excitement. Perinne, also in brown, kept watch on the riders, ready to judge the moment that they could slip away without being noticed.

The sea was choppy and the tide wooshed along the shore with foamy ripples. Sam was chasing a stick thrown by Nathan. Other dogs dipped in and out of the sea as people walked along the sands. The wind had picked up and some were holding on to their hats. Danny's hands were thrust deep into his pockets as he watched the edge of the cliff for Perinne. Will had wandered ahead and was looking into an old boat shed. He beckoned his friends over.

'We can meet in 'ere. We'll be shoutin' o'er the wind an' waves outside.'

Nathan threw the stick again and made his way up the beach. Danny arrived first.

'I'll stand outside, watch for Perinne.'

'No need,' Nathan said. 'She's by the trees. But she's not alone.'

'Oh,' Danny groaned. 'It's no good if her governess is with her.'

'She's young for a governess.'

The boys stepped aside from the front of the boat shed and scanned the cliff. Perinne waved and started her pony down the nearby gravel path followed by another girl. Perinne slid down from her saddle.

'It is good to see you all. This is my friend, Kitty.'

Kitty raised her gloved hand in a wave. She was forcing a smile.

Will took Pierre's reins and helped Perinne tether him to a nearby tree. Kitty remained in her saddle.

'Are you not getting down?' Perinne asked her.

Danny moved over and offered the girl a hand.

'I don't think we should dismount, Perinne. We shouldn't be with these boys alone.' Kitty had her hand on her hat and her scarf was blowing about her face.

'They are my friends, Kitty.'

'You said we were going for a ride. If I knew we were meeting boys, I shouldn't have come.'

Nathan stifled a laugh.

'It is not funny, Nathan. Kitty lives in a school, she is taught these things.'

'Come on, Kitty, ye'll be all right,' Will smiled. His dark eyes sparkled. Kitty blushed.

'We need to talk, we can't leave it too late. How long have you got before you have to go back?' Danny asked.

'Not too long, we need to return with the hunt, so no one will know we have been away.'

'Come on, let's go into the boat shed out o' the wind,' Will said, making to the doorway.

'Perinne, no,' Kitty warned. Danny offered his hand again. 'Oh, all right.' Kitty dismounted her pony and Danny helped her tie it alongside Pierre.

There were lobster pots and boxes in the boat shed and they all found somewhere to sit. The door was left open to allow in light. Sam joined them, curling up beside Will's feet.

'I can't believe we're all together again,' Danny's voice quivered. 'Uncle John needs help. I know he hasn't been coining, he wouldn't.'

'What have ye found out?' Will asked.

Danny took a breath and closed his eyes, as if playing the events back in a dream. He shuffled on the pot he'd settled on and toyed with the marker corks. He began. 'Two weeks ago, Uncle John and Caleb Brown were arrested. They were on the river late at night and the revenue men were waiting for them. I found out coming home from school, there was a crowd outside the revenue officer's cottage. Everyone was shouting. They were taken on a cart. There were dragoons and Joshua Stevens was there and another man – I'm sure it's the same one as I've just seen, Will.'

Will nodded. 'Go on.'

'Uncle John and Caleb were taken away, to Winchester gaol. My Aunt Mary's seen him. It's cold and damp, but they're well.'

'What 'bout Edmund? Ye said he's involved.'

'He was there. He mentioned coins. I ran home, then went to get Aunt Mary. We took her to town and to Mrs Brown. She said men had searched the forge and stables and found moulds. The house was a mess, they'd turned everything over. She said that Uncle John and Caleb had been accused of coining, making coins, when they were arrested. We went to see Joshua Stevens, but he's disappeared.' Danny scowled. 'I'm sure it was Edmund who put the moulds there.'

'You cannot say that, Danny, not without being certain. Edmund would be in a lot of trouble if it were true.' Perrine pulled on the ribbons of her riding hat.

Nathan spoke. 'That's what the man in Ringwood said, but why would he do dat? Does he know Massa Brown and Danny's uncle?

'Ringwood?' Danny narrowed his eyes.

'Finish your story an' we'll explain,' Will said.

Danny shrugged. 'I've no proof of it. I started asking questions. Isaac told me a man called Byng had asked Henry Lane to set up a delivery of barrels to a pool at Avon. Uncle John, Caleb and Isaac just delivered them, left them in the pool. They'd already dropped Isaac off before they were arrested.' He stopped and took a breath.

'Moonrakers,' Will said. 'Barrels are left in ponds an' pools. They wait 'til the time's right an' rake 'em in. It's another way of hidin' smuggled goods.'

'Why are they called Moonrakers?' Kitty asked.

'It's said that a gang in Wiltshire were rakin' in barrels o' brandy from a pool one night when the revenue men caught 'em. It were a bright night with a full moon. The men said they were tryin' to rake in the moon for the cheese.'

Everyone laughed. 'Did the revenue men believe them? Surely not,' Kitty scoffed.

'That's the story. The revenue thought they were simple men believin' the moon to be made o' cheese. But they were fooled an' the smugglers kept their brandy.'

'Isaac will know where the pool is then,' Perinne said. The others muttered in agreement.

Danny carried on. 'Mrs Brown saw Mr Sweetland the attorney, he said that because they were caught with the coins, he thinks nothing can be done but plead their good character. I went to Sopley to, er...' Danny went quiet. Perinne moved over and put her hand on his arm. 'To talk to grandpa. It was then I saw Edmund Tarrant with Meekwick Ginn. I could hear them arguing. Edmund wants a reward and he mentioned coins, some gold. He had the letter my mother wrote to his father. He threw it at Ginn. No one said the coins found with Uncle John and Caleb were gold.'

'So Edmund is talking about different coins?' Perrine asked.

'I think so,' Danny answered.

'Is dere anything else?' Nathan asked.

'On Christmas Eve, er after my fight with Edmund, I called in the revenue officer's cottage. There's still no sign of Joshua Stevens. The officer there...'

'Toby Cox, Guy Cox's cousin,' Will put in. 'Been workin' at Poole Customs, but brought to Christchurch 'til Joshua Stevens turns up. Isaac told me.'

'He, Toby Cox, said Edmund wanted a reward, but as none had been set he couldn't have one. He said Edmund was really angry. He also said Uncle John's trial was now going to be on January the third.

'That's only just over a week away,' Kitty said.

'What about you, Will what is it you know?' Perinne asked.

'The coach from London took us to Ringwood. We were

waitin' fer a lift on a cart to Christchurch an' overheard Meekwick Ginn talkin' with another man.'

'What was he like?' Danny asked.

'Ye saw 'im better than me, Nathan.'

Nathan pressed his lips together. 'Hmm, he was a-sittin', so me can't say how tall. He wore a hat, but I remember his eyes, dark like he was a-starin' hard. He had a long nose, a wart or mole, round on the side, and a cleft on his chin.'

Danny gasped. 'That's like the man next to Joshua Stevens and the one I just saw with Mr Jenkins. What did they say?'

'The moulds were planted. The man said Edmund saw to it.'

Danny's face reddened and his fists clenched.

'That's all we know.' Will let out a breath. 'Except what Isaac told me. They didn't know what were in the barrels. They just took 'em to Avon, dropped 'em in the pool an' he found the purse o' coins as payment under a stone. They'd done it before.'

'And those coins were forged,' Danny spat.

The friends sat quietly as the words sunk in. Nathan broke the silence.

'We saw your daddies, remember, Will? We saw dat coach?'

'Aye, I'd forgotten. About the same time the arrests 'appened. They were in a coach, drivin' very fast.'

'In London?' Danny perked up.

'Aye, but they could've been goin' anywhere.'

'We should be going, we do not want to be caught riding outside the hunt,' Perinne said. 'Shall I tell you what I know now?'

'Yes, please, Perinne.' Danny gave her a smile.

'I have spoken with Danny when he came to our house, so I knew about his problem. I overheard Maman and Uncle Charles. She asked him about Danny's letter. Maman said that people were saying that someone had put the moulds in Mr Brown's stable. Uncle Charles said that coins were being smuggled into Christchurch. They are being forged and then brought in through the harbour. Then Uncle Charles said Edmund had come to him and said he knew who it was and the revenue men needed a warrant, so he signed it.'

'On Edmund's word?' Danny jumped from his seat and hit the side of the boat shed so hard it shook.

'Well, that's simple,' Kitty said. Everyone looked at her. 'If the coins are coming in through the harbour, then they are not made in the moulds from the stable.'

'Aye,' agreed Will.

'Then there are two mysteries,' said Perinne. 'The coins that are being smuggled in and why the moulds were in the stable.'

'Uncle John and Caleb are charged with forging coins, but not gold ones.' Danny slumped back on the pot he'd been sitting on. He shook his head. 'Oh, we'll never work it all out.'

'Aye we will, Danny.' Will scrunched his face as if forcing thoughts from his mind to his mouth.

'Let's think. Edmund wants a reward, what for? Who were he talkin' to when he said he'd get the warrant?'

'Ginn?' Danny suggested. 'Or the revenue man, it could be anyone, we don't know.'

'An' what did he tell 'im? He must have known somethin'. Maybe he saw somethin' at Cliff House. Maybe 'bout the gold coins? There'd be big rewards fer catchin' gold smugglers.'

'Where does Byng come in?' Danny asked.

'If he's a smuggler, it might be 'im bringin' in the coins.'

'It is certain,' Perinne said, 'that Mr Brown and your Uncle John, Danny, have nothing to do with the gold. They did not know what was in the barrels, and the coins they had were given to them by the smugglers.'

'Aye, that's true.'

'We have to go. What can I do?'

'We, Perinne, I'll help,' Kitty added.

'Try to find out more 'bout the coins, a letter or somethin'. Maybe it's somethin' to do with why yer father an' Danny's father are away. Try to find out where they are. An' Edmund. He's a show off, has he said anythin' - why does he want money?'

'And what should we do?' Danny asked.

'We'll go to Avon. Try to find out about Byng and the Moonrakers.'

Chapter 25

Shocks for Perinne

Danny dressed quickly. He yawned. He thought he'd sleep better after meeting with his friends, but so many thoughts still spun in his mind. Will and Nathan had talked about their time in London as they walked back yesterday. It was lucky, because Aunt Mary was with his mother when he'd returned home and they asked him all about it. He didn't say anything of what he'd found out about the coins and moulds. His mother would have been angry and he wanted to make sure of everything first. He knew it was important they found the truth and told the court. He was sure they were close, but things still had to be worked out. Perinne needed to find out why Edmund thought he could get a reward. Why did he need money in any case? His family had plenty. Aunt Mary had told them about the feast provided for the tenants at Cliff House on Christmas Day. Her friend had boasted to her about what they'd eaten and that they'd all been given two shillings.

Danny looked out of the tiny bedroom window. Last night the sky had clouded over and the snow had come again. He hoped it would thaw quickly like it did yesterday, but it looked to have fallen thickly. Will and Nathan were

to meet him on the stony lane and they'd carry on to Avon.
If the snow stayed, it would be a difficult walk. They said
around nine o'clock. He pulled a woollen jacket around
his shoulders and climbed down the stairs. Mother, Sarah
and Jack were close to the fire and the kettle was steaming
above it.

'I need flour and butter, Danny, will you go to town?'

'Can't Jack go?'

'I've got to go to work.' Jack was biting on a crust and
dipping it into hot milk.

'All right.' He had to keep calm, not give away he was
going to Avon to try to find out about the Moonrakers. If
Will and Nathan were on the way he'd see them, if not
he'd get the shopping and call at Will's house.

Kitty tapped on the door to Perinne's room and opened it.
Perinne was pacing the floor. She was dressed in a green
woollen frock and held a shawl of the same colour around
her arms, despite there being a fire lit.

'What are you going to do, Perinne?'

'I do not know. I will have to try to look this morning.
I thought we were to stay for another few days. It was a
surprise when Maman said we were going home today.'

'I shall miss you. This has been the best Christmas ever.'

'It has been good to have a friend. And thank you for not
telling anyone where we went to yesterday.'

'We were lucky that we caught the hunt returning. It
was very exciting. I like your friends.'

Perinne slumped on to her bed, throwing herself flat.
'If I cannot find a chance today, I will not be able to help
Danny.'

'There are games this afternoon, so everyone will be in

the drawing room. My father said that Sir Charles went away last night after the hunt and won't be home until tomorrow or longer, so he'll not be in his study.'

'But we will be leaving this afternoon.'

'Then this morning is your only chance.'

'Will you help me, Kitty?'

'Yes. Shall we go now?'

The girls made their way down the staircase and into the hall. Voices and clattering could be heard from the back of the house. It was coming from the kitchens. All the doors leading off the hall were closed, keeping in precious heat from the fires. The smell of coal burning hung in the air. The hall was chilly. Perinne pressed her ear to the study door.

'It is quiet. Let us go in.'

The library study was as cold as the hall. Ash lay in the grate waiting to be cleared and the window shutters were closed. Perinne dropped her shoulders.

'It's impossible, Perinne. It's too dark, we need a candle.'

'Oui. I shall bring the one from my room. We can light it from the fire there.'

'We'll be seen.'

'I know another way, come on.'

The girls returned to the hall and ran up the stairs. Once the candle was lit, Perinne showed Kitty the narrow back staircase used by the servants. These stairs were dark, but sconces were lit giving off a pale, yellow glow.

'How do you know this way?'

'Do not forget, Kitty, I lived here for over one year.'

'The boards are creaking, someone will hear.'

'Come on, it is brighter at the bottom.'

They reached a circular hallway.

'Where are we?' Kitty's puzzled face looked around.

'See this break?' Perinne pointed to a line down the wall. 'Hold the candle.' Kitty took the candle as Perinne ran her fingers into the gap and, with her shoulder pushed at the wall, the wall opened into the study. Perinne stepped inside, then gasped.

'What do you want? Why are you coming in here?'

The shutters had been opened and Edmund was behind his father's desk rifling through a pile of papers.

'Er, I was showing Kitty the servant stairs.' Behind Perinne Kitty stood with her mouth agape.

'Well this isn't a staircase, this is my father's study. Why have you a candle?'

'The staircase, it can be dark.'

'I don't believe you, you came to pry, and you've always been a meddler. You shouldn't be in here.'

'And nor should you, Edmund.'

'Tell me what you wanted, or I'll tell my mother you were spying.'

'Then your mother will know you were in here also.'

'Hmph. I just wanted to find out where father has gone.'

Perinne held back a grin, Edmund had given her the excuse she needed. 'I also wish to find out where Papa is. I miss him. I know he is doing a job for Uncle Charles.'

A smirk crossed Edmund's face. 'I know where he is.'

'Please tell me, Edmund.'

'It's secret.'

The smell of wax caught Perinne's breath as she held it, trying not to give Edmund any clues that she was looking for more. It had been Kitty snuffing out the candle. She was now standing beside Perinne and cast her a glance, then spoke.

'I think I know where your father is, I overheard him talking to mine.'

'Where? W-where is he?'

'First tell Perinne where Monsieur Menniere is and I will.'

Perinne widened her eyes, Kitty was getting braver by the day. This was perfect. Edmund had gone pale at being outsmarted.

'Oh, all right. They'll be home soon I'm sure, then it won't matter. Who can you two tell in any case? He's in France. James Clarke's with him.' Edmund slumped into his father's chair.

'Why?' Perinne asked.

'I don't know. Something to do with coins. They're being smuggled in through Christchurch Harbour. I think they're trying to find out where from.'

So, it was true about the coins, Perinne thought. They still needed to find out what part Edmund had played in the men's arrests.

'Ah, Mr Brown the blacksmith and Danny's Uncle John. They've been smuggling these coins?' Perinne pushed.

'Er, moulds were in Brown's stable.'

'People in the town are saying that they are innocent. If coins are being brought in, then the moulds are not the ones that were used to make them, are they?'

Edmund was shifting in the seat. His face gave away a look as if he'd realised something. Perinne sensed he'd say no more. She needed to have a look at the papers, see if there were any clues. How could they make him leave?

'I've told you where your father is now tell me where's mine,' Edmund suddenly demanded.

'He was going to see your head teacher. I thought you'd left school?' Kitty told him.

'I have, are you sure? Why would he go there?'

'Something about a fire in the school boat house and what had been found in the remains.'

All the colour drained from Edmund's face. He leaped up out of the chair and sped out of the study. The two girls looked at each other.

'I only said what I heard.'

Perinne smiled at Kitty. 'And you have given us the chance to seek what we are looking for. But we need to be quick - and quiet.' Perinne tip-toed over to the desk and began looking through the papers. They were mainly bills.

Food for Christmas, candles, a repair to a cartwheel and for coal.

'Is there anything about the coins?'

'Come and help me, Kitty, there must be more.'

'Look in the drawers.'

The sound of a door opening in the hall stopped them. They ducked behind the desk, each holding their breath. Footsteps sounded, then another door opened and closed.

'Perhaps I should stand by the door and listen.' Kitty crossed the room.

'There is nothing here.'

'Try a drawer.'

Perinne tugged at the handle of the first drawer, it was locked. The next one held paper and her uncle's seal. The lowest drawer also held papers.

'Shhh,' Kitty whispered and peered through the gap, grateful Edmund hadn't properly closed the door. 'It's all right.' Kitty looked over to the desk. Perinne had disappeared. Then she spotted the top of her friend's head. She'd crouched down. Kitty's heart began to beat faster. A clock ticked somewhere nearby in time to her pulse.

'Have you found something?'

Perinne peeked over the edge of the leather-topped desk and waved a paper.

'What is it? What have you found?'

'You won't believe it, Kitty.'

Chapter 26

The mystery revenue officer

'I'm freezing and my feet are wet,' Danny complained as they reached the town hall.

'Me too, I hope Mr Oake has a good fire going. See you later.' Jack slipped through a nearby door.

The road was rutted with chunks of grey ice as horses dragged carts through the snow. There'd been no sign of Will and Nathan. Few shops were opened, so Danny decided to go straight to Will's cottage. He wondered if he was staying with his mother, he hadn't said anything about taking rooms like he did when he came home in the summer. The track to the cottage had drifts, some as high as Danny's knees. Normally he loved the snow, but not today, it was sure to stop them from trying to solve the mystery of the man called Byng. He scooped a handful of snow and formed it into a ball. He snorted a deep breath, holding it as he threw the snowball hard against a nearby tree, making powder fall like dust from the bare branches. It would takes ages to get to Avon, too long in this weather, he knew they wouldn't go.

Smoke from the Gibbs' chimney meant someone was home. No one would go out unless they needed to, or their mothers needed butter and flour.

'Hello, Danny. What in the world brings you so far on a mornin' like this? In ye come.'

'Thanks, Mrs Gibbs.' Danny kicked the snow from his boots and took off his hat.

'Danny.' Will appeared from the rear of the cottage. 'Nathan's not well. He had oysters last night.' Will tapped his stomach and pulled a face.

Danny grimaced. 'Poor Nathan, is he all right now?'

'He won't be goin' to Avon.'

'I don't think we could get there in any case, the snow's pretty deep.'

'Ye didn't come all this way to tell me that, did ye?'

'No, an errand for mother.'

'Well, we saw Toby Cox last night. An' we 'ave another mystery.'

'Oh?'

'I asked 'im who the man with Joshua Stevens was. He said Guy 'ad asked 'im the same. Said he'd tried to find out. One o' the other officers there on the night yer uncle were arrested said the man were called Buchan an' 'ad been sent over from the Commissioners at Poole. Toby said he was sure no one 'ad been sent. He were the only one sent from Poole, an' that were only after Joshua Stevens 'ad gone missin'.'

Danny sat on a nearby chair, eyes wide.

'Guy'd been there when the men were taken away. He hadn't seen much of him, but what he 'ad he described to Toby. Toby said there was no one like that at Poole.'

'So who is he?

'I don't know.'

'I am pleased Maman allowed you to come to stay with us.'

'So am I, Perinne. Yesterday was so exciting. We need to get a message to Danny about Edmund.'

'That is difficult. The snow is deep and Miss Ashton returns tomorrow.'

'Perhaps we should just tell your mother what's happened.'

'Then she will know that we went to meet the boys.' Perinne stared across the bay. The snow had settled high up the beach and on the cliff top. It was as if the whole view had been painted in shades of silver and grey. An icicle hung down from the lintel of the window. Her breath misted the glass and she drew a *P* with her finger. Out at sea, ships in full sail made their slow progress, maybe returning to port, or perhaps going to France. Papa was in France. She had never been told what his work was, but trying to find out about people who were making coins sounded dangerous. Smugglers were dangerous also. Kitty was now standing beside her. She had a new dress, blue with blue ribbons. She put a hand on Perinne's shoulder.

'I wish I could think of something we can do.'

Perinne closed her eyes, then a smile moved her lips. 'I have an idea, simple too. I shall write Danny a letter. Lucy can to take it to him, she knows where he lives.'

Ethan Byng looked out across the valley. The river appeared as a curving line drawn on a sheet of white paper. No one was about. Mokey and Ambrose should have been here by now, but they must have decided against trying to travel the Avon Cross Way today.

A log on the fire tumbled as the one below gave way to ash. He liked the cottage, it would soon be his. His father was now 80 years old. It was incredible how he'd stayed well all these years. He watched as the old man slept in the chair. Now he grew weak and Byng feared it wouldn't be long before he passed. He put more wood on the fire. His own home was close to Christchurch where his workshop was. He allowed himself a tight-lipped smile, then changed it to a frown. Bringing in the barrels from France was well-paid, but that had to stop. Mokey, Ambrose and the gang fighting with the revenue men at Parley had been dangerous too, but at least he was able to say he was at work when they made their attack to get those goods back. The customs wondered how the gang had known where and when the goods were being transported, but he made coats and shirts for lots of people and many had loose tongues. He let out a sigh. With the recent problems, things might have to go quiet for a while.

Edmund guessed his father might return today, though the weather could delay him. What did the headmaster want? What had been found? The fire had razed everything to the ground. Had it? His palms began to sweat. He played over in his mind what had happened. He'd been in bed when Jacob Screever had sneaked into his room and laughed in his face. 'I know what you're trying to make Edmund Tarrant, give me half and I'll keep quiet', then he ran off. He hated Jacob Screever, weasel boy. After that he'd dashed to the boat house thrown everything he had into the sack and set the fire. He was sure nothing had been left behind. He'd been to the sack since he'd got home, when he'd fetched the two moulds and dies to put in the blacksmith's stable. There were two other moulds and a few more dies, some tools and some metal. He'd better check them and maybe move them to a new hiding place.

Chapter 27

The boys go to Avon

Danny sat on his bed holding the paper. Lucy's brother had brought it. Danny's mother had thought it to be a friend calling by. No one had seen the message being handed between them. Perinne had been clever to think of writing and passing it to him this way. She'd found two letters in her search at Cliff House. One was from London asking if her father, and someone else whom Charles Tarrant could trust, could go to London. Coins were being smuggled into England through Christchurch harbour. Her father was to go to France to try to identify the culprits. It also said there was a large reward for giving information leading to the capture of those responsible. Her father and whoever went with him would be paid well. They might also receive the reward if their discoveries led to the arrest and conviction of those responsible. The men should not be told this, everything would be explained when they were in London. The second letter was the one that had given Danny the biggest jolt. His hands had shaken as he read. It was from Edmund's head master asking that his father go immediately to the school. It said items had been found in the ashes of the burned-out boathouse that suggested someone was trying to make coins and it all pointed to Edmund.

It had been four days since he'd been to Will's cottage. More snow had fallen, but yesterday it had begun to thaw. He'd had to go to the church and, on his return he'd decided to call on Mr Jenkins in Stanpit again. The idea just came to him. He decided to be bold. He'd said he'd wanted to apologise. He told him he was sorry to have disturbed him and hadn't thought he might have company. He was worried about his uncle. Mr Jenkins replied it was good of him to travel through the snow to say sorry and that it had only been a visit from his tailor, Mr Baker, who was measuring him for a new suit.

Will and Nathan would be calling soon. They'd agreed that when the thaw began they'd all go to Avon. Danny'd done his chores for the day and he'd told mother they were all going to the beach. He fingered the letter. He'd read it again and again. If Edmund had been trying to make coins, then the moulds placed in Caleb's stable must be his. It made sense. If he'd seen the letter about the coins from France, then that would be the reward he'd been asking for. But where did Byng come in to it all? Edmund could have planted the moulds and gone to Joshua Stevens himself. Even if he had, which he was certain was true, Edmund would deny everything. Joshua Stevens would know, but he still hadn't been seen since the day his uncle and Caleb had been taken away. Only he would know what had happened. Tomorrow would be the start of a new year, 1782, and it was just three days to Uncle John's trial. He could hear voices below, his friends must have arrived.

183

James Clarke watched as the French countryside passed by. He hadn't travelled much in coaches, but it seemed the English ones were far more comfy. The cabin lurched again as the wheels banged against ruts in the road. 'Is our job done, Yves?' he whispered.

Yves Menniere gave a brief nod of the head. 'Oui. It will now be up to London to capture any culprits. Hopefully nothing will come back to me.'

'Yes, your friend the Comte.'

'He will not get any blame, he will pass that on, or deny any knowledge of what was happening on his land.'

'As with Meekwick Ginn, he always appears to have done no wrong. People like him and gentry seem to have a way of avoiding punishment. Whether in France or in England.'

Yves, frowned. James, realising what he'd said, opened his mouth to apologise, but Yves raised his hand. 'Let us get to Le Havre. There will be a ship to Poole and hopefully we shall be home in two or three days.'

'I wonder if there's been snow at home?' James pressed his lips into a line. It had been difficult to keep track of time. Three days would be the third of January. He closed his eyes. He'd missed Christmas, but could imagine what had happened. Danny would have been reluctant to go to the church. Jack would have been working most of the time and Sarah keeping her mother busy with endless questions. There'd been plenty of wood in the yard for the winter, so they'd be able to keep warm. Hopefully the time he'd been away from them all had passed quickly and without any problems.

Yves responded. 'If there has been snow, it could slow our journey. But let us wait. Look, ahead, the sea and the harbour too. It will not be long now.'

The coach pulled into an inn and the men dismounted. The air was wet and cold so they moved swiftly inside. A fire was burning brightly in the grate and over this, on the mantelpiece, a garland of holly and ivy was laid. Removing their hats they scanned the room. It was full of people. Like them, they were most probably waiting for passage across the channel. The air was thick with smoke and smelled a mixture of tobacco, sweat and of the wood crackling on the fire. Some people were eating, others simply sitting chatting. Then James stopped in his tracks.

'What is it?' Yves asked.

'Over there, under that painting on the wall, I'd swear that's Joshua Stevens. The revenue officer at Christchurch.'

James led as they wove their way through the packed room.

'Joshua?'

'James. What brings you here? Have you been sent to find me?'

'Find you? Are you lost?'

Stevens allowed himself a wry smile. 'You don't know, do you?'

'Don't know what? What's happened? Monsieur Menniere and I have been on a task for Sir Charles. We've been away almost three weeks.'

'Then you'd best sit down. I have to tell you what happened and why we need to get home as soon as possible.'

As Stevens told his tale James could feel anger rising, as if he were a clock being wound. He feared he would snap. He was fond of his brother-in-law, John Hewitt. He knew he'd been involved in landing goods, but it would be tea or brandy. He would never get involved in something as serious as coining. Nor the blacksmith. He clenched his fist beneath the table to try not to betray his feelings.

'I don't know where the moulds came from, but I'm certain that Tarrant's son, Edmund, isn't it? Well he put them there.'

'And the officer?'

'That's what's had me confused. He said he'd been sent

from Poole and the arrests were part of a wider search. He seemed to know a great deal about the gang, far more than me. He also appeared familiar with the boy and I was sure I'd seen him somewhere before.'

'Can you remember where from?' James asked.

'I couldn't at first, but I've had a lot of time to think these past weeks.'

'Who do you suspect?'

'He said his name was Buchan, I believe that a lie. He was tall, wore a wig and his hat was low and collars high. It was dark most of the time, but the nose and his dark eyes are so like Elias Baker, a tailor from Hern. I haven't used his services, but people speak highly of him. I've seen him in town collecting parcels of cloth sent from London. I'm told he has a fine house.'

'Could he work for the customs as well?'

'I think not. If it is him, his tailoring services are in much demand.'

Yves, who had so far said nothing, spoke. 'Are you certain it is the same man?'

'I can't be sure, but I knew he wasn't with the customs the moment he put a pistol to my back.'

The track was wet and muddy. It was easiest to walk in the ruts left by carts making the same journey. It took less time than they thought, though the damp had seeped into Danny's boots and his toes were pinching. Spikes of bare hawthorn poked through drifts of snow which lay against the hedgerows. Danny thought the spikes looked like spiders.

'What we goin' to do, just knock on a door?' Nathan asked.

'There's a smithy, we'll ask there,' Will answered, pointing to smoke rising from a small, brick building.

'What happens if the blacksmith is one of the gang?' Danny frowned. They should have planned this better.

Will's eyes glinted. 'I 'ave a plan.' He strode cheekily into the forge. 'Good day, blacksmith.'

'Hello, young man. I see you've no beast, how can I help?'

'I'm lookin' for Mr Byng.'

Nathan and Danny held back, waiting beside the wooden door. Danny breathed in and slowly out, trying to stay calm. Will looked unworried as he spoke more.

'I've a watch 'ere.' Will pulled a watch from his coat pocket and showed it the man. Danny recognised it, it had belonged to Will's father and Will treasured it.

'I think it's Mr Byng's.'

'You sure, lad?'

'It's what I've been told.'

'Tis not likely, but I suppose you can ask. His cottage is the first one riverside, just past the Avon Cross Way.'

'Thank ye, sir. I'll show it to 'im. If it's not, then I think I'll keep it.' Will smiled as he tucked the watch back into his pocket.

As the boys drew closer to the cottage a figure could be seen chopping wood beside the whitewashed wall.

'Does that look like the man you saw in Ringwood, Nathan?' Danny asked.

'Can't tell from here,' Nathan answered. 'He doesn't look old enough.'

Danny shook his head. 'It's not the man who was outside the revenue cottage either. We're wasting our time. The blacksmith said it was unlikely to be Byng's watch.'

'Why would he say dat?' Nathan shrugged.

'Come on, we're nearly there. That could be a son, or a servant.' Will marched ahead. 'Hello.'

The face of a boy looked up from his task. He set the

187

head of his axe onto the top of a block he was using to chop firewood. His eyes were as red as the hair poking from under his damp hat.

'Who are you? What do you want?' The boy called out.

'We're lookin' fer Mr Byng.'

'He's laying down. He'll be asleep.' He examined the boys in turn, saving his last and longest inspection for Nathan.

'Are you all right?' Danny asked. 'You look like you've been crying.'

The boy sniffed. 'My father's died. Three days ago. I'm on my own now. I'm staying here to look after Mr Byng.'

'I'm sorry. Were ye father ill?' Will stepped forward. As he did so, Danny spotted a face by the window. Whoever it was, they dodged aside as their eyes almost met.

'No. His leg was bad. He got a fever.'

Will rested a hand on the boy's shoulder. 'My father died the same way.'

'Why do Mr Byng need lookin' after?' Nathan asked.

'Don't you know?' The boy picked up his axe and ran the handle up and down his palm. 'Why are you here? What do you want?' The boy stepped back and stood stiffly, as if he'd got a sudden burst of strength and he was ready to defend the man.

'Er... we, er... ,' nothing would come to Danny. He didn't want to mention Will's watch.

'Mr Byng's nearly eighty years old. He's not well.'

'Eighty?' Danny's eyes widened. The face hadn't looked so old.

'I think we're mistaken an' 'ave come to the wrong place,' Will said. 'Come on, let's go.' He motioned to Danny and Nathan.

Ben Lambert watched Danny, Will and Nathan as they faded down the track, then he dashed into the cottage.

'Mokey, Ambrose, there were three boys asking about Mr Byng.'

'Yes, we saw,' Mokey said.

'Who were they? Why did they want Mr Byng?'

'Nothing for ye to worry about, Ben,' Ambrose said, sucking on his pipe. 'We heard, too. Ye did well an' you're doing a job looking after old Mr Byng.'

'We've seen one of those boys before,' Mokey added. 'We'll let young Mr Byng know, he'll be most interested.'

Chapter 28

Danny's hunch

'Where are the moulds now, Edmund?'

Edmund stood in his nightshirt and bare feet with his hands behind his back, head down. A newly-lit fire struggled to burn in the grate across from him. He shivered. He hadn't had time to put on a dressing gown. He didn't know his father had returned home until he'd stormed into his room and demanded he go to the study with him. It was late. The guests who remained from Christmas had all retired. His father slumped into one of the leather chairs set beside the fireplace. His face was red and deep furrows of wrinkles crossed his forehead in waves. He wasn't wearing his wig and his wispy grey hair had been combed across the top of his balding head.

'Speak, boy, are there more?'

Edmund sucked in air. He had two hidden and some dies, if he gave them up, he'd not be able to make the coins he was planning to.

'Making coins is treason, boy. Do you understand?'

'Yes, father.'

'I've been to your school. The headmaster showed me remnants of a mould from the boathouse. Someone had been trying to forge coins. It was you, wasn't it?'

'No. I just lit a fire. It was an accident, father. I was trying to keep warm.'

'Some of the boys say otherwise.'

'They're lying to save themselves.'

'Hmph. And the head teacher too?' Sir Charles took a deep breath and looked directly at his son. 'Was it you who put those moulds in the blacksmith's stable?'

A jolt ran through Edmund as if he'd suddenly turned to stone. 'N... n... *no.*'

'Two men could hang. And so could you.' Sir Charles ran his stubby fingers across his head sending a long strand of hair down over his ear. 'Your mother and I can no longer cope with your behaviour. You are to join the navy.'

'*What*?'

'You heard. And not as an officer, you'll join as a seaman.'

'But, father.'

'It's done. You'll go to Portsmouth the day after tomorrow.'

'It was the same one who was fighting the Tarrant boy in Christchurch on Christmas evening.'

'And he mentioned my name? What did he say?' Ethan Byng, stood beside a large table. On it were pieces of cloth, a tape and scissors. Rolls of fabric lay like scrolls on shelves close by, lit by candles along a shelf. A large window, which faced to the street was hidden by a heavy velvet curtain. Mokey and Ambrose rarely came here where he lived his life as Elias Baker, a tailor. Byng studied their faces. The candle light made them appear sallow and glum. Why were they so worried about a boy? But they were good men, he'd trust their instincts.

Mokey started. 'He yelled at him, '*Who's Byng? Tell me. I want to know where to find Byng*'. Why would he be looking for you? How did he know to look at Avon? He found your father's cottage too.'

'You've no idea who he might be?'

'No, Mr Byng.'

'Describe him and his friends.'

'He's about thirteen maybe fourteen, not that tall for his age. Fair curly hair, real temper on him.'

'One's a black boy, can't be too hard to find him in Christchurch,' Ambrose added, feeling for his pipe. 'An' the other's tall, dark haired. Good coats, all of them.'

'A black boy?'

'Do ye know of him, Mr Byng?' Ambrose asked.

'There was a black boy at the inn in Ringwood. I didn't notice who he was with.' Byng grunted. 'And, five days past, I was with a customer, Mr Jenkins. A boy like the one you describe called. Jenkins said he was with a black boy and one other. It has to be the same boys.'

Mokey's eyes widened. 'Was he asking for you?'

'Jenkins didn't say.'

'What we going to do?'

'We need to silence the Tarrant boy, luckily he'll do anything for money. As for the boy who's been snooping, we need to do something about him too, he's getting too close. See what you can find out.'

Danny lay in bed wrapped in his covers like he'd been rolled in a rug. Jack's breathing was keeping a calming rhythm unlike his own racing heart. Will had talked about his father on their journey back from Avon. Seeing the boy upset had brought back memories for him. His father had been shot in his leg, it had become bad and he'd died of a fever. Will had been just eleven years old and had since worked hard to help keep food on the table. He'd spoken of his guilt at leaving his mother and sister to go to America. He and Nathan had let Will talk. It had taken Danny's mind off everything and made him feel fortunate to not only have a father, but to have been able to go to school.

As Will's story rolled in his mind a thought had struck him. Will's father was also William, so there could surely be more than one Mr Byng. Maybe that was who he'd seen at the cottage earlier. There was something else, it was niggling at the back of his mind refusing to come forward. He pushed his knuckles against his brow trying to nudge his brain. So much had happened in the past few weeks. Perhaps if he thought about something else it would come to him. What else was there to think about though? He pulled his arms from inside the blanket. Tomorrow would be Tuesday and the trial was on Thursday. Mr Reeks was to take people to Winchester in his waggon. Mr Sweetland had found many townsfolk prepared to stand in court and swear that Uncle John and Caleb Brown were good people and it had all been a misunderstanding. There was no one from the town who would speak against them, just some of the officers who'd been at the river on the night of the arrest. Joshua Stevens could have spoken, but was nowhere to be found. The attorney had put a small notice in the *Chronicle* newspaper asking for people to come forward if they had any information that might point to the real culprits.

'The *Chronicle*, that's it.' Danny gave the bed a satisfied thump. There was a story in the *Chronicle* weeks back about a gang at Parley. They'd attacked customs officers to claw back tea and brandy that had been seized. The newspaper said the gang had used disguises. Toby Cox had told Will that there was no one called Buchan at the customs office at Poole, nor anyone who looked like the man seen with Joshua Stevens. Danny was certain the man he'd seen at Stanpit was the same person, yet he was Mr Jenkins' tailor, Mr Baker. Maybe Byng was the tailor, maybe he uses disguises and different names. His shoulders sagged into his mattress. This still didn't explain Edmund's meeting with Meekwick Ginn and why he was asking him about a reward. Ginn knew the smugglers and there had to be a link with Byng. Ginn was clever, why would he take a boy like Edmund Tarrant seriously? He took a deep breath, perhaps it didn't matter. It was getting too close to the trial. He had to tell Mr Sweetland everything he knew, it was Uncle John's only chance. It would be best if they all went together. Will and Nathan could tell him what Toby Cox had said and what they'd heard in Ringwood. Perinne would tell him about the letters and he'd explain all he'd found out. It had to be soon - but how could he get the friends all together again?

Chapter 29

January 1st, 1782

'Don't set the fire. I don't want it lit yet,' Edmund yelled at Clara.

Clara put down the bucket with coal and kindling and shifted quickly through the door. Edmund was out of bed and dressed in his good shirt and breeches. His best coat lay like a brown puddle on the floor next to saddle bags, stuffed until they were plump. He listened for the maid's footsteps to fade and went to the fireplace. He had one last thing to pack then he'd go to see Simon Slate, ask if he wanted to run away with him. He pushed his arm up the chimney, his fingers probing for the bag he'd placed there. A fluttering noise echoed down the flue. A bird, he thought. Then a low rumble grew louder and a great blast of blackness burst into Edmund's face covering him from top to toe with soot.

The fire was barely alight, but enough to use to light the candle. Danny set it in front of him as he sat to write his message. The rest of the family were sleeping. The clock tapped out the seconds passing by, every one stealing the time he had left to carry out his plans. He would go to Lucy's brother just as it was becoming light. He'd slip away when he went to collect the eggs for breakfast, it wasn't far and if he ran no one would know he'd been gone. He took his father's wax, melted a red blob onto the folded paper, blew it until it dried and pushed it into his pocket. He'd asked Perinne to try to get into town tomorrow morning, Wednesday, when he would go with his friends to see Mr Sweetland before he left for Uncle John's trial. He had to go into town today to collect Uncle John's cart from the Browns' stable. Whilst there, he'd slip to Will's house. Will and Nathan said they'd speak with Guy Cox and Adam Litty again, see if they'd found anything more about the night the men were arrested and of the man named Byng.

His mother had been very quiet over the past few days. Danny's heart tugged seeing her. He hadn't told her that father was in France; that would have given away what he'd been doing. He'd tried hard to appear he was carrying on as normal and not interfering. He wished father would come home. Mother would be going to Aunt Mary's tonight then travelling to Winchester with her for the trial on Thursday. Jack was to stay at home and look after Sarah, helped by Danny. He bit on his lip. That wouldn't happen, Jack would have to manage alone, for he would be at the trial.

Edmund spat soot from his mouth, sucked in from the shock of the fall. His clothes were streaked with black smears. It was lucky that he had others. He'd not been able to pack everything. He bent forward, riddling his fingers angrily through his hair to remove the dirt, then undressed. Lifting a candle from the mantelpiece he crossed to the dresser, leaving dirty footprints in a trail across the carpet. After tipping water into the basin and soaking his cloth, he wiped his face and hands, rubbing hard. He held the candle to his looking glass and inspected his work, then found clean breeches, shirt and stockings. He felt the moulds and dies in the bag, they wouldn't fit in the saddle bags. He opened the wardrobe and reached to the back, pulling out a linen haversack. His nurse had made it for him years ago. His name had been embroidered onto it and the letters were now red and faded. He found another coat and then rummaged in a drawer for a shirt, breeches and stockings, laying them all flat on top of each other in the bed. There was room only for one mould and two dies and the tools. He rolled the clothes around them and pushed them into the haversack. He left it untied. If he could sneak into the pantry, he'd take some food. He picked up his coat from the floor, lifted his saddle bags and the haversack and crept out of his room.

The servants were about, he could hear clattering in the kitchen. He tiptoed down the main staircase and into the hall. Passing through the doorway into a rear passageway he could see a rush light glowing in the courtyard and a light coming from the laundry, but no one was there. The stables were in darkness, he moved towards them and slipped inside. The horses snorted and rustled in their stalls. 'Shhh,' he commanded. He lifted a saddle from the rack and chose his father's best horse, a sturdy stallion. Just before dawn he was ready and rode off silently into the frosty morning. He would go to London. If the Gibbs boy could manage there, then so could he. What would he do if Simon wouldn't go with him?

'Danny, are you with the hens?'

'Yes, mother.' Danny reached under another bird, feeling for eggs, her feathers brushing soft warmth over the back of his hand. There was just enough light for his task. His plan so far had worked, his mother hadn't noticed he'd been out to take the note. The lamp he'd taken was back in its place and the candle snuffed. He breathed steadily. He hoped Perinne would be able to do as he'd asked. He allowed himself a smile. Of course she would, she was Perinne. Inside the cottage the fire he'd set was glowing in the grate.

'You were up early,' Hannah said.

Danny's heart skipped, but saw his mother smile. 'Yes, I woke and couldn't get back to sleep.'

'I need you to get a few things in town when you fetch the cart, so you don't have to go again. I want both of you looking after Sarah, she might fret with both me and your father away.'

A shiver ran through him as he set the basket of eggs on the table. He found telling lies difficult, but if he didn't say anything, then he couldn't lie.

'There's some money for Mrs Brown, to pay for feeding Uncle John's pony. Make sure she takes it.'

'Yes, mother.'

'And I need you back here as soon as possible, I'm leaving this afternoon. I need it to be light, I'm not as used to driving carts as your aunt is.'

It was light outside now and by the time he'd walked into town and sorted the pony and cart the shops would be open. Jack went with him. Jack had to work today, then Mr Oake was allowing him two days off work to look after his sister. His way, he said, of helping Uncle John and Caleb.

Mrs Brown was grateful for the money and didn't argue when Danny passed her the coins. He studied her face. She'd lost weight, her normally jolly, round face was long and the colour had gone. Inside her cottage looked neat and tidy with all the furniture, tossed about uncaringly by the revenue men, back in place.

'I'm goin' today, Danny,' Bessie said. 'Takin' a good shirt an' coat fer Caleb.'

'Has Mr Sweetland found anything out?'

Bessie shook her head. Danny bit his lips together. The urge to tell her all he knew was surging in his chest.

'I'm sure it was Edmund Tarrant.'

'Aye, that's what's bein' said, but Mr Sweetland says it needs the lad to be there an' confess.'

'Or someone who saw him do it.'

'An' who be that?'

Danny hunched his shoulders. 'Mr Stevens is still missing and no one knows who the officer with him was.'

'Mr Sweetland says that it might be possible that the judge will ignore the moulds, Danny, but they had the coins an' were on the river.' Bessie's eyes began to fill and a tear tricked down and onto her apron.

'I'm sorry, Mrs Brown.'

'We can only hope their good character saves 'em.'

'No, Edmund. Where would we go?' Simon Slate toyed with his coffee cup. The coffee house was empty but for two men sitting beside the window. 'What's all the dirt on you?'

Edmund rubbed his hair and inspected his dirty fingertips. 'Just soot. Come on, Simon, it'll be fun.'

'Fun? What will we do?'

'Get rooms.'

'No. Going on a tour with your tutor's one thing, but running away. No, thank you.'

'Then I'll go alone.'

'Don't be a fool, Edmund.'

'But father's making me join the navy, I'm supposed to go tomorrow.'

'Then join, you might like it.'

'I'd have to work.'

'You'll have to work in London.'

'I don't like the sea. Boats make me feel sick.'

'You'll get used to it.'

'Come on Simon.' Edmund sucked in air and glanced around. 'There's more. Father's found out about the moulds. He even said it was me who put the ones in the smuggler's stable.'

Simon's eyes widened. 'And did you?'

Chapter 30

Terror for Edmund

Edmund gave up with Simon and led his horse to the quayside. The fishing boats had left for their day's work and the water's edge lapped against the pier. Gulls were resting on the water which was lit in ripples of blue from the clear sky. He pulled his hat over his ears and drew his coat around him. His father had said he could hang if he were found with moulds, but he knew his father wouldn't give him up to the customs. Perhaps he should make one last attempt to get money out of Meekwick Ginn, but he'd made it clear there was none. He didn't believe him. He lifted the haversack from across his shoulder and sat on an old box next to a wall. He unfastened the strap and rummaged for the cheese he'd taken, dropping the haversack behind him. He sniffed the cheese then bit into it.

'Edmund Tarrant, isn't it?'

'Who are you?' Edmund eyed the man.

'Never mind 'bout that. Mr Byng wants to speak with you.'

'How did you find me here?'

'We have our ways.' Mokey grinned at Ambrose then

pointed at Edmund. 'What's that on you? You're a dirty one for a rich boy.'

Edmund wiped his fingers over his forehead, smearing soot across it. Mokey laughed.

Ambrose lifted his eyebrows. 'That's a fine horse for a boy.'

'None of your business.'

'Two fat saddle bags, going somewhere?' Mokey smirked.

'Go away.'

Ambrose laughed. 'You're coming with us.'

'Do you know who you're speaking to, ruffian?'

Ambrose leaned into Edmund, sending a swirl of rotten-cabbage breath into his face. 'Yes, I do. And imagine what people will say when it gets out that Sir Charles Tarrant's son's been coining and blaming old men for it.'

Edmund gasped.

'Get on your horse,' Mokey spat.

'And don't try anything clever. We can ride as good as you, beside we have these.' Ambrose parted his coat front to reveal two pistols tucked into his belt.

'Henry Lane told Adam in the end. He said he's been paid an' says he knows no more. The last load's gone.' Will was leaning against the fireplace in his cottage. The fire was out and he was wearing his coat, as was Nathan who was sitting next to a small table. Danny was in the middle of the tiny room, hands deep in his pockets.

So, there's no chance of catching them bringing in the goods again,' Danny said.

Will shook his head. 'No.'

'And he was sure he was called Ethan Byng?' Danny

felt they were at last finding out the truth.

'The man on the beach last summer? Aye. It were arranged with the Captain o' the *Glory*. The ship sent a boat into the 'arbour. Caleb an' yer uncle met it, they were given the barrels an' they took 'em to Avon an' dropped 'em in the pool. Their payment were in a purse, left under a large stone.'

'Then Henry can tell that to the court.'

'He's scared. He thinks they work between Avon and Parley. Says he thinks they're the gang that attacked the customs a while back.'

'I read about that gang,' Danny sighed. 'The *Chronicle* said they were dangerous, had all kinds of weapons. It also said they were all disguised and I think that's what Byng does. He changes how he looks. The man you saw with Meekwick Ginn at Ringwood, the customs officer with Mr Stevens when Uncle John was taken away and the man I saw with Mr Jenkins. Byng, Baker, Buchan they're the same man.'

'Dey all begin wi 'B',' Nathan said.

'Yes! And he must be in that gang.'

'The leader I'd wager,' Will said.

'Was it the same face at the window in Avon?' Nathan asked.

'I only caught a glimpse, but no, it was a different one.'

'So where do Edmund come in?' Nathan asked.

'He sees the letter about the gold and coins being smuggled and wants the reward. He thinks it's Meekwick Ginn behind it.'

'So why not tell him daddy?'

'Because he doesn't know, he's only guessing. And his father would know he'd been looking through his things.'

Will held out his arms. 'But why would they plant the moulds in Caleb's stable? You said Mrs Brown told you the customs no longer believe they were his.'

'To give them time to bring in the last barrels. Did Henry

say when that was?'

'Aye. Christmas Evenin'.'

Danny sat on the bottom rung of the ladder that led to the roof where Will slept. He rubbed his face. 'Jack and I saw something strange that night, when we were going home from the church.'

'What?'

'A horse and cart coming from the lane leading to the wharf. It was as if the cart was moving on its own. It was only when it got to the street that you could see the horse. It was a strange grey colour with mottled markings.'

'Davey, de cheesman,' Nathan said. 'His horse was like dat.'

Will grinned. 'I knew he was coming to town for a load. It could be.'

'Not if it's a gang working around Parley.' Danny puffed out from his lips.

'Unless Meekwick Ginn arranged it 'cause Caleb an' your Uncle John weren't there to do it anymore.'

'So, Edmund goes to Ginn. Ginn says he knows nothing about it but tells the gang, Byng's gang. Byng dresses as a customs officer, gets Edmund to plant the moulds and gets Uncle John and Mr Brown arrested.'

'Sounds possible, but Edmund would have to confess in front of the court, and that's not going to happen.'

Danny rubbed the back of his neck. 'I've asked Perinne to come to town tomorrow morning. We'll all go to Mr Sweetland before he goes to Winchester. The only problem will be that her governess, Miss Ashton will be with her.'

'We'll 'ave to find a way to distract her,' Will said.

'That won't be easy,' Danny shook his head. 'I have to go. Mother needs the cart and I'll be in trouble if I'm late. I'll see you tomorrow. Maybe Perinne will send another message. She needs to tell Mr Sweetland what she found out.'

'Where are we going? Where are you taking me?'

'Shut your bonebox.'

'Don't speak to me like that, I'll tell my father. He'll have you arrested. I'll tell him about Mr Byng.'

'I said, shut *up*. Get down from your horse.'

Edmund slipped his boots from his stirrups and swung down to the ground. 'Hey, what are you doing to me?'

Mokey grabbed Edmund's arms and held them behind his back whilst Ambrose pulled a cover over the boy's head.

Edmund kicked out. 'What are you doing to me,' his muffled voice yelled.

'Keep still.'

Edmund felt his legs snap together as they were tied. He would have fallen had he not been held by Mokey. Next, his arms were brought forward and also tied then he felt himself being lifted and thrown on his belly across a saddle. The horse beneath shuffled its legs and Edmund thought he would fall. The horse started off, along with the sound of the other horses. Edmund tried to imagine where he was. They'd set out on the road that led to Ringwood and passed the inn at Sopley where, a few days since, he'd met Meekwick Ginn. It was not far from the Avon Cross Way when the men had tied him up. The horses had left the gravel track and it felt like they were moving over grass. After what seemed an age they'd come to a halt. Edmund felt a tug and he was back on his feet. Silently, he was made to shuffled forwards then shoved down, landing on what he thought must be hay. Everything went quiet, then Edmund heard a twig snap and the cover was snatched from his head, revealing the shapes of three men, Mokey, Ambrose and behind them stood Ethan Byng.

'You.' Edmund looked quickly around. He was in a shepherd hut, bare but for straw on the floor and piled up behind him.

'So, I hear you wanted rewarding,' Byng said, pushing his way forward between the others.

'You're not a customs officer, are you?'

Mokey and Ambrose sniggered. Byng tilted his head to one side and sniffed.

'Maybe I am, maybe I'm not.'

'What do you want? Why am I here?'

'I need something from you. I might even pay.'

'Pay? How much?' Edmund's eyes widened.

'Where were you going with your saddle bags full?'

'My bags, where are my bags?' Edmund tried to push himself up, but it was impossible.

'*Where* were you going?'

'London.'

'You were running away, weren't you? Why were you running away, Master Tarrant?'

'Nothing to do with you.'

Byng kicked Edmund's feet. 'Oh, I think it is. Tell me.'

'My father's sending me to join the navy, tomorrow. I don't want to go.'

The three men laughed. Byng spoke again.

'The navy would suit you.'

'What do you want? You said you'd pay.'

'Oh, no, I've just changed my mind. Your father's obviously a wise man. Getting you out of his way, which is what I want. *You*, out of *my* way.'

Behind Byng a pistol clicked, its barrel pointing his way.

'I, I, I'll go. Let me go. Give me my saddle bags, I'm going to London. I won't come back.' Edmund was shaking. He needed to pee.

'My friends here,' Byng tilted his head in the direction of Ambrose and Mokey, his piercing eyes burning into Edmund. His words were spoken slowly and low-voiced. 'They will find you wherever you are. If I want them to.'

'Why would you want me?'

'I don't. I don't ever want to see you, you snivelling thing.'

'Then let me go.'

'You can go. When I say. Come on, men.'

Byng watched as Mokey pulled the hut door closed and placed a bar across.

'Keep him here for two days. The trial will be over and it'll be too late for him to squeal.' He moved to the doorway. 'I'll take that horse of his, lovely beast. Take mine to the cottage.'

'Yes, Mr Byng.'

'What have you found out about this other boy?'

'The word is, Mr Byng, that he's the nephew o' one of the arrested men,' Ambrose said. 'Lives out Burton way, father works for Tarrant.'

'Been asking lots of questions with those friends of his,' Mokey added. 'He's telling everyone the moulds were planted.'

'He can't prove anything. Though people are saying he's determined to go to the court an' say what he thinks.' Ambrose reached for his pipe and sucked on the stem, despite it being unlit.

'They wouldn't listen to a boy's stories, would they?' Mokey scoffed.

'Best not risk it. Find him, make sure he doesn't get to Winchester.'

'See you tomorrow,' Danny called out to his pals, as he drove the cart away.

Will and Nathan waved, then made their way towards the Priory heading for the quay. They doubted Guy or Adam had learned any more about the gang, but wanted to ask one more time. The men had also promised to get Danny to Winchester and wanted to check what they'd planned. There were no clouds today, making the air chilled. The low sun was over the Head and small boats sat almost motionless on the still water.

'They should be back soon, they'll 'ave gone as soon as the tide allowed this mornin'. It were early, before dawn,' Will said, scanning the harbour. The clear sky meant the Isle of Wight and the white stacks of the Needles could be seen. Smoke rose from a nearby cottage and a man was in the garden trying to dig the frozen ground.

'What's dat?' Nathan pointed to a bundle poking from behind a box by the wall. Will headed towards it.

'Looks like a sack.' Will pushed it with the side of his foot. 'It's an old haversack.'

'It made a noise.'

Will picked it up. 'It's Edmund Tarrant's, look his name's on it.' He chuckled. 'Wonder what it's doin' here?'

'What's inside?'

One of the two straps was undone, Will unfastened the other. 'Clothes.'

'What made de noise?'

Will pushed his hand inside the bag, parted the clothes and peered inside. He gasped

'What? What is it?'

'I think it might be a mould an' other bits – fer makin' coins.'

Chapter 31

Who's following Danny?

'I'm going, Jack. You can't make me stay.'

'I knew you'd been up to something, you've been very quiet. You can't go. I promised mother I'd make sure you stayed at home.'

'I had to do something.' Danny reached for his coat. Underneath was a small bag, which he unhooked.

'What's in there?'

'A few things.'

'What things? Danny, what are you doing?'

Danny slumped on the seat beside the window. The morning was clear and frost speckled the branches of the shrubs outside. 'I'm going into town. I'm meeting Will and Nathan and hopefully Perinne if she can get there. We're going to see Mr Sweetland and tell him what we've found out.'

'And what's that?'

'Edmund saw a letter sent to his father about coins being smuggled in through the harbour. And he set fire to the school boathouse trying to make coins.'

'Are you sure?'

'Perinne saw the letters.'

'Has she got them?'

Danny shoulders sank. 'No.'

'Is that all?'

'Father's in France trying to catch the men who are sending the coins over. He'll never be home in time to sort things out.'

'Father, in France?'

'And the man I saw with Joshua Stevens has been seen in Ringwood and I've seen him in Stanpit too. Each time he's had different names. I think he's an imposter. It must be him who's smuggled the gold and the coins, dressed as a customs officer and blamed Uncle John.'

'Gold?'

'Yes, and there was no gold in the purse found with Uncle John,' Danny's voice had raised. 'Even the revenue men think the moulds in Mr Brown's stable were put there by someone else, Mrs Brown told me.' He let out a burst of breath. 'But Uncle John and Mr Brown still had coins and they were on the river.'

Jack sighed. 'Go to see Mr Sweetland, but come back home.'

Danny bit on his lip. 'I'm going to Winchester.'

'No, Danny, no.'

'I have to.' Danny grabbed his bag and rushed out of the cottage, slamming the door behind him.

'Was Henry sure the boy would come to town today?' Ambrose stamped on the ground behind the thick walls of the old ruins.

Mokey looked through the gap, watching carts and people walking over the bridge. 'He's going to Winchester on Henry's old barrel cart. Henry, three others and three boys.'

'The ones who've been snooping. Maybe we need to take all three.'

'And how do two of us do that? They're not babes, they're big lads.'

Ambrose drew on his pipe. 'True. Mr Byng said the nephew, so the nephew it is.'

'If he comes into town, he'll come this way.'

'And if he doesn't?'

'We find him in Burton.'

When Danny arrived in Christchurch he realised that he hadn't noticed anything on the way. In fact, he'd been so deep in thought he couldn't remember passing the stone cross or seeing if there was still snow on the marshes. And when he passed the old house, he didn't notice two men appear from the shadows and follow him.

The high street was a hubbub of comings and goings. Mr Reeks' wagon was outside the town hall and a group of people gathered close by. He strained his neck to see who was there. He was surprised to see Sir Charles Tarrant. He was talking with the mayor. Will had told him they'd be travelling on Henry Lane's barrel cart, though not leaving until later when Guy Cox returned from fishing on the *Solomon*. Adam Litty also had to work at the brewery until later. There were two other people coming with them, though Will hadn't said who. Isaac was going on Reeks waggon. He said he would tell the court he'd been to Avon with Uncle John and Mr Brown that night, even if it meant he could also be arrested.

Danny wove his way down the street, passing the *Ship Inn*. The attorney's office was close by. The door was closed. As he checked the latch he thought he caught sight of a man darting into the narrow road just after the *Ship,* he let it out of his mind. The days had grown colder since the snow. He thought about going to Will's cottage, but decided to wait. He patted his arms and shuffled on his feet, his breath sending out a stream of mist. Mr Sweetland might come along and he could also watch the street for Perinne. He hadn't had a reply to yesterday's letter, he hoped she'd think of some way to get here. Whilst he waited, people Danny didn't know were saying 'good morning' to him and 'they'll be all right' and 'good luck'. He knew they meant Uncle John, but how did they know him? He jolted. The face again, it popped in and out from the lane and he was certain it was the same one as he'd seen at the cottage at Avon. He was being watched.

''ello.' A finger poked into Danny's back and he spun around.

'Will, Nathan, hello.'

'Any sign of Perinne?' Will asked.

'No, not yet.'

'An' Mr Sweetland?'

'The door's locked.' Danny glanced away from his friends.

'Is there somethin' wrong?'

'Someone's watching me.'

Will and Nathan looked about. Horses clopped and carts rattled, both drivers and animals focussed on their track. Everyone seemed to be rushing.

'Don't look, he'll know I've seen him.'

'Where is he?'

'In the lane. I'm sure it's the one who was looking at us from that cottage.'

Will dashed away stopping close to where the face had shown itself. He disappeared then came out again, shaking his head and returning.

'Can't see anyone.'

'What have you got there?' Danny said, pointing to the

haversack Nathan had just set down on the floor.

'Hopefully more proof for de court.'

'We found it on the quayside yesterday.' Will leaned into Danny's ear and whispered, 'a bag with moulds and dies in.'

'And it has Edmund's name on it,' Nathan said.

A broad smile crossed Danny's face. 'That's great. I saw his father by the town hall, but not Edmund. Why were they on the quay?'

'That's what's strange. We don't know.'

'Excuse, me, boys,' a plump man said, pointing to the attorney's door.

'Are you Mr Sweetland?' Danny asked.

'Er, no, I work for him, I'm his assistant. Why do you ask?'

'We need to speak with him.'

'I'm sorry, he left early this morning. He has a trial tomorrow, two local men. You must know, all the town does.'

The colour left Danny's face. His body stiffened and he stepped nearer to the man. 'One of them is my uncle, we have to talk to him.'

The man pulled a key from his pocket and opened the door. 'Then you need to go to Winchester.'

A carriage pulled up just before the entrance to the Misses Pilgrim's drapery shop. It was new and a dark mahogany colour. The wheels almost shone and, between the polished shafts was a groomed chestnut horse. The driver jumped down and let out his passengers, first Miss Ashton then Kitty followed by Perinne who all went into the shop. As she stepped inside, Perinne paused and checked the street. Spotting the boys, she raised her hand. The boys crossed the road, but Perinne had gone inside.

'What do we do now?' Nathan said. He leaned into the shop window, cupping his hand over his forehead as he peered through the glass.

'I don't know. Perinne won't be able to get to Winchester. Let's wait, catch her when she comes out.'

'She coming.'

Perinne tip-toed over the step. 'I have to be quick. I told Miss Ashton I had left my gloves in the carriage.'

'Mr Sweetland's already left, his assistant told us. We'll have to tell him what we know when we get to Winchester,' Danny said. 'Is there any chance your mother would let you go?'

'No, it is impossible.' The sound of the shop door opening made Perinne turn. It was Kitty.

'Miss Ashton's asking where you are.'

'Tell her that I am talking to Mistress Preston from the poor house and that I will not be long.'

Kitty grinned and closed the door.

Perinne looked directly at Danny. 'Why do you not see if the assistant is going to Winchester also? I can tell *him* what I know.'

'That's a great idea, I'll go and ask.' Danny dashed away just before a cart passed by and barrels tumbled from the back, rolling into the path of a horse and rider. The horse reared and a woman screamed after a small boy who was running away from the scene. Men rushed towards the cart to help calm the horse and help the driver rescue the barrels. It was all over quickly. Kitty had appeared again.

'Miss Ashton wants the driver to help carry the boxes.'

'He is there, helping to lift the barrels,' Perinne pointed.

'I'll get him,' Nathan said.

Soon the cart was on its way again. Across the street the man who worked for Mr Sweetland came out of the building, locking the door.

'Where is Danny?' Perinne asked.

They stepped into the road looking all around, but Danny was nowhere to be seen. Will ran to the man.

''Ave ye seen our friend? The one who asked ye 'bout Mr Sweetland,' Will asked.

'No, I haven't,' the man answered and walked away. Will pushed his knuckles to his hips and scowled. Nathan and Perinne joined him just as Simon Slate appeared.

'What are you doing with that?' He pointed to the haversack.

'Have ye seen Danny, Simon?'

'Oh, it's you.'

'Well, 'ave you seen 'im? He were 'ere a minute ago, now he's gone.'

'That's Edmund's,' Simon said, pointing to the haversack. 'Why've you got it?'

Will had to think quickly. 'We found it. His father's by the town hall, we were takin' it to him.'

'He's just gone up the road towards Fairmile. He was on a horse with another man and there was someone else with them.' Simon pushed the boys apart and strode away.

'Will, Will, lad,' Isaac appeared, running and out of breath. 'I just saw Danny, he were in our road, two men,' he puffed and took a deep breath. 'They had his hands tied and then put him on a horse. They've taken Danny.'

'Who were they, Isaac?'

'Don't know.'

'What'll we do?' Nathan gasped.

'Can you drive a carriage?' Perinne asked.

The boys looked at each other, and the three dashed over to the waiting horse. Perinne climbed into the coach and the boys jumped onto the driver's seat. Will grabbed the reins, tugged them and the horse set off apace.

Chapter 32

Where is Danny?

The carriage reached Hern on a downhill slope and Will tugged at the horse to slow him down. Ahead the road forked left and right. There'd been no sight of the two riders Isaac had seen.

'Which way?' Nathan asked.

'Don't know.' Will stood upright on the foot well, craning his neck. 'It's 'ard to see, trees everywhere.'

The glass window behind the driver's seat slid across and Perinne's face appeared.

'What is it? Why have we stopped?'

'The road splits, east an' west, not sure which way to go.'

'Where are the men from?'

'From what we know, Parley,' Will pointed to the left then right, 'or Avon.'

'Dey could have gone either way.'

'There is a man over there, look, he is coming this way,' Perinne said. 'Ask if he has seen anyone.'

'Good day, sir,' Will said, touching the brim of his hat. 'We are lost. We were following some, er friends. Two men an' a boy on 'orseback.'

'Ah, yes, I did see them.'

'An' which way did they go?'

'Over the Cross Way. Not sure you'll get across in that fancy carriage.'

'We'll 'ave to try, thank ye.'

It took nearly an hour to get across the valley. The ground was hard from the recent snow and frosts and the ruts in the road tossed the cart about. At one point the road dipped into a muddy ditch and Will and Nathan had to lay logs and stones to help the wheels over. They stopped again when they reached the Ringwood road, pulling up beside a crop of fir trees.

'What we do now?' Nathan said. 'Dey could be anywhere.'

'We will have to give the horse a rest,' Perinne said, from inside the cabin.

'Look, down the road. Isn't that the boy from Byng's cottage?' Will climbed down from the driver's seat.

'What yu a-doin'?'

'Stay 'ere, I'm goin' to follow 'im.'

Perinne and Nathan watched as Will crept up the road, keeping close to the hedgerows and ducking behind trees, then he slipped out of sight.

It seemed an age before anything happened. They saw the boy first. The bag he'd been carrying earlier slung flat across his back as he walked up the road away from them. Then Will was there, checking for the boy then dashing back to the carriage.

'There's a shepherd hut. He went inside. I could hear voices, one was Danny.'

'Yu found him.'

'Come on, let's go. Perinne, stay with the carriage.'

Perinne scowled as the boys ran off.

There was no sign of anyone. The ground brushed damp across the boys' stockings as they crept towards the hut. There was a wooden bar across the door and footprints in

217

the mud below, there'd been more than the boy here. Will and Nathan pressed their ears against the wooden wall. All was quiet. Will looked around and spotted two chunks of tree branch, handing one to Nathan and grasping the other, holding it above his head. He lifted the bar, tossing it to one side and flung open the door.

'Will, it's you, how did you find me?'

'Never mind that, let's get you out of here.'

'And Edmund?'

The gloomy hut was strewn with yellow straw and, propped in the corner covered with a blanket, Edmund Tarrant sat. Both boys were tied at the feet and hands.

'Are you rescuing me? Those ruffians stole my father's horse. I need to get home.'

'What should we do with him?' Nathan asked, untying Danny.

'We take 'im with us. Keep 'im tied up.'

'Take me where?'

'Winchester. You're goin' to tell the court the truth, Edmund Tarrant.'

The crowd around the town hall had grown. The horses at the head of Reeks waggon were shuffling and snorting. A barrel cart was immediately behind it. A bell rang and the mayor stepped forward. Behind him Sir Charles Tarrant stood in a green coat that almost reached the floor, his round face red and scowling.

'Two of our young people have gone missing. First Master Tarrant has not been seen since yesterday along with Sir Charles' best stallion.'

'He's run off,' a voice shouted. The crowd tittered.

'And only just a few minutes since a carriage belonging

218

to Mister Menniere of Mudeford has been stolen from the high street. Mister Menniere's daughter, was inside. It might have been taken by William Gibbs and his friend, the black boy. We think they were chasing two men who have snatched Daniel Clarke.'

'They were,' Isaac shouted. 'It's a gang from Avon, Moonrakers. They're villains, they're why John an' Caleb are in gaol.'

'Are there any men who can help to find these children?'

'We need to get to Winchester,' Isaac said. 'Will's a good lad, he'll make sure the girl comes to no harm.'

'I'll help,' Joseph Martin shouted. 'But only until it's time to go.'

'Me too,' David Preston stepped forward with his hand raised. 'I'll get a few others, though most are going to the trial later.'

'Can everyone going to Winchester with Reeks board the cart, the others for the search come with me and Sir Charles.'

'See, the coast,' James said. 'We should be in Poole before dark.'

'Do you think that we can find a coach to Christchurch at that time?' Yves asked.

Joshua Stevens shook his head. 'Not usually, but we'll go to the customs house. They'll help. We have to get a message to Winchester. Hopefully the trial won't be for a while, but those men don't deserve to be where they are.'

Nathan appeared at the edge of the road.

'We found Danny. Edmund Tarrant is there too. We bringin' him.' Nathan climbed onto the driver's seat and took up the reins.

Perinne looked across to the field. Danny was holding Edmund by the legs and Will was holding him under the arms. Edmund was shouting. When they reached the carriage both had sweaty beads tricking down their faces.

'Untie me now, ruffians.'

'Shut up, codshead.'

'Let's put 'im inside.'

'Where do we go now?' Nathan asked.

'To Winchester. I'll sit inside with Perinne an' Danny. Put Edmund on the floor, keep 'im quiet. We'll go to Ringwood then across the Forest.'

The three boys bundled a struggling Edmund into the carriage and everyone took their places. By the time they reached Ringwood it was mid-afternoon. Nathan looked for somewhere to pull up.

''Ow much money 'ave we?' Will said. 'I've three shillin's.'

'I have none, I am sorry.'

'Same, three shillin',' Nathan said.

Danny reached into his bag, 'four shillings and these pennies,' he lifted a small purse and rattled it. 'I haven't counted them.'

'Then we're all right. We'll get some oats fer the 'orse and something to eat. Once the 'orse has rested, we'll go again.'

'We will travel in the dark?' Perinne asked.

'Aye, we should have a good hour or more daylight first. This is a new carriage. The lamps'll cast a good light.'

'Where du yu think the men will be now?'

'Who knows - did they say anythin', Danny?'

'No. They must have known who I was or why take me?'

'Did Edmund say anythin'?'

'All he's done is complain. Wants to know how we've got his haversack and to give it back. What about him? We'll have to feed him too. He's bound to have some money.'

'Leave 'im fer now.'

'Someone needs to stay wi de coach. I'll do it, people remember me, best I keep away.'

'Good idea. Perinne can stay with ye. We'll go an' get food.'

Meekwick Ginn probed the fish searching for bones then took a fork full, chewing noisily.

'So both boys are out of the way, Mr Ginn.'

'Hmph. And Byng?'

'He left for Winchester earlier,' Ambrose sucked on his pipe.

'There's been no word from France. This has been a bad business,' Ginn sneered, then lifted cabbage to his mouth.

'Folks are travelling from Christchurch today. They're pleading good character,' Mokey said.

'I heard they're not charging them over the moulds. Is that true?'

'I think so, Mr Ginn, though they're still in trouble, smuggling and they had your coins.'

'My coins? My coins?'

A wigged man on a nearby table turned and gave Ginn a puzzled look. The inn was quiet, the log fire glowed in orange spits and snaps.

Ginn lowered his voice. 'I've finished with Byng and his gang, you'd be wise to find another way to make a living.'

'We trust Mr Byng.' Mokey narrowed his eyes as he stared at Ginn.

'Hmph.'

'We're going. We'll be back for the payment,' Ambrose said, lifting himself from his seat.

'I told you, I've heard nothing from France. This weather's holding things up.'

Mokey and Ambrose stepped out from the inn. Mokey rubbed his hands together and blew into them. Some shops were getting rush lights ready and others with their doors and windows closed had signs in the windows saying '*open*'. The men pushed by on the way to Davey Brook's dairy where they'd left their horses. Their instructions were to travel to Winchester, watch out for any sign of the other boys or anyone who might get in the way of Ethan Byng's plan.

'Look, Mokey,' Ambrose pointed with his pipe stem. 'One o' those new carriages. There was one in Christchurch earlier.'

Mokey strained his eyes. 'And look who's sitting on it.'

'That pie was good,' Nathan said to Perinne, wiping his mouth.

Perinne leaned from the driver's seat and peeped through the window into the carriage. Danny and Will were sitting with their feet on Edmund's legs. They were handing him bits of food which he put to his mouth with his tied hands.

'Is everyone all right? We will go soon?'

'Yes,' Danny said, before letting out a gasp, spreading pie crumbs across Edmund. He shrieked, '*it's them*, the men who took me, they're coming, quick, Perinne, *go, go, go*!'

Chapter 33

Friends in peril

'Yu can drive?'

'I know how to, Nathan, but I do not think that I can drive as fast as Will.'

'Turn here, here, dis one. I remember de road, we came dis way.'

Perinne guided the carriage and cracked the whip as the horse's hooves and the wheels of the carriage crunched and juddered on the road. Danny poked his nose through the small panel of the cabin as they were tossed from side-to-side.

'Are they chasing us?' He raised his voice. 'Nathan, Nathan, can you see anyone?'

'No, not yet. But dey sure to come. I think dey want to stop yu a-gettin' to de court.'

'They'll soon catch up on horses, is there another road?' Danny shouted.

'I do not know this way,' Perinne called out. Her hat had blown onto the back of her head and her hair was streaming behind her.

'Do yu know which road to take?' Nathan called back.

'I know we came on this road last week,' Will replied.

'We cannot go for too long without resting the horse,' Perinne said.

'There must be other ways. Do ye know 'ow to get there, Danny?' Will urged.

'No, no. Oh, what are we going to do?'

'I know,' Edmund said. 'I come this way to school.'

'Why would you help us?' Danny snapped at him. 'You're working with those men, we know what you've been doing, Edmund.'

'Yes, 'ow can we trust ye?' Will sneered.

'How did dey see it was yu, Danny?' Nathan bellowed into the cabin. 'Did yu see them, what do dey look like?'

'They covered my head, but I did see one of them. It was the face I keep seeing. It was him and another man in a big hat. That was all.' Danny pulled a face. 'And they smelled. I'm sure they didn't see me just then, it must 'ave been the carriage, we were all beside it in Christchurch.'

'Aye, they were watchin' ye.'

Danny said, 'did you see them, Edmund?'

'Only for a moment, they covered my head too.'

'Which way do we go?'

'Danny, we can't trust him.'

'We have to, we don't know the roads. Where do we go, Edmund?'

'Keep on this road, then there's a fork and you take the left, towards Romsey.'

'What about de men? Dey'll be a-comin'.' Nathan was leaning his face against the panel now.

'We'll hide the carriage an' take the 'orse,' Will said.

'Hide this?' Edmund laughed.

'He has a point, Will,' Danny said. 'And there are five of us, one horse is no good.'

Danny looked ahead. The clouds had gathered again, sucking the colour out of the heath and swathes of forest, leaving an expanse of silver grey. They should stop, he thought, swap drivers. Perinne and Nathan would be freezing outside with the icy air blowing into their faces.

'Come on, Danny,' Will gave his arm a touch. 'There's no sign of the men.'

'We're making so much noise, we wouldn't hear them 'til they were next to us.'

'Nathan's watchin' out.'

Danny rocked to and fro on his seat. 'Maybe they won't follow us.'

'Of course they will, Shorty.'

'Shut up, Edmund.' Danny leaned to the window again. 'Nathan, Nathan, make sure you look back. Watch for the men.'

'I will, Danny, I will.'

'We will find her, Jane. We know she's with those boys and there are plenty out looking for them.'

'Oh, Charles, I thought with getting her a governess and then letting Kitty come to stay, Perinne would stop these adventures.'

'She's certainly got spirit.' Sir Charles was still wearing his thick coat and riding boots. He looked around the room. He was pleased that the Menniere's had their own home now, and it was good that it kept Yves close by. He put a hand on Jane's shoulder. 'We know the boys, rascals they may be, but they won't hurt her.' He swished brandy around the glass he was holding. 'She has a generous heart, I expect she was just helping out. Unlike Edmund, who does everything for himself and nothing for others - unless there's payment.' He let out a long sigh. 'The Clarke boy wanted to help his uncle and with his father away, I suppose it's to be commended. It seems he's come to the notice of villains and his friends were trying to help.'

Jane paced the room. 'But she's in danger again. You're very calm about it. Edmund is missing too.'

'I think he ran away. He'll be with a friend trying to scare us, his mother especially. He'll be safe, he always puts himself first. It's my horse I want.'

'Charles, that's an awful thing to say.'

'He's become a burden to us, Jane. I've arranged for him to join the navy. He should have been in Portsmouth today. That's why he's run off.'

'Surely he can't be so bad?'

Sir Charles raised his eyebrows, though his face gave away a hint of sadness. 'He was trying to forge coins, Jane. He was almost caught and I've no doubt now that he's had something to do with this business with the two smugglers. If that's true, he could hang with the rest of them. Best he be sent away, if we ever find him.'

'How long we been ridin'?'

'I do not know, but the horse is tiring. We must stop soon.'

'My fingers are frozen, what about yu?'

'Yes, my gloves are not helping anymore. Look, there are lights, over there.' Perinne pointed to the distance. 'It must be big enough to put out rush lights. I shall go there.'

Nathan pulled the glass across the window. 'We stoppin' soon, there's buildin's ahead.'

'I wonder what the place is?' Danny said.

'If you let me see outside, I could tell you,' Edmund smirked.

'I wonder why the men didn't follow us.'

Edmund chuckled. 'You're supposed to be smart, Clarke. They'll have gone another way. Be waiting for you ahead.'

'Come on, Danny, let's get out.' Will opened the door and jumped onto the hard gravel. Nathan was helping Perinne down from the driver's seat. They moved away from the carriage and huddled.

'Edmund has a point,' Will said. 'This aint Romsey. That were a much bigger place. They'll know we'll go that way. I'll wager they'll be waiting fer us there.'

'So what do we do next? It's dark,' Danny asked. 'If we're not even at Romsey yet, we'll never get to Winchester in time.'

'We carry on.'

'But it is so dark, the lamps will help a little, but only if you drive slowly,' Perinne said.

'We need to think about it. If dey be a-waitin' maybe we need to do what Byng does.'

'What, Nathan?' Danny perked up.

'Well, dey a-lookin' for three boys maybe a girl too if dey saw Perinne. We're four boys, if we count Edmund. Perinne could do with bein' a boy too.'

'Moi? A boy, non.' Perinne's mouth fell open.

The boys laughed, Perinne gave a scowl, then joined in.

'Nathan's right. And we'll need to get rid of the carriage,' Danny said.

'Non, Papa will be furious. It is new.'

'I've had an idea,' Will said. He whispered into Perinne's ear, then spoke again. 'Look, there's an inn, follow me.'

'Sir, can ye 'elp us?'

The innkeeper narrowed his eyes.

'Yes, boys, er miss.'

'That barrel cart outside, is it yours?'

'And what if it is?'

'We were wondering if you'd swap it for our carriage for two days.'

'We are going to Winchester. My papa said to leave it somewhere safe.' Perinne crossed her fingers behind her back.

'It's worth a lot more than a barrel cart,' Will said. 'If we don't bring back yer cart, ye could sell it and buy two with what ye'd make.'

'Let me see it.'

The innkeeper followed the friends outside and looked around the cart.

'The horse has come a long way, we will leave him also and take yours,' Perinne said.

'All right, I'll agree.'

'Is dat yu son?' Nathan said, pointing to the door of the inn where a boy was watching.

'Yes, it is,' the innkeeper said, returning to the doorway. Nathan followed him.

'Him clothes look a bit small, how would he like new ones?'

'Ah you're trying to sell me…'

'No, sir. We have a bag of good clothes. We just need some smaller ones, clean and warm for this weather.'

'Show me.'

Nathan called to Will. A few moments later he fetched Edmund's haversack.

'Hey, what are you doing with my …'

'Who else have you in there?' the man asked.

'Oh, that's Edmund, he can't walk very well. 'ave you some blankets we could borrow? We'll pay.'

Danny and Perinne stood aside, trying not to laugh at Will and Nathan's antics. The man disappeared into the inn and returned with breeches, stockings, a jacket and a thick woollen coat and hat.

'Hitch the cart for these lads,' the man instructed his son. Then take the carriage to the stable and feed that horse.

The man gave the boys one last look and went inside the inn, closing the door behind him. Then the boy ran around the side.

'Danny, put the moulds back in the haversack and untie Edmund's legs. Nathan, follow the boy, get the carriage lamps,' Will ordered, handing the boy's clothes to Perinne. ''ere, change into these, tie yer hair up in the hat.'

Soon they were on their way again. The lamps were fitted to the barrel cart and cast a low glow ahead. Will and Edmund sat at the front. Edmund's hands and legs had been retied and covered with a blanket. Nathan, Danny and Perinne hunched inside under the canvas.

Will sucked in the freezing air making his teeth ache. The men had seen him, Nathan and Danny, but they wouldn't know they had Edmund and, hopefully, hadn't seen Perinne. 'They'll be lookin' for three boys an' a carriage,' he thought. 'Now we're five boys an' a barrel cart, but will it fool 'em?'

Chapter 34

Can Will's plan work?

The lights of Romsey appeared in the distance, flickering like fireflies. It was now deep into the evening.

'Get Edmund inside, we don't want 'im shoutin' out,' Will called. 'If we get stopped, cover yerselves wi' the blankets an' keep as still an' quiet as ye can.'

Nathan and Danny pulled a complaining Edmund backwards into the cart. Perinne took his place at the front.

'Wrap ye scarf o'er ye face and pull the hat down,' Will commanded, his voice firm. 'Listen, ev'ryone, I'll drive in, then keep on, we'll stop once we're through the town, don't forget, keep quiet.'

'All right,' Danny called from inside.

'If Byng's men see the cart an' guess who we are, I don't know what we'll do,' Will muttered under his breath.

'My bones are aching,' Mokey shivered. The street where they stood was in shadows of rush and candlelight, though a short way off the lights from an inn flooded the road with a warm glow.

'Tis bitter. How long shall we wait?'

'Mr Byng said stop them at all cost. All night if we must.' Mokey stamped his feet and banged his gloved hands against his arms. 'Not many about. If they come this way, we'll get them.'

'Look, lights.'

'A barrel cart. Could be goods bein' taking somewhere.'

'Make it look as if we're coming out of the inn, come on let's get by the door.'

'Why? It's not them.'

'We can ask if they've seen anything. A carriage like that should have been here by now.'

The barrel cart moved steadily towards them.

'Looks like a man and a boy,' Mokey said.

Will spotted the two men. One was taller than the other, but that was all that could be seen. They too were wrapped up for the freezing weather. They were simply black shapes against the background of yellow glow from an inn.

'Two men ahead,' he whispered through the canvas of the cart. 'Get under the blanket, Perinne huddle down, pretend to be asleep.'

Will's teeth gritted and his hands squeezed the reins tight as the horse continued its steady progress. He had to stay calm. One of the men had moved a little further ahead on the road. 'What were they doing? Was it them?' Will asked himself. He took a deep breath and concentrated his eyes on as much of the scene as he could. The nearer of the two men was approaching. He heard Perinne take a deep breath.

'Bitter night to be on the road,' Mokey said, his voice light and friendly.

'Nearly done,' Will said, using a low voice that almost growled. 'Delivery, not far to go.'

'Your boy asleep?'

'Pretendin' more like,' Will grunted. 'Must be gettin' on.'

Mokey followed the cart's wheels as they ground into the frozen dirt of the road. The horse pulled forwards passing Ambrose. Flakes of snow had begun to trickle onto everyone's clothes.

'Have you seen a carriage? My employer was due some time back.'

'Seen nothin'.'

'You can't miss it, a new one.'

'Sorry, not seen anythin'.'

'Oh, all right, thanks.' Mokey stopped.

The cart had reached Ambrose and, as it drove by, a yelp sounded.

'You got someone in there driver?' Ambrose asked.

Will gulped, then an idea sprang quickly into his head. He laughed. 'The lad's puppy dog. Needs feedin', so do we. A good night to ye, sir.'

Will's heart raced like a hare being chased by a hound. He dared not look back. He couldn't tell if the men were following, the crunch of the cartwheels masked any sound four boots might make. Soon the rush lamps of Romsey were replaced by occasional candles in cottage windows. The coach lamps were fading, they'd have to stop soon.

'Danny, Nathan. Can ye see anythin'? Are they followin'?' Will said leaning back and talking as quietly as he could.

'Can't see anything, they'd need lamps, it's so dark,' Danny said. 'Were they the men? Did they hear Edmund?'

'Told 'em the noise were a puppy. Don't know if it were them. One taller than the other, didn't see much of his face. The other had a pipe, not lit.'

'I remember the pipe. It must have been them,' Edmund offered.

'You nearly gave us away, Edmund,' Danny snapped.

'Phew!' Will blew out his cheeks. His eyes were watering

after keeping them on the men, the wet was freezing. 'We must've been goin' two hours or more, will the 'orse be all right, Perinne?'

Perinne's teeth were chattering. 'We w-w-will need to s-s-stop soon. We all need to rest.'

'We'll stop at the next place. Get in the back with the others. Ask Edmund what the next town is after Romsey.'

'Why not ask me yourself?'

'Just tell us what it is, Edmund?' Danny groaned.

'It's a village, Hursley. Then we're near Winchester.'

Danny wondered what Edmund's face was like. It was too dark to see whether he was looking afraid, smug or if he was planning anything.

'Why did you do it? Why did you put those moulds in the stable?'

'I never said I did.'

'Why, Edmund? Did you know my uncle's a hero? He saved dozens of lives. What have you ever done?'

'Leave me alone.'

'How did you get involved with Byng?'

'The customs officer? Mr Ginn, he got him to meet me. He said they knew the men were smuggling and they were bringing in coins, but no one would believe them.'

Danny wasn't going to tell Edmund what they suspected. 'What happened to Mr Stevens?'

'I don't know.'

'You don't know anything, Edmund. You're so selfish. You wanted the reward, didn't you? You saw the letter about the gold.'

'How did you …? Oh, yes, it was you Perinne, you *were* snooping.'

Danny was pleased Perinne ignored him. 'Well you'll tell the court everything.'

'You *can't* make me.'

'I think this is it,' Will called from the front. 'We need to get somethin' to eat an' drink, then find somewhere to 'ide, those men will be comin' this way. They'll be watchin' out fer us an' be waitin' again. Next time, we might not be so lucky.'

'We couldn't wait outside anymore, Ambrose, we'd have frozen to death.'

The two men sat across from each other watching out of the window of the inn. Two empty plates lay on the table in front of them and, to their side, the last embers of a fire made a feeble job of thawing their frozen limbs. 'Pah, why didn't we do this before, Ambrose?

'Aye.'

'What is it?'

'Don't know, something's niggling me about that barrel cart.'

'What about it? Just be a man on a run.'

'Can't just … '

'The puppy?'

'No.' Ambrose rubbed his forehead with the heels of his hands. 'No, er, er ... that's it. The lamps. Did you notice the lamps on that cart? They weren't right. They were new, they were the type from…'

Mokey's eyes widened and finished Ambrose's sentence. 'A carriage.'

Chapter 35

Danny's despair

Danny woke. They'd huddled together in the back of the cart, apart from where the boys had made a bed across the top end for Perinne. They'd given her an extra blanket and the boys' bodies had kept each other warm. He ached. He hadn't slept. Every crack and hoot had made him jump, thinking the men had found them. He knew it was animals, a deer or a rabbit, but he couldn't shake it from his mind. He lifted the canvas with his finger. It was nearly dawn. It seemed bright. He raised it a little more and sighed. Snow, it had snowed again. That was good and bad. He'd gone out with Will after they'd eaten and brushed over the cart tracks with fallen branches. The good thing was that the fresh snow on top meant the men wouldn't have a trail to follow. Will also said he'd told the innkeeper a story, so should the men call in and ask questions, it wouldn't sound like them. Edmund said they would easily get to Winchester from here, so the bad thing was that the snow might hold them up. But even if they could carry on their journey, somewhere out there were the two men who wanted to stop them.

'We just don't know, Mr Byng.' Mokey held out his arms.

'They were three children, they can't have got here,' Ambrose tutted.

'You let the boy escape,' Byng sneered at the two men.

They'd agreed to keep quiet about the lamps. Just coincidence they'd decided. They'd followed the cart's trail to Hursley. Once there the snowy road was lined with other tracks. Footprints peppered the snowy floor. They'd all seemed to come from the inn, then out towards nearby cottages and eventually stopped – or had been covered by further snow. A carter had called at the inn for food and drink, two beers, two pies and some cheese, the landlord had said. The carter had told him that the cheese was for the morning before his journey back home. It sounded like the driver they'd spoke to, so now they were sure it wasn't the three boys. The landlord also told them there'd been more than the usual number of carts and waggons passing by that day. What if the children had turned back and come across one of those?

'Make sure that they don't get to the court,' Byng hissed. 'The plan's working here. Are you both ready?'

'We need to get changed. Even if they turn up, what can they say?'

'They haven't passed us we're sure of that, Mr Byng,' Mokey said. 'And we've put our other plan into place.'

'A good one,' Ambrose added, 'and if it works *no one* will get into the city.'

'Do we know where de court is?' Nathan said as the cart set out.

The road stretched ahead like a white river. Nathan sat with Will at the front. They'd decided the men would have gone on to Winchester by now and would try to catch them there. They'd made up their minds that they would stop outside the city and work out how to get to the court. They might need to split up. Danny and Perinne would walk together. Perinne had changed into her dress again. Will would walk with Edmund, keep him tied at the wrists and Nathan was to run on ahead. The journey dragged on. The snow stuck to the wheels and built up into clods of ice on the cart's axles. Will and Nathan had to get down lots of times and kick off the chunks before they could carry on. Finally, smoke from many chimneys could be seen rising in columns into a blue sky. Buildings began to line the road. The air smelled of wood, coal and brewing. It was Winchester.

'We need to stop, leave the cart somewhere,' Will said.

Perinne poked her head through the canvas. 'We should look for an inn, the horse he will need food and rest.'

'There's one,' Will said. 'Let's try it.'

'How far are we from the court?' Danny asked.

'We need to find out where it is,' Nathan said.

'Do you know, Edmund?' Danny stared at the boy. He'd not spoken since they'd woken. Edmund stared back and smirked.

'What time is it? We don't even know what time the trial is.' Danny stood, his legs unsteady, and sat down again pulling his hat on and off.

'We'll find out soon,' Will said.

'Do not worry, Danny. We can ask at the inn, we are here now,' Perinne said putting her hand on her friend's arm.

Will drove into the yard and an ostler came to meet them.

'Good morning, do you need stabling?'

'Aye, we do. How much for the day?' Will asked.

'A shillin'.'

Nathan dug a coin out from his purse and handed it over.

'Take it through, leave it over there with the others, I'll get the boy to tend the horse.'

'Look,' Danny gasped, 'that's Uncle John's cart and Aunt Mary's.'

'You here for the trial?' The ostler asked.

Danny gave Will a worried glance, but Will nodded. 'Yes, do you know where it's being held?'

'Aye, the great hall, by the castle. Though it might be difficult to get there now.'

'What do you mean?' Danny's body tensed.

'Why, they locked the gates and the roads are blocked. A call went up an hour since, escaped prisoners.' At that the ostler walked off.

Danny stood, mouth agape, the others didn't know what to say. The stable boy appeared and began unfastening the breeching and detaching the cart's shafts.

'What did the ostler mean?' Perinne asked him.

'There's French and Spanish prisoners in the castle. Sometimes they escape. The gates are guarded. No one can go in or out of the city until the dragoons say so.'

Danny slumped onto the frozen stones of the yard. 'No, *no*, I *must* get to the trial.'

Chapter 36

The trial begins

'Why?' the stable boy asked. He looked at the friends. Tears were falling down the red cheeks of Danny's face.

'It is his uncle, he is to go before the judge,' Perinne said.

'But he's not done what they say, an' we know who did.' Will glared at Edmund. 'We must get there or Danny's uncle will hang for certain.'

The court clerk, in his dark cloak and wig, bellowed, 'the King against Caleb Brown and John Hewitt.' He pushed the spectacles that were riding down his long nose back in place and lifted the sheet of paper he was holding.

The hall bustled with people shuffling into seats that were tiered to either side of the hall like a theatre. The hall was wide and its ceiling lay high above them. Cold draughts whispered along its stone floor and around the ankles of those coming inside. Hung flat against the west wall was a large, round table top and beneath this was the bench soon to be the seat of the judge. In front of the bench men in grey wigs and black gowns shuffled papers on a long table. To one side of the bench was a stand, which seemed more like a deep box. In the seats the townsfolk of Christchurch sat in silence. Some were looking about the vast hall, others deep in thought. On the front row sat Bessie Brown and Mary Hewitt and beside Mary was Hannah Clarke. The women were dressed in coats and hats against the chill of the hall. Lines of worry were etched on their faces. Mary stared blankly across the floor. Isaac Hooper, red faced, took off his hat and rested it on his knees. He closed his eyes and bit on his lips. His hands were shaking. Meg Gibbs took one of them and gently squeezed it. Other familiar faces took their places. Adam Litty, Guy Cox, David and Judith Preston from the poor house, Joseph Martin and Henry Lane. The Reverend Jackson sat on the highest tier with John Cook and Edward Allan. Across the floor, the jury sat. All were strangers to the people opposite. Close to these two customs officers stood chatting, their backs to the room. Towards the back of the seating was a further stand.

'Bring in the prisoners,' the clerk called out.

Two men in heavy coats appeared followed by Caleb and John, both with their hands tied and their feet chained. They were led to the box where they were ordered to stand. The spectators mumbled, Mary gasped. The clerk coughed.

'Silence. All stand.'

A rumble of shuffling feet welcomed the judge, tall, slightly stooping. He scanned the scene and sat down, pulling his gown around him.

'Go ahead,' he gestured to the clerk, who faced the court and spoke slowly and clearly.

'In the name of God, amen. Before you, the worshipful George Fielder, find Richard Beattie, of His Majesty's customs in Poole in Dorsetshire against Caleb Brown of Christchurch and John Hewitt of Hinton, both of the county of Hampshire. Also find Mr Philip Sweetland of Christchurch who will speak on behalf of the defendants.

The judged nodded.

'May the court hear that Caleb Brown and John Hewitt are accused of the following offences. First, that of coining, keeping moulds and dies for the making of coins, the filing of coins for the metal then using that metal to make coins, the possession of coins and putting them into circulation. Such conduct is an act of treason against His Majesty, King George.

Secondly, that Caleb Brown and John Hewitt did transport goods to others without proper duties being paid.'

'Mr Beattie will open on behalf of His Majesty and his customs,' the judge said.

'Thank you, My Lord.' Beattie turned towards the jury. 'On the night of 13th December last, officers conducted a search of the stable belonging to Caleb Brown. In a sack, hidden at the rear of the building was discovered moulds and dies. Officers at Christchurch had been watching both men and it was decided to make an arrest. The men were captured later that evening and were found in the possession of forged coins. We have the said moulds and coins here for the jury to see.'

'Do you have witnesses for the court, Mr Beattie?

'I have two officers who were sent from Poole to assist and were both present and will describe how the blacksmith's home was searched.'

'Is the chief revenue officer not here?'

'No, my Lord, he has not been seen, but I notice that the mayor of Christchurch is present, I will also call him to the witness box.'

A rumble of chatter echoed around. A mix of surprise and puzzlement flashed over Edward Hooper and John Cook's faces.

'Mr Cook was made aware from customs in London that coins were coming in through the harbour. I will ask him to swear this. Edward Allan is the Commissioner for Customs, he was in London, but can swear there was gold and other coins being smuggled into Christchurch.'

The judge turned to Philip Sweetland. 'And the defence?'

Sweetland stood. 'My Lord, Caleb Brown knows nothing of the moulds and I have a letter and report from a Mr Richard White, who works for His Majesty's customs in London. I am surprised Mr Beattie hasn't been made aware of this. Mr White has examined the moulds and dies presented by Mr Beattie and he states in his report that the coins in the purse held by John Hewitt were not made in these.'

Beattie rose. 'But they still had coins and moulds.'

The judge gave Beattie a scowl. 'Continue, Mr Sweetland.'

'I will bring forward many witnesses to the good character of the two men.'

'And that is all?'

'It is, sir.'

The red-coated dragoons lifted their muskets as three horses approached the south gate.

'Halt,' one of them shouted.

'We need to get to the Great Hall for a trial.'

'No one can go in, prisoners have escaped.'

'I am Joshua Stevens, Chief Revenue Officer at Christchurch. The trial needs my witness, I have been delayed. These men also have evidence.'

'Can you prove this?'

'Please, officer. It is most important. It is also thought

242

that our children are here.'

'It's a Frenchie,' the second dragoon shouted, pointing his musket at Yves.

'Officer, do you really think your escaped prisoner would be in good clothes, riding a good horse trying to get *into* the city?' James Clarke said, shaking his head and frowning.

'I will get the captain.'

'Don't delay,' Stevens called after him.

'Here, this is it, I often come this way.' The boy had led them through a maze of tumbledown cottages then showed them a narrow space. 'The city wall is behind here, there's a hole.'

The boy pressed himself into the gap, Perinne went next, then Danny. Nathan followed, pulling Edmund as Will, with Edmund's haversack strapped across his chest, pushed him forward. His feet had been untied, but not his hands. The hole was low to the floor, which was wet with snow. One after the other they squeezed through. Their clothes damp and smelling of earth were now smeared with green moss. They emerged into a small garden then followed the boy to the street. He pointed.

'That's the east gate, follow the path and you'll find the hall. I have to go before the ostler misses me. Good luck.' At that the boy scrambled back through the hole.

'Quick,' Danny shouted, 'Let's *go*.'

Chapter 37

Is Danny in time?

Judge Fielder pressed his hands to make a steeple and rested his chin on the top. 'We have heard from two customs officers, who swear that the moulds and dies were found in the stable. They were also witness to the arrest and seizure of the purse with the forged coins. Mr Allan confirmed that indeed counterfeit coins were being brought into England through Christchurch and with many of them being gold it was harming the country's economy. We have heard from Mr Cook that forged coins were being passed at the market in the town. The men were found on the river at night. Christchurch is well-known for its criminals. They may well be good men to their friends and family, but the smuggling of goods and evasion of duty costs our country dear. I ask you now, the jury, have you made up your minds?'

The man on the front row nearest the bench stood. 'We have.'

'On the first charge of coining, possession of forged coins and passing these on…'

'Stop!'

Danny burst into the hall.

'What is this?' The judge scowled.

'Danny, what are you …?' Hannah Clarke cried out. There were gasps of surprise all around the hall.

'The men, they're innocent.'

'I'm afraid the jury has decided, young man.'

'You have to listen, please.' Danny stared directly at the judge. His legs began to shake and his mouth dried. He could feel rage rising as his face reddened like flames creeping up his body.

Perinne appeared at his side followed by Nathan and a stumbling Edmund. Philip Sweetland turned around and looked at Danny, then the others, shock on his face. At the back of the court, Caleb and John both gasped.

'It's not Mr Brown and Uncle John, it's a man called Byng, he smuggled in the coins. They were from Avon, they had them left in a pool for the Moonrakers. He dressed as a customs officer and had the moulds put in Mr Brown's stable. The coins, they were given to Uncle John to get him into trouble.' Danny was panting, he took a breath.

'Ah, one of the accused is your uncle. Mr Sweetland? Do you know this boy?' Sweetland shook his head.

'I do,' Reverend Jackson stood. 'It is Daniel Clarke, a pupil at the grammar school at the Priory Church. He's one of my best students.'

'Me also, John Cook added getting to his feet. 'The boy's from a good family.'

'Mr Beattie? Beattie was looking at the floor.

'A boy's fantasy, my Lord.'

'It's not. Ask Edmund, he has moulds, he gave them to Byng. He wanted the reward. Tell them Edmund.'

'Is that boy tied up?' Judge Fielder pointed at Edmund.

'He'd 'ave run away from us,' Will spoke. 'He were running away from his father when Byng's men caught him. We found him. He left these.' Will pushed Edmund forward and put the sack on the table, taking out the moulds. The hall door opened, but no one heard as the room burst into a rumble of shock at what Will had revealed.

'They are Edmund's,' Perinne said. 'Look, they are the same as those. She pointed to the moulds on the bench.

'And you are, miss?

'Perinne Menniere. Edmund is Sir Charles Tarrant's son, my mother is his father's cousin. Edmund was expelled from school for setting fire to the school boathouse. He was trying to hide that he had been making coins. His father found out, that is why he was running away.'

'An' he wanted the reward for catchin' the smugglers,' Will added.

Danny looked at Edmund who had fallen to the floor trembling and with tears dripping from his face. Something pulled in Danny's heart. 'And Byng tricked him into planting the moulds. He's tricked lots of people, some people think he's a tailor.'

The judge breathed deeply and leaned back into his chair.

'It's true,' a voice called from the back of the hall. There were more gasps as Joshua Stevens made his way to the front of the court. People began muttering 'it is' and 'he's here' and 'where's he been?'

'I'm Joshua Stevens. The customs officer was called Buchan. It took me some time to recognise his disguise, he's known in Christchurch as Elias Baker, a tailor. The day the men were brought to the gaol, I was hit, knocked out, again and again. I was taken across the English channel to France, then left to die in a lane miles from anywhere. I was very lucky to be found alive.'

Judge Fielder looked to the leader of the jury. 'Has what you've heard changed your verdict?'

The man leaned into the eleven other men who exchanged words, heads nodding.

'We have.'

'And do you find the prisoners guilty or not guilty of counterfeiting and passing coins?'

'Not guilty.'

A great cheer rang around the court. The judge banged his gavel hard on the bench. The clerk shrieked 'silence'. Beattie sat down and put his face in his hands.

'And of the second charge, transport of goods to others without proper duties being paid, smuggling, what is your verdict?'

The head juror checked with the others. 'Guilty.'

'*No!*' Danny shrieked.

'Quiet boy. I'll have you moved from the court.'

'Danny, *Danny*.'

Danny turned to see his father. 'You have to help father, you *have* to.'

'Don't get yerself in trouble, lad,' Uncle John called out.

Danny spun on his heels and faced the judge again. 'What was the proof?'

Philip Sweetland put his hand on Danny's shoulder. 'They were caught, on the river.'

'Who says?'

'Young man,' Judge Fielder said. 'The court has heard from witnesses.'

'I want to ask them something.'

'Mr Beattie, will you allow your witness to repeat what they saw?'

Beattie stood, his back to Danny. 'It's not usual my Lord.'

'What was found on the boat, that's all I want to ask,' Danny pressed.

'Nothing,' Joshua Stevens shouted. There was nothing on the boat.'

'Then how can anyone prove they were smuggling?'

There were calls of 'yes' and 'there's no proof.'

'You are a clever young man.' Judge Fielder took a deep breath aiming his words towards the men in the dock. 'Caleb Brown and John Hewitt, you have been found not guilty of the charge of coining, but guilty of smuggling.

However, after listening to those vouching for your good characters and the words of this young man. I am granting you both a pardon. You are free to go.'

A cheer so loud filled the great hall that no one heard Danny shout out.

'It's *him*, it's Byng, he's not Beattie, it's *him*!'

Will and Nathan dashed after Byng who was throwing off his wig and heading for the door.

'*Stop 'im, stop 'im.*'

Nathan caught hold of Byng's coat. The two gaolers sprung to his help.

'And those two, they're with him, Danny pointed at Mokey and Ambrose who were wearing customs officer's uniforms. 'They chased us, get them too.'

Adam and Guy leapt forward and joined James and Yves who grabbed the men. Soon Byng, Mokey and Ambrose were being led away.

Chapter 38

Twelfth Night

'Here we are, small beers for you two.'

Joseph Martin, red faced, carried tankards to the table where Will, Nathan and Isaac were sitting with Caleb, Guy Cox and Adam Litty. Meg Gibbs was chatting to Bessie beside the fire. Laughter rolled around the *George* in bursts and howls.

'On me, my treat for the celebrations.'

They all lifted their ale, clanking the metal together, splashes spilling onto the table.

'To Caleb and John,' Joseph called out. A great 'hurray' whipped around the smoky room.

'Just this an' we must be a-goin',' Nathan said.

'You boys did a great job,' Adam said to nods and 'ayes' from the others.

'It was scary at times,' Nathan said. 'But Danny in court, he was great.'

'Yes, we heard Philip Sweetland's givin' him an apprenticeship,' Caleb said. 'That's a good job.'

'Aye,' he'll do good,' Will said.

'What about you two? Are you staying this time?' Guy asked. 'Will you be coming back on the *Solomon*?'

Will looked at Nathan who smiled, widening his eyes.

'Nathan an' me, we're goin' to buy a cart. We're goin' to set up a yard an' sell coal. They do it in London.'

'Coal?' Isaac said. 'Who can afford coal?'

'More an' more people. We'll buy it from the coastin' vessel, take it to the yard an' sell it in bags, all weighed,' he paused grinning at the men, 'an' all the duty paid.'

Everyone laughed.

'What about the girl, Perinne?' Caleb asked.

'I feel sorry fer her,' Will said. 'She can't do anythin' she wants, but she'll 'ave Kitty stayin'.'

'An we takin' coal, once we started,' Nathan said. Massa Menniere said he'd be happy to be our first customer.'

'And Cliff House, will you sell there?' Adam chuckled. 'Edmund Tarrant's face when the judge said to have him locked up in the gaol.'

'Why not? He was only there a few days, but he's in the navy now, out of the way,' Nathan said.

''opefully get shipwrecked somewhere,' Will cackled. 'Come on, Nathan, Isaac, let's get to Danny's, he says Twelfth Night's always fun at his 'ouse, this year should be e'en better.'

Danny finished his piece of twelfth cake. It had been a great evening. He was pleased Will and Nathan had come and Isaac and Uncle John had shared some funny stories about their time at sea. He hadn't been in trouble for what he'd done. Everyone was happy and smiling, Uncle John was saved. His father said he was very proud of him, though he'd to promise to steer clear of the smugglers in future. It was great that he'd be going to work for Mr Sweetland. He looked across the room, Will and Nathan were telling father of their plans for their new venture. He picked up his glass and went through to the kitchen, poured himself another cordial and went outside into the garden.

The freezing air of the past weeks had moved away and the night was mild, even though there wasn't a cloud in the sky. He looked up at the stars. Orion, Taurus the Seven Sisters. The universe was so big, how far did it go? Would anyone ever find out? A bit like the future, though he now knew what his apprenticeship would be. He smiled. He hadn't thought about being an attorney. Though he'd been scared, it had felt good to talk in the court and show how Uncle John and Mr Brown were innocent of coining. Once he'd learned all about it, he could help more people. The thought warmed him.

'Danny?'

Danny took his gaze from the sky. 'Uncle John.'

'Ye not enjoyin' the party?'

'Yes, but I just wanted to think for a few minutes.'

'I done a lot of thinkin' these past weeks.'

Danny threw his arms around his uncle. 'I'm so happy you're free.'

'And I am, thanks to you - and your friends.'

'Why didn't you tell me?'

'Tell you what?'

'About saving all those people – and Isaac.'

'I don't like to talk 'bout it, that's all, it were a frightenin' time.' Uncle John pulled Danny close and hugged him.

'You're a hero, Uncle John, my hero.'

'And you, Danny Clarke, are mine.'

END

About *The Moonrakers of Avon*

The Legend of the Moonrakers

Will Gibbs explains the legend of the Moonrakers in Chapter 24. The legend of the Moonrakers is based in Wiltshire where it is said that a gang of smugglers were retrieving barrels hidden in the water of a pond. When revenue officers came across them the smugglers told them they were trying to catch the moon for its cheese. This was, apparently, believed and thus the name Moonrakers came into being. There are legends of Moonrakers in Hampshire and there's a Moonrakers Way in Christchurch.

Counterfeiting

Counterfeiting and clipping of coins was a huge problem in the 18th century with many forged coins in circulation. The crime was seen as treason and those found guilty hung.

Smuggling in Christchurch

Christchurch was an epicentre for smuggling in the 18th century. Its out-of-the-way location sandwiched between long stretches of beaches to both east and west, its large harbour – reached through a narrow channel, marshes, two rivers and the town from which to disperse the goods, made it an ideal place. It was certainly watched by preventative officers, customs and the navy and in 1784 the famous Battle of Mudeford took place.

Incident at Parley

The incident where a gang of smugglers fought with revenue officers to take back seized goods was reported in the London Gazette on 24th November 1781 where Customs House announced a reward of £100 for their capture and that anyone captured could earn £50 for the capture of each accomplice.

Glossary

Ankers – Small barrels, usually carrying spirits, such as gin or brandy.

Baccy – Tobacco

Bonebox – Mouth

Controller – The Controller of Customs was in charge of collecting payments of dues at ports and was in charge of the controllers.

Fo'c's'le – Forecastle. The part of a ship at the bow where the crew live.

Free Trading – Another term for smuggling used mostly by the smugglers themselves.

Landers / Landsman – Once contraband had reached the shores, smuggled goods became the responsibility of the lander. The lander organised the transport onward, arranging for ponies and carts and for men to carry the good ashore.

Spotsmen –The man on board ship responsible for ensuring the vessel reached the correct point on the shore to land.

Ostler – The person in charge of the stables at an inn.

Poor House – or workhouse – A place for the people unable to look after themselves.

Preventatives – Waterguards stationed around the coast

Side saddle riding – Perinne would have ridden her pony side-saddle and would have had a special ladies' saddle for this purpose.

Places in Christchurch

Here are places in Christchurch mentioned in The Moonrakers of Avon that you can still visit (v) or see:

Christchurch Priory & St Michael's Loft (School room) (v)
The Red House Museum (Poor House) (v)
Place Mill (v)
The Castle (v)
The Old House (the Constable's House) (v)
The George (v) public house
The Eight Bells (v) shop
The Ship (v) public house
The Ship in Distress (v) public house
The Marshes (Stanpit Marsh) (v)
Mudeford (v)
Quomps (v)
Sopley Church (v)

There remain some old cottages in Burton similar to the one Danny would have lived in.

Will's old cottage would have stood near to the by-pass where a car park now stands.

There was no such place as Cliff House. There was a building called High Cliff and this was replaced in the early 19th century by Highcliffe Castle. Bay House is also an invention. New houses were being built at Mudeford at that time and fine examples remain.

The Bargate was destroyed in 1744 but there is a road, Bargates, in the town centre

Poole is an ancient port and the customs house of the story was replaced with the current customs house. Also close by is the museum.

Bournemouth did not exist in 1781 but Kinson, Throop and Holdenhurst were villages at this time

Bibliography

White, Allen – Christchurch through the Years – Church Street
    and Castle Street
Day, Malcolm – Voices from the world of Jane Austen – David
    & Charles 2007
Olsen, Kirsten – Daily life in 18th-century England –
    Greenwood Press 1999
Picard L – Dr Johnson's London – Weidenfeld & Nicholson
    2000
Platt R – Smuggling in the British Isles – Tempus – 2007
    Quennel M & CHB
Howard, J – The State of the Prisons in England and Wales –
    William Eyeres 1777

Other sources

The internet
www.localhistories.org
http://blog.mikerendell.com/
http://www.daviddfriedman.com/Academic/England_18thc./
England_18thc.html
http://www.oldbaileyonline.org/static/Crimes.jsp#coining